COURAGE IN MAGIC

IN MAGIC SERIES
BOOK FOUR

KJ WARAWA

MYSTIC
CITY
PRESS

Edited by Jennia D'Lima

Proofread by Taylor Gonzales

Cover Designed by Sunset Rose Books

"Stop!" Rowena yelled to the voice in her head. She pressed her palms into her forehead, as if she could push the voice out. "Stop! It's too much; let me think!"

The words and visions in her mind disappeared. She let out a long breath and conjured a glass of wine, taking a seat in the large armchair in her living room. The huge gulp did little to wash away the bitter taste of anxiety coating her tongue. Lifting the glass to her lips again, she took only a small sip. Trying to ground herself, she concentrated on savoring the light, fruity flavors of the pinot grigio—her favorite wine.

She'd consumed too many glasses of the beverage lately to try and dull the voices in her mind and the hallucinations. If she wasn't careful, she could easily drown herself in wine until even it wasn't enough.

As a psychologist, she knew the signs and symptoms of a mental disorder. Although no one was immune, she didn't think it would ever happen to her. At least, she'd hoped it wouldn't.

She looked around her apartment, seeing her favorite

things—items she'd collected over the years. Framed pictures covered the walls, and books and other cherished items lined the two enormous bookcases flanking the end wall. There were candles and crystals, and several packs of beautiful tarot cards. Perhaps strange things for a psychologist to collect, but she loved the look of them and the symbolism behind them, whether they were real or not.

Her collection soothed something inside her as she continued to visually scan each item. She took another sip of her wine and felt a calm finally settle over her.

Only a year ago, she'd been spellbound and hadn't known people with magic even existed. Then her world, and that of her three cousins, had been upended in the worst possible way.

The hallucinations had started a couple of months after the spellbinding that had locked her magic away for twenty years had been broken. They were subtle at first—just fleeting blurry images, like a memory—and as her magic grew more powerful and the more she perfected it, so did the hallucinations. Then the voices started.

They weren't really clear at first—a word here, a word there—but nothing that made any sense. She'd gone to a doctor and had every test under the sun to rule out nervous system problems, such as Parkinson's disease, epilepsy, and brain tumors. That left a whole host of mental health disorders as probable causes.

She'd seen a psychiatrist, but her symptoms didn't present as a mental disorder, and her psychiatrist finally told her she needed to lower her stress levels. Now she knew how her own patients felt when she told them that—frustrated.

Putting her empty wine glass on the coffee table, she conjured a small charcuterie board. She'd been as giddy as a teenage girl on a first date with the high school quarterback when she'd figured out she could conjure one.

Chewing a piece of cheese, she thought back to the last hour. She'd rushed up two flights to Morgana's apartment when she'd heard something was wrong, only to discover Morgana wasn't actually Morgana. She was her cousin Molly, who they thought had been buried over twenty years ago. They hadn't known Morgana's true identity because she'd been disguised by a spell.

The relief that Molly was still alive was more than she could put into words and yet with the relief came so many questions. Her two brothers, Mirek and Taren, as well as her cousin Dylan, had been killed in the same fire thought to have killed Morgana. Her dad and uncles had also died in that fire. If Molly had been spellbound, could Dylan be as well? Even though a small amount of hope bloomed inside her, she was afraid to feed it

Mirek and Taren were dead—she knew that in her heart, although she couldn't have said how. It was likely connected to all the hallucinations she'd been having and the strange words popping into her mind.

She reached forward and picked up another piece of cheese, sandwiching it between two crackers, when something fell off a shelf. Placing her snack back on the board, she got up and walked over to the book that had fallen to the ground.

Kneeling on the soft carpet beside the book, she pulled it up on to her knees and lovingly ran her hand over the cover. It was a photo album her mother made of her and her brothers—the last one she made before she died.

She put her fingers under the cover to lift it when the book was pulled out of her hands. A gasp tore through her throat but before she could do anything, the book slammed down on the carpet, with a soft whooshing noise. The album's stiff pages flipped open one after the other until reaching the book's final page. There was only one picture on the page—a large eight-by ten-inch portrait of her brother Mirer. It'd been taken when he was ten, just before he died. She and Taren had each sat for a similar photo. She'd been eight and Taren six. She ran her fingers along her brother's image, his thick blond hair mussed, like he'd run his fingers through it. She remembered her mother hustling them all off to a photo studio and her brothers grumbling because they weren't allowed to get dirty.

She chuckled as she remembered—so bittersweet. She was the only one left of her immediate family. Her father and brothers had died in the fire that took the lives of seven members of her family… well… six, since Molly was actually alive.

Her mother died a few years later, and it wasn't until the previous year that Rowena discovered it was because her mother had spellbound her and her cousins.

Sounds burst into her mind, like static on a TV channel without a signal. The album slid off her knees as she slammed her palms against the sides of her head. "No! I don't understand!" she yelled into the silence.

Images swam in front of her vision. This time, they were more clear than they'd ever been. She saw Mirek on his bike, Mirek kicking a soccer ball in their old backyard, and Mirek swimming at the lake. But it was as if she was seeing the scenes through someone else's eyes, like they were someone's personal memories.

Alive.

The word was spoken into her thoughts as more images of Mirek popped into her mind, like someone slowly flipping through an album. These images were like the others—someone's memories. It wasn't until she saw the third image of Mirek that her hands trembled. He was sitting on a couch, but he looked like he was in his late teens. But that was impossible. Mirek died when he was ten.

IT WOULD BE A GOOD DEATH. Connor Davis's fingers flew across the keyboard as he wrote the gruesome details of the poor man's demise. Connor used the heavy metal music pouring through the stereo speakers at an unsafe decibel to fire his creativity. He could see the man in his mind's eye as the poison took hold and consumed his character from the inside out—a quick but painful death. One best suited for an enemy. Oscar Ford, his series' detective, would have his work cut out for him with this one, just the way Connor liked it.

When he finished writing the chapter, he glanced at the time on his computer. It had been a productive morning. After hitting save, he pushed back from his desk, the sound of the chair's wheels on the floor drowned out by his music, his phone's vibration caught his attention. He let out a groan and pushed his magic out the tips of his fingers, turning the music off and accepting the call. His dad's picture had lit up on his screen, eliciting a curve of his lips. He enjoyed hearing from very few people in his life, but his dad was one of them.

"Hey, Dad."

"Morning. Are you in the middle of writing?"

"No, I wouldn't have answered the phone if I was. It's perfect timing; I'm just taking a break."

"Good. I thought I'd come up and visit you. "It's been a while."

Connor stiffened and flopped back in his chair. "What's wrong?"

His father blew out a breath. "That obvious, huh? I've lost my touch."

If his father had meant for him to laugh, he'd failed. "You were here last week, and you know you're always welcome, but you said you'd come back at the end of the month. What's changed?"

When Connor had first moved up to the family lake house almost at eighteen, he'd expected to receive bad news at every turn. He'd been in such a dark place, he couldn't see a way out. Any phone call prompted a worry that the call was being made to deliver more bad news. It had taken him years, but he'd slowly been able to answer a phone call without thinking something horrible had happened—or mostly.

This wasn't one of those times. He knew every nuance of his father's voice. Had even imitated it in his characters.

"No one has died, son."

Connor blew out a breath as he relaxed his shoulders, a habit he knew was an exact replica of one he'd picked up from his father. "Okay. When are you coming?"

"I'm not sure exactly, but in a couple of days. I'll let you know when I know. But in the meantime, make sure your protection on the house is secure."

"So… no one died, but it's still bad?" Connor felt his old friend anxiety rear its ugly head as the beginnings of a headache loomed.

"No… I'm probably making more out of this than I should. It's nothing new."

That was like his father and he suspected that his dad was downplaying whatever had happened. Connor's headache took a firm hold as the realization of his father's words sunk in. "It's Drew."

"Yes. It's not so important that I need to go into it over the phone; just make sure your spells are in place."

"I will. I love you, Dad."

"I love you, too, son. I'll text you when I'm coming."

They said their goodbyes and Connor pressed the end button before shoving the device in his back pocket. He needed to get outside to clear his head.

He looked over at Doyle, who was doing his usual impression of a couch potato.

"Ready for a walk?"

His seventy-pound greyhound bounded off the cushions and came over to him, nudging Connor's hand. He gave the dog a hearty rub and grabbed his leash from the hook on the wall. Sometimes he'd let Doyle run free, but because of the phone call Connor didn't have the patience to wait around for Doyle to frolic in the water. He needed to move. A restless energy overcame him whenever he had to think about the past. Mentions of Drew could throw him into the past in a heartbeat. Maybe he'd been right to think that phone calls brought bad news.

They went out the back door and through the gate, heading toward the lake. Doyle did his business and then came into a heel position by Connor's side as they headed along the well-worn path around the lake.

Connor took off at a fast clip to burn off some of the restless energy that had settled over him with his dad's call. At the two-mile mark on the trail, he stopped and conjured a bowl of water for Doyle and put it down in the middle of the path. He conjured a bottle for himself and downed it in a few gulps. If he got dehydrated, a headache would set in for days and he wouldn't be able to write.

When Doyle finished, Connor disappeared both his water bottle and Doyle's bowl, then set off at a much more leisurely pace.

The beautiful area had soothed him more times than he could count in the almost twenty years since he'd permanently moved up to the family property. He looked out over the lake to the trees on the other side and soaked in the calm. It had taken him almost that entire first year to appreciate what lay in front of him. He'd wallowed in his grief for so long that it had almost consumed him.

It was his novels, writing about death and grief and solving the mysteries he created in his head, that had helped him finally come to accept his past and move on. Well... if he was honest with himself, he hadn't really moved on; he'd just come to accept things the way that they were.

The passing years had made life easier by making the memories not as fresh, and now there were entire days where the past didn't consume him. His dad and his uncles and aunt had moved on, or as much as anyone could from the loss they'd endured. And now no one brought up the past around him anymore, unless it was to relive good memories.

The mention of Drew was not one of those good memories. The man's name brought a flood of grief with it. Connor tried to shake the thought off, and when he reached the three-mile fork in the path, Doyle turned around and started walking toward home.

Connor chuckled to himself. He was obviously predictable if his dog knew when to turn around. He and Doyle had been a team for three years now, when his father had given him Doyle as a present. Connor's last dog had died a year before that. It had almost been more than he could handle, even though in dog years, Conan had lived a good, long life.

Conan's death had reawakened his grief and he'd settled into a depression he didn't think he'd ever get out of. He thought he'd come to terms with his mistake from years ago; he would never forgive himself, but he had accepted it. Or so he told himself. His dad had given him a year to grieve and then one day showed up with a wiggly, gangly looking greyhound puppy, his ears flapping over, with the biggest brown eyes.

Between writing and training Doyle, Connor had slowly pulled himself back out of his despair. Years ago, before he'd graduated from high school, his dad had forced him to see a counselor, but now he chose to walk out his troubles. It wasn't perfect, but it was enough.

He wondered how many miles he'd have to walk to deal with whatever his dad was going to tell him about Drew. Connor hadn't seen his former best friend in over twenty years because seeing him had brought back too many memories. And several months ago Drew's true nature was revealed, so that was likely what his dad wanted to talk about.

Just like always, the walk back to his house always seemed shorter than the walk out. The fresh air and the time with Doyle had been a good break, but not enough to calm all his thoughts.

After removing Doyle's leash, Connor waved his hand toward the sliding glass doors off the deck to open them so Doyle could get to his water bowl. Connor pushed his too-long bangs out of his eyes and sunk down on the cushioned wooden swing he kept for when his aunt Stella visited. She'd sit out here for hours.

Connor couldn't understand why his aunt and uncle, but especially his aunt, didn't hate him for what he'd done. He'd never had the courage to ask her why, and when he'd been in his deepest grief, she would sit beside him on the swing, their thighs pressed against each other, and drink their coffee in silence. She was the one who gave him his first cup of coffee and taught him how to make it the non-magic way.

Over the years, it had had become their thing—strongly brewed coffee and soaking up nature on the deck swing. Maybe that's exactly what he needed today, and maybe it would help prepare him for whatever news his dad was going to bring.

2

*R*owena closed the video chat and typed up her notes from her patient's session. She'd done video chat appointments in the past, but they were becoming more frequent with so many of her patients now located across the country. They were effective, yet sometimes she worried that she'd miss something by not being in front of her patients, like a nuance in their expression or body language.

She stared at her laptop and closed her eyes. The drive to help people and to make sure she was worthy of the life she'd been given pushed at her every day. Years ago, she'd watched the old war movie, *Saving Private Ryan*, and the end scene became her motto to live by. Matt Damon's character, now years older than he was during the earlier parts of the movie, stood in front of the gravestones of the people who gave their lives to save him. He turned to his wife and asked her to confirm for him that he'd led a good life and was a good man.

Rowena's family hadn't given their lives for her in the same way, but like Matt Damon's character, she was the only one left. When the end credits of *Saving Private Ryan* appeared on the screen, she'd made a promise to herself. She'd vowed to help every person she could. Not only because she felt called to, but to ensure that she was a good person and living the life she'd been given in the best way she could, when the rest of her family hadn't been given the chance.

Over the years, she'd learned how to go days without thinking about the movie, but never did she go a day without reminding herself of her promise. Changing her practice in the last few months was helping her fulfill that promise even more than she had been.

She was loving her practice's new direction—working with magic people—magics for short. When she'd made the decision to switch her practice's focus, she thought it would take a while to rebuild her patient list, but it hadn't. Magics were coming out of the woodwork, wanting to work with a psychologist who understood what they were going through. Her calendar had very few openings.

She saved the document before closing her laptop and pushing it to the side.

Rowena.

The sound of her name had her turning to look behind her, even though she knew that she was the only one in the apartment. In the week since the word *alive* was spoken clearly in her mind, she'd heard nothing from the voice that she could truly grasp, only static.

Rowena.

"Yes?" She spoke aloud, but wondered if she should be speaking in her head. It was so different than telepathically talking to someone, like she did with her cousins. Why it was different, she didn't know; it just felt that way.

You hear me? The voice held a tone of surprise.

"Yes. Who are you?"

Laughter bubbled up in her thoughts—such a strange sensation.

Taren. He laughed again, and the suddenly familiar sound made her heart ache. *I can't believe you can finally hear me.* Even after all this time, she'd recognized his voice, but it hadn't entered her mind as a possibility that it could really be Taren.

"Where are you?"

Here.

On reflex, she looked around her apartment again. "I can't see you." For a brief moment, the realization that she was talking to someone who wasn't there flittered into her thoughts before she dismissed it. As strange as that was, it was a relief to know it wasn't stress and that she didn't have a disorder. This was a magic specialty of some kind; that was the only explanation. Or she was truly having a psychotic episode, but she wasn't going to go there yet.

You'll need help for that.

"You're dead?" Rowena let out a breath and closed her eyes. Deep down, she'd known her brothers were dead. She'd been convinced until the photo album incident, but now she wasn't so sure about Mirek since Taren had said he was alive.

Yes.

"Why now?" Taren had been six when he'd died in the fire. At least she'd thought he'd died then, and maybe he had. She opened her eyes and stared at the photos lining one of her living room walls. She focused on one picture of Taren making a goofy face, taken a few days before he died.

You were bound so I couldn't get through to you.

"I've been unbound for a year and a half."

And I've been trying for months.

"Do you mean that the static and undistinguishable voices I've been hearing for months were you?"

Yes.

"What's different now?"

I don't know for sure, but I think your magic might be stronger now.

"How do I know you're really Taren?"

Ask me something.

She scanned the photos and her shelves, wondering what only Taren would know. "See that photo of you laughing on the wall, beside the family photo?"

Yes.

"What were you laughing about?"

Taren laughed again—it was a young boy's laugh, one of glee. *Mirek told a joke and Dad snorted his coffee out of his nose!*

Rowena chuckled at the memory, even as sadness swamped her. She'd lost Taren, Mirek, and her dad that week. Pushing away from her kitchen island, she walked over to her bookcase to see if there was anything else that reminded her of something only Taren or her family would know. They'd been so young and it was decades ago, so it was hard to remember specifics.

Believe me now?

Did she? The voice sounded like Taren, and he knew something no one else did, but she'd seen all types of strange magic in the past year. "I'm trying to."

What about that time when we were canoeing? It was boys against girls and Jo cheated.

"Funny you should mention that one. I only remembered it after the spell was broken. Mom got rid of any memory that had to do with magic. It was one of the memories taken when we were spellbound."

But you remember now?

Staring at Taren's photo, one she'd looked at for years, felt surreal with his voice in her head. "What was your favorite show to watch on TV?"

That's easy. Teenage Mutant Ninja Turtles.

All at once, more memories came to her, like she'd been given permission to look into the past. "Remember that time you snuck out of bed in the middle of the night and hid in the family room in the basement? You watched almost every DVD we had of that show and ate a couple dozen cookies."

Oh yeah. She heard Taren's child-like chuckle. *Mom was so mad. The cookies were for a school bake sale. She conjured some more, but she was still mad. I didn't get to watch TV for two weeks!*

"What about the time that you and Reece put worms in the toes of my and Jo's shoes?"

That was awesome!

Rowena flopped down on her couch and closed her eyes as she and Taren went back and forth with their memories. There were so many that had been blocked because of magic, and others that she'd blocked because they'd been too painful to revisit.

After a while, their laughter died out and they were both quiet for a few minutes.

Ro, I need you to do something.

"What?"

You need to go to Connor Davis.

Rowena's eyes sprung open, but Taren still wasn't visible. "Connor Davis, as in Frank's son and Ben and Stella's nephew?"

Yes, him.

"I haven't seen him in years. Most of his family comes to our weekly dinners, but he doesn't." Dinners that Taren would never get to go to. She shoved the thought down; she couldn't keep thinking that way or she wouldn't enjoy the time she had with him now. Instead, she tried to picture Connor in her mind. She'd hear about him from his family now and then.

He must have been around eighteen when he left Blue

Mountain and moved to his family's place by the lake. Still in Colorado, but not close. Connor was about eight years older than her, and she remembered looking up to him when she was a little girl. He'd seemed so big—larger than life. Would she even recognize him since it's been so long?

Rowena?

Taren's voice brought her back to the present. "I'm here."

I know. Taren giggled. *I can see you.*

Rowena sat up and stared straight ahead, so wishing she could see her brother. "Can you always see me?"

Yeah... oh, you mean when you're in bed or something? Gross! I could, but I leave. I don't want to see that"

"Okay." Another thought occurred to her, giving her a shiver. "Can others see me?"

You mean, others like me?

"Yes."

Probably, but they'd have to be stuck here like I am.

She heard a sadness in Taren's voice. "Why are you stuck?"

You need to go see Connor.

Rowena wasn't sure if Taren meant he was stuck here until she went to see Connor, or if he was changing the subject. "Why?"

Because he needs you and you need him.

She settled back on the cushions and let her gaze wander over the pictures on the wall. "He needs me as a psychologist?"

Yes, and more.

"More?"

Just go and I'll help you.

"Taren, I haven't seen the man in years. I'm not about to go to him and say. 'Hey, my dead brother'—" She broke off as the words sank in. He'd been dead for years, and yet she was talking to him. Taking a deep breath, she pushed through. "I can't tell him you told me to talk to him. His dad and uncles have tried to get him to move back to Blue Mountain for years, but he lives like a recluse. He might not even talk to me."

He will.

"Can I think about it?"

I'll come back. Bye.

His last words sounded just like the little boy she remembered. Rowena sat up and conjured a small glass of wine for comfort. She took a sip and looked up at the picture of Taren laughing.

Seeing the spell break on Morgana and realizing that she was Molly had awakened a small spark of hope in Rowena. If Molly was still alive and just spellbound to look like someone else, then perhaps her brothers were still alive too. She'd told everyone that she knew her brothers were dead. Somehow, she'd known the voices and sounds in her head were from one of her brothers—it had been a gut feeling, no matter how hard she'd tried to deny it.

Now she knew for sure he really was a ghost. The spark of hope had fizzled out and turned to ash.

She took a sip of wine and grimaced. It wasn't that the wine was bad, but it wasn't bringing the comfort it usually did. Disappearing the glass, she stood and walked over to her computer.

Rowena checked her schedule and pushed all thoughts of her brother, ghosts, and the reclusive Connor out of her mind for now. She'd decide later if she'd go see him.

ROWENA SMILED as Javier pulled out a chair beside her. "I wasn't sure you were going to make it tonight," she said.

Javier reached over and gave her a quick hug. When Jack had first introduced him to their group to help with the unbinding, she'd hoped there could be something between them. Besides being one of the kindest people she'd ever met, Javier was easy on the eyes. He was tall and muscular and she'd always been a sucker for darker coloring like his, but they'd discovered early on that there weren't any sparks between them. It hadn't taken them long to realize that they'd never be more than friends.

"I'm working on a case with Jack, and he said he had some news to share tonight and that I should come. I hate it when I have to miss the family dinners, anyway.

"I like it when you're here too. Do you know what the news is?"

"No, he didn't say, but I got the feeling that it was council and not FBI related."

"I don't know how Jack finds time to do both. Or Meredith either." Rowena's mind briefly flashed through all the events that had taken place over the last year and a half. Besides the spell on her and her cousins breaking, Jack and Meredith had fallen in love and were now co-leaders of the new North American magic council. They both had a bit of a type-A personality and liked being busy and organized, so the council fit their personalities.

Javier shook his head as he laughed. "Maybe Jack stops time and gets shit done."

"Now, that would be fabulous!"

"Hey cousin, how you doing?"

Rowena grinned at Reece as he pulled out a chair across from them. Her cousin could always bring a smile to her face. He was another one of those bigger-than-life type of people, like their fathers had been. And with the muscle he'd put on since the spell that almost killed him had been broken, his physical size now matched his personality.

"I'm good, and you look like you've put on even more muscle. Not eating your own baked goods?" she teased.

"There's no calories in my cupcakes." Reece winked and flexed his right arm, eliciting a laugh from her and a scoff from Javier.

"Then I want one after dinner."

Reece winked again. "I'll bring out an entire tray."

Rowena, Javier, and Reece made small talk as the week's designated helpers brought out the meals from The Magic Plate's kitchen. Rowena usually got up to help whether it was her turn or not but stayed to chat this time as she'd been so busy lately that she wanted to sit and catch up. With the family restaurant closed early, and just her magic family and friends around her, it was the one time each week where she could chat with everyone and just be herself.

She was halfway through her meal when she clued in that even though there was a large group present, it was smaller than most weeks. Some of the restaurant staff that often joined them were absent, as were some of Meredith's personal staff who were considered like family. Rowena turned to Javier to ask him about it but noticed Jack stand up before she had the chance.

"Can I have everyone's attention?" Jack asked from the end of the line of tables, his voice penetrating through the other voices until a hush fell over the large crowd.

"Consider this me putting on my leader of the North American council hat." Jack paused as nods and agreements passed among those at the tables. "You all know that Jo and Simon retrieved an ancient magic book, but you may not know that it is rumored that there are seven of them in the world. I say rumored because the council leaders only know of the whereabouts of two—the one from Jo that we now have and one held by the council in Eastern Europe."

Jack paused again, and Meredith reached out and gripped

his hand. "The book in Europe was stolen by Andrew Skalbeck, also known as Snake, and Drew Bartley, a former FBI agent who used the nickname Bullseye."

"You're kidding?" Reece scoffed. "Rather obvious, don't you think?"

Jack gave a humorless laugh. "Yes, Simon and Jo thought so too."

Rowena raised her hand and didn't comment on the chuckles around her. "Bullseye? I don't get it."

"I didn't either as I've never been much into comics, but apparently Bullseye is the nickname for a character known as Benjamin 'Dex' Poindexter, who is an evil FBI agent in the Daredevil comic series," Jack said.

"Jack dear," Fiona called, getting his attention, "I was under the impression that Drew was still pretending to be on the FBI's side and going undercover with his father, Andrew."

Ben stood and nodded at Jack, indicating he'd take over. "Once Drew revealed the connection between himself and Andrew… Snake… we knew immediately that Drew had been our mole all along. We were in a bind, needing to rescue Jo and Simon, and because Drew swore up and down that he hadn't been working with his father, we let him think that we believed him. In the end, he did help us, but after that, we dropped all pretenses. Drew is evil, end of story."

"Now what?" Reece called out.

"Andrew and Drew killed a powerful magic—"

A sudden dread spread through Rowena. "No! Not Mary?" The Emissary was the only powerful magic she could think of that Jack would mention because she had become a friend to all of them recently.

"The Emissary—Mary—was injured in the attack but will be okay. I didn't know the person who was killed. The two magics guarding the ancient book mentally reached out to her when they were attacked. She flashed there just in time to save one of them, but Skalbeck and Drew got away. Now Skalbeck has the knowledge to find the magic box." Ben gestured to Jack to pick up the mantel again.

Jack stood beside his mentor and looked at everyone seated around the tables. "All of you here today have in one way or another been affected by the search for the magic box that started with my father more than twenty years ago. Whether it be because of family you lost or through the FBI, we're all connected through the tragedies we've endured."

Rowena understood why Jack wanted only certain people present for his announcement. Twenty years was long enough for them all to suffer because of the box; she wondered when it would ever end.

Jack continued. "After Jo and Simon found the ancient book, we—Meredith, myself, and some leaders from other councils—were able to identify the spell that would locate the map to find the magic box. We found the map, but not the box. Everything we've tried with the map has been a dead end. By now Snake and Drew will have a map too."

"I've heard about the magic box, but what does it do?" Morgana asked.

Jack turned her way. "It's believed that when it's opened, evil unlike anything we've ever seen before will be released, and it will take a strong magic council of fourteen members to contain the evil and close the box."

Javier shifted and Rowena turned to him. He leaned forward and directed his gaze at Jack. "How many council members do you have now?"

"Four. Myself, Meredith, Jo, and Simon. And as much as I'd like to immediately initiate more members into the council, it doesn't work that way. When it's time, members are revealed to us. For now, all we can do is look for the box and hope we find it before Skalbeck does."

Rowena got the sinking feeling that Taren hadn't told her everything that he knew. The timing of Taren wanting her to see Connor, who at one time had been best friends with Drew, just seemed too coincidental.

AFTER JACK'S ANNOUNCEMENT, there were some questions before Reece brought out desserts. Rowena grabbed a cupcake and made an excuse about having to catch up on patient files.

She flashed into her apartment's foyer.

Are you going to see Connor? It's been three days!

Rowena fumbled her cupcake and just managed to get it on the kitchen island before it could land on the floor. "Crap, Taren! Don't scare me like that."

Sorry.

She squeezed her eyes shut at the sound of her little brother sounding contrite, just like he had as a little boy. "It's okay. I'm just not used to it. Telepathy is bad enough." She turned around. "Where are you?"

Here.

"I can't see you, Taren, so I don't know where 'here' is." She walked to the couch and sat, facing her loveseat. "Why don't you sit in the loveseat?" she said, pointing at it.

Okay, I'm sitting there now.

She smiled across at where she assumed he was. "Does going to see Connor have something to do with what Jack just told us? Wait, were you in the restaurant?"

I was, but it got boring.

"Can you go anywhere you want?"

Only where I have a connection to the place or the people.

Although it was difficult smiling at an empty loveseat,

Rowena made sure she kept a smile on her face, hoping Taren knew she was trying to sort through all the information. "Will you come to Connor's with me?"

Yes. You need me there.

"Why?"

Because I need to tell you and Connor something.

"Can you tell me now so I'm prepared?"

Taren was silent for a moment, and she imagined her brother shaking his head as she continued to look at the loveseat.

No.

She'd had a feeling he was going to say that. "So what do I say to Connor?"

That he needs to talk to you about the day Julia died.

Rowena sucked in her breath and slowly let it out through her nose. "I don't think that will go over very well. I heard at one of the family dinners that Frank, his father, and both his uncle Ben and uncle Joel still haven't been able to talk with him about that day. Why would he tell me anything?"

Because I'm going to help you.

"I've got some patients tomorrow morning, but I can go in the afternoon. I'll drive since I won't know where to flash to and it just might be safer since I don't know the area. Do you have his address?" She could just imagine the look she'd get from Ben if she asked for his nephew's address out of the blue. The senior FBI agent would have some questions of his own that she wouldn't be ready to answer.

Check your phone.

"Why?" Rowena pulled her phone out of her long skirt's pocket. When she unlocked it, she saw her map app was open with a location listed. It was less than two hours away. She looked over at the empty loveseat. "How'd you do that?"

It's just energy. Like when I pulled the photo album off the shelf.

Rowena bit the inside of her lip to stop from laughing at the implied 'duh' she could just imagine her little brother adding to the end of his sentence.

She looked down at the map, still open on her phone. Tomorrow would be interesting.

3

Connor finished typing a scene and debated moving on to the next one or stopping for a break. He glanced at his watch. It was later than he thought and he hadn't eaten yet.

We're here.

The telepathic message from his dad made the decision easy.

Come on in. He threw the message back at his dad and walked out of his office. The 'we' was probably one or both of his uncles. Even though they would have flashed to Connor's, they never entered without an invitation and would be waiting for him at the front door.

His dad and his uncle Joel both appeared in the foyer as Connor walked in, Doyle bounding ahead of him when he saw the visitors. Uncle Joel crouched down and petted the dog vigorously, his tail wagging in bliss as Connor gave his dad a quick hug. Uncle Joel stood and also gave him a hug before all three of them turned and walked into the kitchen. The routine was long ingrained in each of them.

Connor grabbed three mugs from the cupboard and

conjured coffee before floating the mugs over to the kitchen table.

"Pull out some plates too. You probably haven't eaten." His father knew him well. He grabbed three plates and some cutlery and took them to the table.

"Sandwiches okay?" his dad asked, looking at him and Uncle Joel.

"Sure."

"That works."

A sandwich and a pile of potato chips appeared on each plate. Connor smiled. He couldn't count the number of times he'd sat with his dad and uncle—sometimes his Uncle Ben too—chatting about nothing significant over sandwiches and chips. No matter how often he'd tried to retreat from the world, they hadn't let him.

Doyle came over to his side and put his head in Connor's lap. He petted Doyle and then picked up his sandwich. "So, what's Up?" This isn't a normal social visit, is it?" He took a bite of the sandwich, waiting for his dad to answer, and realized how hungry he was. At least he'd remembered to feed Doyle earlier. Like usual, his own needs always came second.

His dad put down his sandwich, and Connor knew the news wouldn't be good.

"We wanted to let you know some things that have happened recently. First, you remember me talking about Morgana? The woman who we rescued when Jack Knight killed Louis Copeland?"

Connor had just taken another bite of his sandwich and nodded, looking at his dad as he chewed.

"She didn't know anything about her own identity, and Ben's team wasn't able to find any trace of her in missing persons records. We suspected Morgana Smith wasn't her real name, but she didn't match any of the age-progression photos of missing children either. But that's because she'd been spelled and her appearance had been altered."

Connor swallowed his last bite as he met his dad's gaze. "I'm guessing the spell broke. Who is she?"

"Molly Williams."

Dropping his sandwich onto his plate, Connor glanced between his dad and his uncle. "Meredith's twin? The one who died in the fire with half of the three Williams families?"

"Yes, that one. When she was rescued, she didn't remember anything, but the spell broke, and now some images have come back to her, but no solid memories. We're hoping she'll remember more in time, like the other Williams children did after their spell was released."

Connor ran a hand through his hair, pushing the long strands out of his eyes.

"There seems to be a lot of that going around." They chatted about what they'd been up to recently while they finished their meals. Afterward, Connor magically cleaned and put away the dishes while his uncle topped up the mugs.

He ran his fingers through Doyle's fur, using the familiar sensation to ground himself. As an FBI agent, his dad had an excellent poker face, but Connor knew him too well, and his sudden silence, combined with his unreadable expression in a family setting, meant he was holding something back. "What else? It's good that Morgana or Molly—what name is she going to use?"

"Morgana; at least for now, I think."

"Right, Morgana—it's good that she's been reunited with her family, but there's more, isn't there? Were the other family members not killed either?"

His dad leaned back in his chair and clasped his hands together on the table. "The Williams fathers did die in the fire, but we don't know about Morgana's three cousins. She can't remember if they were taken when she was or if they actually died." He paused and took a sip of his drink.

Fitting his leadership role in the FBI, his dad was direct and never beat around the bush. At least not usually. The only time he hesitated was when he talked to Connor about the past, like now. "Spit it out, Dad. It's about Drew, isn't it?"

"Yes. I told you he was our mole in the FBI and that he disappeared with his dad a few months ago... Well... he's resurfaced. In Europe."

Connor frowned. "If he's in Europe, why worry? And if he does come back here, do you really think he's a threat to me?"

"I'm not sure, but I want you to be cautious. He and Snake or Andrew whatever we call his dad—killed someone for a copy of the ancient book."

"I thought Jack had the book."

"He has one copy. Drew now has the other known copy. He needed the book for a spell to locate the map to the magic box."

Connor looked down at his mug and then disappeared it. He conjured a shot of whisky and downed it in one gulp.

Uncle Joel frowned. "What's going through your head right now?"

"I don't know." He met his uncle's eyes. "I guess I'm not surprised. Drew always figured he could take whatever he wanted, by whatever means necessary. I'm sorry someone died, but it doesn't affect me, and I try not to think about what happened."

"That could be the problem." Uncle Joel's voice was matter of fact. "Maybe you need to think about the past so you can finally let it go. There was nothing more you could have done."

"You don't know that. You weren't there."

His dad reached across the table and gripped his forearm.

"Connor, Joel's right. We've been over this. You need to let it go. Holding it in for half your life is long enough. I don't expect you to suddenly move back to Blue Mountain, but you need to stop blaming yourself for what happened. I know that you don't like thinking about Drew, but you need to be on guard, just in case."

"I will, but I don't think Drew has anything to gain by showing up here." Connor hadn't seen his former best friend since the day his world fell apart, and he didn't expect to see him anytime soon.

Rowena shut down her laptop. "Okay, I'm ready." It was strange how fast she was becoming used to talking to an empty room. But then, it wasn't really empty. She'd come to an agreement with Taren after the family dinner last night, that he'd let her know when he was in the room by talking or, if she was on a call, by moving something. Just as she was finishing her last call for the day, he'd moved the coffee mug beside her computer.

About time. I thought you'd never be done.

"I have to work, you know. I can't just drop my patients so I can go on a wild goose chase for you."

It's not a wild goose chase.

"Maybe not to you it isn't, but since you won't give me details, it seems that way to me."

"Knock knock."

Rowena looked up to see Javier poking his head in the apartment door.

"Are you busy? On a call?" he asked

She smiled as he walked into the room. "No, I finished a few minutes ago and shut down for the day."

Javier looked around as if he expected to see someone. "Who were you talking to?"

"No one." She hated lying, but she wasn't ready to tell anyone about Taren yet because she wanted to know about her magic specialty first.

Javier furrowed his brow. "I heard you talking when I opened the door."

Rowena forced a chuckle. "Just talking to myself. A bad habit I've picked up recently." She heard Taren laugh but didn't visibly react.

Javier's frown made her think he didn't believe her. He probably thought someone had been there and they'd flashed out, but she didn't need to explain herself. "So what's up?" She redirected the conversation, hoping he'd let it go. "I just saw you last night. Not that you're not welcome, of course."

Javier walked around the kitchen island and pulled her into a hug. He held her tight for a moment before pulling away. "Are you alright?" His gaze looked concerned but she couldn't say for certain that it was.

She stepped back. "Of course. Why would you ask that?"

Taren giggled. *Because you've been talking to a ghost.*

She so wanted to throttle her little brother.

"Because you've been acting differently lately. You never used to talk to yourself either."

Rowena picked up her laptop and shoved it into the bag before she faced him again. "I'm fine. Just a lot on my mind, and I'm going to see a friend this afternoon." Saying that was bound to raise flags with him, but she couldn't tell him she was going to see someone she didn't really know. Even though she and Connor had been close as kids, the years apart had made them strangers.

"Anyone I know?"

She shrugged. "I don't know. Connor Davis."

"Frank Davis's son? *The* Connor Davis who lives like a recluse and writes mystery books with macabre killings?"

Maybe she should have lied again, but she hated lying. And she felt saver with someone knowing where she was going. "Yes, the same Connor. "He's a couple of hours away, so I've got to get going." She threw her bag's strap over her shoulder and headed for the door.

Javier walked around her and opened the door. "Maybe I should go with you. The guy could have a few screws loose."

"That's not a diagnosis I'm familiar with."

"Ah, Rowena, you know what I mean."

She waved her hand at the door to magically lock it and turned to face him. "No, Javier, I don't. Connor is a long-time friend of my family and I'll be fine."

He looked deflated but didn't fight her as she walked to the elevator. "Are you headed to your car? Why aren't you flashing there? You flash everywhere."

Keen observation skills—one problem that came with being friends with an FBI agent. "I just wanted some time to myself, and it's a nice drive," she said, hoping he'd drop the subject.

They said their goodbyes and he flashed away as she stepped into the elevator. She hadn't lied when she'd said Connor was a long-time friend of her family, but it had definitely been a stretch. She still hoped she'd get a warm welcome.

4

The drive was relaxing, just what the doctor ordered. She laughed at her own joke.

What are you laughing at?

Rowena swerved on the road, but quickly corrected. "Shit, Taren! Don't scare me like that when I'm driving."

Why did you laugh? he asked again.

"Just thinking about a doctor joke." She glanced at the passenger seat before putting her eyes back on the road. A longing to see her brother welled up inside her. As she'd talked with him over the past few days, she realized he didn't sound much older than he had when she'd last seen him. In her mind, he'd always stayed six years old, but now that she was talking to him, she expected him to have aged like she had. So strange how minds worked.

That guy didn't believe you.

"Javier?"

Yeah.

She shrugged and spared another glance at the passenger seat. She might not be able to see Taren, but he could still see her and she wanted him to know she was looking at him out of respect. "Maybe not, but it doesn't matter. I can go where I want."

I wanted to go to Disney World.

Rowena could hear the longing in his voice and had to think about what to say. As a psychologist, she'd worked with many patients to help them realize their dreams. It was never easy, but she'd seen so many people achieve their goals and have the lives they'd always dreamed of.

"I'm sorry you didn't get to go there." A physical ache spread through her chest. She rubbed it with one hand, but nothing could alleviate the pain of knowing she couldn't do anything for Taren. His life had been cut short years ago, and as horrible as it was, maybe this state was even worse for him. When he didn't say anything else, she decided to change the topic. "Have you always been able to see people? Since you died, I mean."

He didn't respond for several minutes, and she thought maybe he'd left.

No. I was away.

"Away where?" She turned her head just enough to see the passenger seat before paying attention to the road.

Not here.

She had no idea what that meant. Some type of afterlife? Heaven? She wanted to ask him more. Ask if he'd seen their dad and mom. Had he talked to them? Did he know where Mirek was? Maybe, in time, he'd answer these questions. Did he even have time? How long would he be around? So many questions without answers peppered her thoughts as she tried to come up with one that he'd maybe answer.

"Do you remember your time after you were taken?" she asked as she flicked another quick glance to the side.

Yes.

Well, that was new. No one had ever had to drag words out of Taren when he'd been alive. He'd been a chatterbox as soon as he'd learned to talk and had never stopped. Time and experience changed all people to a degree; perhaps the change happened shortly before he died or even after. What actually happened in the afterlife was something she'd never given much thought to before. She'd just assumed people were happy and at peace after they died.

"Can you tell me something about the time after you were taken?"

Not now. When you talk to Connor, I can show you.

"Show me? Like a memory?"

You'll see.

Okay then. She knew when to let things go, at least for a while, and this was one of those times.

Rowena pulled in a long, calming breath and let her shoulders drop as she stared at the open road in front of her. She'd never been a nervous driver, but she needed to pay attention since, according to her GPS, the road curved for the next several miles. Huge evergreens lined one side of the highway, while a steep drop-off lined the other. Rowena gave it a quick glance, but couldn't see anything but a wide-open space where the road ended. There weren't any guardrails and she gripped the steering wheel tighter.

Finally, the road straightened out and Rowena loosened her grip on the steering wheel and let her mind wander again. She tried to picture Connor from when she knew him as a kid. Since he was quite a bit older than her, she hadn't hung out with him, but he'd been around with Jack and Damon at family events when all the council members and their advisors got together. Connor had seemed like an introvert, but he'd always been kind and friendly. He'd been tall as a kid, with shaggy brown hair that fell onto his forehead and into his eyes. She couldn't imagine what he looked like now, but she thought about the reception she would receive, and hoped once more that it would be friendly.

Whatever the reception turned out to be, it would be sooner, rather than later because she was almost at his house. The GPS gave her two more commands to follow and then she was pulling up to a large single-story house, not the cabin she'd been picturing. Trees lined the sides of the property, providing privacy and a sense of coziness.

She shoved her keys into one of her skirt's pocket and her phone into the other. Looking at the passenger seat, she lowered her head in case anyone could see her talking to herself. "Taren, are you coming with me?"

Yes.

"Anything I need to know first? I don't even know what to say to him."

You'll know.

She doubted that but got out of the car. Ear-splitting, obnoxious heavy metal music penetrated the quiet calm. She walked the short distance to the front door, up the two steps, and rang the bell. There was probably little chance Connor could even hear her over the pounding and wailing of the noise he likely called music.

She rang the bell again, and a dog barked once. Less than a minute later, the music cut off abruptly and the door was yanked open. She stood facing the handsome Connor Davis, who towered over her with a frown.

CONNOR'S FINGERS flew across the keyboard. The killer waited in the darkened corner of the room as the victim walked in. The words flowed onto the page at a tremendous speed as the scene unfolded in his mind and his fingers captured the thoughts as fast as they formed.

Doyle's bark penetrated his consciousness over the loud

percussion of the music that pumped through speakers on either side of the room. "Damn." His concentration was broken now, and if he didn't answer the door and get rid of whatever annoying salesperson had made it to his deserted neck of the woods, they would probably come back and disrupt his progress again. He hit save on his document, then went to the front door and yanked it open with more force than needed, jerking his arm with the movement.

The woman in front of him threatened to take his breath away. She was beautiful in a natural way, with long wavy blond hair and large hazel eyes. A hippy type of skirt concealed the rest of her figure.

She twisted her hands in front of her and glanced to her side before meeting his gaze. "Hi."

"Hi" She'd ruined his creative flow and now he was going to be thinking about her mesmerizing hazel eyes and the way her hair lay around her shoulders, like a soft blanket, for the rest of the night. Unfortunately, he'd been brought up with better manners and could never be mean just to benefit himself.

"I'm Rowena Williams. Do you remember me?"

The image of a skinny little girl about age seven popped into his mind. The person in front of him was definitely no little girl. He wrote murder mysteries, sometimes with graphic sex scenes, and he could definitely write a sex scene starring her. He gave himself an internal shake. Not thoughts he needed to be having right now when he had a murder scene to write.

He pulled himself out of his head as Rowena took a step down and tilted her head up to look at him. What had she said? Remember her, right. "I think so, and I'm Connor. But I'm guessing you know that."

"Yes." Her gaze snapped to the side and she frowned before looking up at him again. He leaned on the door jamb, crossing one ankle over the other, and waited as she paused. It was like she was listening to someone, but they were too far away from any neighbors for anyone to be talking telepathically to her. Maybe she was just one of those people who took a long time to formulate sentences. "He'd written a character like that once and he'd liked the guy but couldn't save him from his fated demise.

He watched emotions shape her expression, perhaps sadness or resignation, before she physically straightened herself.

"Sorry, I just had to think for a minute. I—uh—need to talk to you."

"About?"

She stared at him, and his manners finally kicked in. He moved back, lifting his arm to indicate the foyer. "Would you like to come in?"

"Thank you." She walked in, and he closed the door behind her before leading her into the living room.

Once more, he extended his arm and indicated one of the two comfy sofas angled toward the large stone fireplace. He briefly considered showing her into the kitchen. The living room was his favorite place in the house, besides his office, and he didn't need to associate the room with bad news. He didn't know for sure that she was bringing bad news, but he didn't know what else could have brought her out here unannounced.

They sat kitty-corner to the bookshelves that flanked either side of the fireplace. They ran from floor to ceiling and were filled with old books he'd collected over the years. He even had a few first edition Sherlock Holmes that were his pride and joy, and he wondered if she would think them too nerdy. He was nerdy, but something in him wanted Rowena to like him. He wondered if she liked mystery books.

When they were seated across from each other, he leaned

forward with his forearms on his knees. "What would you like to talk about?"

"I want—"

She paused again, and this time he was almost positive she was telepathically communicating with someone. "Who are you talking to?"

"What?" She shook her head. "No, I mean, I'm not talking to anyone. I want to talk to you about Julia."

He sat up and pushed his hair out of his eyes, taking a moment to compose himself. "That was a long time ago."

"I know. She died around the same time as my family, and I'm sure it's difficult to talk about, but I need you to revisit your memories from that day."

He frowned. "That's a very specific request. Why?"

She looked sideways and then snapped her head forward. "I'm hoping that will become apparent when we look at the memories."

"What do you mean, *look at the memories?*"

Rowena twisted her hands in her lap, but her gaze didn't stray from his this time. He still wasn't sure that she wasn't talking to someone, and she had a nervous air about her. Her mannerisms were the spitting image of how he'd write an uncomfortable character. If he was writing about her now, he might have her character take a tissue out of her pocket and twist it to shreds with her fingers.

"I'll help you pull up and examine memories from the day she died. There might be information that you've forgotten that could help… help the new council that is forming."

Connor wished they could talk about anything else, such as books, like they were on a date and getting to know each other. Talk about anything but what she was requesting. "No." Those memories were buried deep for a reason, and he wasn't about to let an almost stranger unearth them. "Why you? Are you a shrink?"

"I'm a psychologist, and I've been advised that I'm the best person to help you remember."

Strange wording—*she'd been advised*. She was hiding something. He wondered how far she'd push her agenda and he decided to test her, just like he would one of characters. "No," he said again, and stood, feeling both a sense of relief when she did the same and followed him back to the foyer, and a sense of disappointment that they wouldn't get to know each other. "Sorry you wasted your time coming all the way out here. Next time you might want to call first." He really was sorry that he couldn't give her what she wanted. For a moment he even considered asking her to stay for coffee. He'd like that if he could get her to agree to not talk about the past, but he expected that was just wishful thinking.

Rowena stopped, her hands shoved into her skirt pockets and faced him. "I know this came out of the blue. It did for me too, but I think looking into your past will help all of us." She paused and looked to the side, like she was listening to someone again. "And if it doesn't, maybe it would help you. I'd like to help you if I could."

"Why?"

She paused again as if carefully considering her words. "Because no one's past should haunt them, and I expect yours does."

Connor knew she was right, at least about his past haunting him, but not about looking into it. He couldn't imagine ever examining it and forgiving himself. He let his silence speak for itself.

She stared him in the eyes and he could have sworn he felt a connection with her. "Did you know that Drew Bartley recently killed for an ancient magic book?" she asked.

Now she was going down a path he really didn't want to travel. "Yes." He pulled the door open and felt like an ass for pushing her out. "Look. Why don't you give me your number in case I change my mind?" A part of him said to take the plunge and talk to her, but he wasn't ready. Though if he wasn't ready after twenty years, he wasn't sure if he'd ever be ready.

She pulled out her phone and he held out his hand to magically retrieve his from his office. She entered his number when he recited it and he looked down when his phone pinged. Even though he wasn't going to change his mind about revisiting the past, it couldn't hurt to have her number. On his walk last week, he'd contemplated getting out more. Maybe this was his chance.

They said their goodbyes and he watched her until she drove away. He glanced at her number in his phone and attached her name but wondered if he'd really use it. She didn't need someone in her life who got people killed.

5

"*S*tupid, stupid, stupid." She shook her head as she drove, humiliation and defeat beating down on her.

You have to go back and talk to him.

"What?" She flicked her gaze to the passenger seat, still expecting Taren to visibly be there. "No. He probably thinks I have a psychosis. Since you won't tell me what we need him to find, I couldn't tell him much. And… I couldn't tell him I'm talking to my dead brother."

Why not?

She called on every ounce of professionalism she'd learned over her career not to screech at her dead kid brother. Taking one hand off the steering wheel, she twirled a stray curl near her face and slowly breathed through her nose. Good question. Why not? She so wished she could see Taren, his facial expressions and his body language, as she explained. She glanced to her left. "Well, it's not normal for people to talk to ghosts."

You're magic.

Occasionally, she'd forget that since it was still so new to her, but not this time. Being magic had taken some time to get used to after being bound for twenty years, but in the last eighteen months, she'd fully embraced her magic. Even her career centered around magic now, and she'd learned about many different types of specialties.

There were as many magic specialties as there were non-magic ones. But instead of being great at playing the piano, someone might be able to turn into someone else, like Jo's boyfriend, Simon. Or have a gift of persuasion, like their friend Damon. Yet not once had she heard about people being able to converse with ghosts.

She gripped the wheel tighter and eased up a bit on the gas pedal as she reached the treacherous section of road but felt more confident than the first time she'd driven it, as she knew what to expect now. "I know. But I don't think talking to ghosts is a common magic specialty. Besides, how am I supposed to convince him I can talk to you when he can't see or hear you?"

That's why you need to talk to him.

"Can you explain that?" She flicked her gaze to the passenger seat.

Look out!

Whipping her head forward, she saw someone standing in the middle of the road. She slammed on the brakes as she cranked the wheel to the right. The wheels gripped the pavement until she hit gravel. The steering wheel shook in her hands, and she tightened her grip until they were white.

The car skidded toward the embankment, the open space of the drop-off taunting her, and she course corrected, yanking the wheel to the left.

The man flashed in front of her car a second time, but only a few feet away this time. She was going to hit him.

Rowena cranked the wheel harder and instinctively gave the car some gas as she tried to avoid hitting the man. Gravel kicked up under the tires and the car tilted toward the cliff.

Life seemed to slow down as movement out her driver side window caught her eye. She turned her head and screamed. The man seemed to be suspended in the air, his arms extended and his body almost parallel to the ground as he pushed her car toward the cliff.

Rowena felt the moment the car lost traction with the road. She no longer had control and let go of the steering wheel. The car slid off the road and angled toward the cliff. She closed her eyes and wrapped her arms around her head.

TAREN LIKED how Rowena kept looking at him, even though she couldn't see him. She was like that before too. Whenever they spoke, Rowena always gave him her undivided attention. She didn't play on her phone or pretend to listen—she truly heard him. It didn't matter that he'd been a little kid; she'd always been there for him. Now that it was his turn to be there for her, nothing had gone as planned.

The seer had told him to make Rowena talk to Connor and that everything would be okay. All he had to do was get them together and they'd use their magic. Then he could explain what he'd heard and what they needed to do. The seer had been adamant that he had to do things in that order.

The energy shifted around him and he went on alert. Facing the front, a familiar face flashed in front of the car.

Look out! Taren screamed into Rowena's mind as terror gripped him. The seer hadn't told him this would happen. He toggled his vision between Rowena and the man outside the car.

Taren hadn't been old enough to drive when he'd been taken and couldn't offer any advice. The familiar feeling of uselessness washed over him.

He looked between Rowena and the guy outside the car. Eddie. He was far older than Taren remembered, but he'd never forget him. Not in all of eternity.

Dissolving through the car door, Taren floated over to Eddie.

Taren pulled in some energy from around him and sent a blast toward Eddie. Eddie wobbled and shot a look over his shoulder. He'd clearly felt Taren's force, but it hadn't been enough. His only guess was that Eddie had erected some type of a magic shield around himself.

Eddie flashed to the side of the car and started to push. His feet didn't touch the ground, like Taren's didn't, but Eddie wasn't a ghost. Eddie must have a special power. Taren sent him another blast, but this time Eddie didn't react. The muscles in his arms bulged and his jaw hardened as he pushed the car toward the cliff.

Taren dissolved back inside the car. He looked around frantically to see if he could do something just as the car started to slide. Rowena let go of the steering wheel and wrapped her arms around her head. She couldn't give up.

Going back outside again, he watched helplessly as Eddie pulled away from the car. It tilted toward the cliff and rolled over the embankment as Eddie flashed away.

Taren sped down the cliff. Rowena's car rolled over and over as it picked up speed. Taren sucked in energy and threw it at the car. He sent blast after blast, pushing the car up the hill as he followed behind it. It was a slow process but he pushed the car back up the cliff inch by inch.

The driver's side lay against the cliff as it scraped over rocks and broken trees. He couldn't see Rowena and talking to her would be futile because he wouldn't be able to hear her answer from inside the car.

When the wheels flopped over onto the gravel, Taren gave the car one more blast of energy, pushing it further onto the road. The car tilted up, the passenger side lifting with the momentum, causing the vehicle to roll.

Taren sped over to the vehicle and laid a thin layer of energy against the driver's side to level the car out. The passenger side wheels hit the road, gravel and dust spewing into the air. He raced back to the cliff side and pushed the car further away from the edge.

Thinking the car was stable, he went back inside and leaned over his sister. Her face was covered in blood like in the macabre horror film she'd seen one night when he'd snuck down to the family room to watch TV. One of her arms hung by her side but he couldn't see the other.

Rowena?

Rowena!

A sensation he hadn't felt since before he died welled up within him. Panic? Fear? It had been so long since he'd felt human emotion like that, he couldn't place it.

He ran his finger along her arm, but it disappeared through her skin.

Pushing through the car's shattered front window, he looked up and down the road. There had been so few cars on the road when they'd gone to Connor's and now it was dark with the moon as the only light source.

Taren went back into the car and searched for Rowena's phone. He'd never sent a text before, although he'd seen it done hundreds of times. If his energy could move items, it could send a text. After searching for what felt like hours, he found it in the back seat.

He couldn't pick it up but was able to float it closer to himself. Directing his energy, he unlocked the screen and called up Connor's contact information. Taren directed his energy to the individual letters and typed out two words.

With the phone hovering in the air, he waited and worried. Would that be enough? He typed the message again and pressed send. And then many times more. Dropping the phone, he hovered over Rowena and waited.

6

The murderer stood in the middle of the room with the victim in his clutches. And that's where she stayed because Connor couldn't force the words. An image of Rowena, her blond curls floating around her face, kept distracting him. He picked up his phone and looked at the screen. No messages.

"Shit." He was an idiot. Did he really think after pushing her out the door that she'd text him? To do what? Just to say hello? Try to talk him into delving into his past?

Tossing the phone on his desk, he turned off the music and stood up, stretching out his back. Doyle was curled up on his couch. "Come on, let's go for a walk." He glanced out the window as he attached Doyle's leash. The sun was just starting to set. He thought of Rowena driving on the mountain roads in the dark, then opened the door for him and Doyle. Rowena was a grown woman and would be fine.

He took a shorter path around part of the lake and kept his pace leisurely, letting Doyle sniff whatever he wanted to his heart's desire. Had he been wrong to push Rowena away? His father and uncles had been trying to get him to revisit the past for years. Maybe they were all right, but the thought of doing so was almost enough for Connor to break out into hives, and a shiver snaked down his spine.

When they'd been out for about a half hour, he turned them around. Doyle was just as happy to walk back, but they still didn't rush. When they reached his property, he let Doyle off his leash and picked up the large stick he'd found for throwing. Avoiding the water, he tossed the stick as far as he could and laughed as Doyle almost toppled over his own feet to change directions and fetch the stick.

He lost track of how many times he tossed the stick as his mind rewound and replayed his conversation with Rowena. She'd been hiding something, but he wasn't sure what. The constant glances to her side and pauses made him sure she was talking to someone, he just didn't know who.

Doyle dropped the stick at his feet and collapsed with his tongue hanging out. Connor bent down and petted him vigorously, loving how simple things could make a dog happy. For him, happiness was so much more elusive. He'd tried to convince himself for years that he was content and maybe he was. But happy? He wasn't so sure anymore.

The moon lit his way as he walked up the back steps to his deck with Doyle trailing behind him. Doyle knew the routine and waited while Connor took the towel hanging over the railing and wiped the dog's paws before opening the sliding glass doors to let him in. Connor left his shoes by the back door and made his way to the front door, turning on a couple of lights as he went. He hung the leash on its hook and looked at his watch. Maybe he could get in a few more hours of work.

His phone pinged from where he'd left it by his desk, but he ignored it. He'd get something to drink and then maybe a sandwich before tackling the scene again. But then his phone pinged again. And again.

An uneasy feeling crawled along his skin. There weren't many people who texted him. The phone had pinged eight or ten more times by the time he picked it up. He unlocked the screen and his uneasy feeling increased tenfold. Rowena had texted two words over and over again.

Rowena: Help me

Connor shoved his phone in his back pocket and flashed to his front lawn when the realization hit that he didn't know where to go.

He retrieved his phone and called Rowena's number. After five rings, it went to voicemail. He figured he had two options: he could flash a few hundred yards at a time, looking for her at each place he flashed, or he could drive. The first option meant he could miss her and he'd be fucked if he needed to drive her back.

Flashing to his SUV, he landed in the driver's seat and hit the button to raise the garage door. There'd been a time when he'd been a dumb teenager and had spent two weeks flashing into the front seat of his car, just to see if he could. His dad hadn't been happy with the bruises, the concussion, the broken arm, and smashed sideview mirror, but Connor was grateful for it now.

He put his phone in the holder on his dash and was on his way in seconds, scanning the sides of the road as he went. After an hour he began to worry that he'd missed her. But he didn't want to turn around in case she was ahead of him.

Channeling his character Oscar Ford, he mentally calculated how far she could have driven. After she'd left, he'd tried to work for maybe ten minutes, and then he'd been gone for over an hour. His driving was likely slower than hers because he continued to scan the road. He would keep going.

He'd driven another thirty minutes when he saw a car on the road up ahead. Pulling in behind it, he could see the damage—roof smashed in and windows broken. It looked like it had rolled, yet it was on the side of the road and sitting upright.

Flashing to the driver's side door, he looked through the cracked window and could see Rowena slumped in her seat. Her face was covered in blood.

He yanked on the door handle, but it wouldn't budge. He could flash inside the car, but then he'd have no way of getting her out. He tried the handle again but lost his grip and stumbled to the side when something pushed him out of the way.

The door creaked loudly as it was ripped from its hinges. The metal door flew through the air and thundered as it landed about twenty feet behind the car. Connor didn't know who had helped him, but he'd figure that out later.

"Rowena?" he called as he leaned into the open doorway and placed his fingers on her carotid artery. She had a pulse, but besides the blood he could see, he didn't know what else was wrong.

If he moved her, and she had spinal damage he could make it worse. But whoever had hurt her could come back, and he couldn't take that chance. He knew there were magics who could heal spinal cords, and if he needed to find one because her spine was damaged, he would.

"Rowena?" She didn't even stir. Reaching over, careful not to jostle her, he undid her seatbelt. Carrying her wouldn't be difficult but getting her out of the smashed in seat without hurting her more would be tricky. Fishing one arm behind her back and the other under her legs, he maneuvered her so her closest shoulder and her head were against him and lifted her while backing away from the car. She moaned and he stopped. Her eyes were still closed.

"Rowena, it's Connor. You're going to be okay, but I have to get you out of the car." He spoke to her as he backed up and freed her from the car. At his own car, he used his magic to open the back door. Standing with her in his arms he stared at the backseat of his SUV, hoping for an answer on how to get her in without hurting her. He came up with nothing.

Calling up as much energy as he could, he turned sideways so Rowena's head was at the opening of the door and used his magic to float her onto the seat as gently as he could. He conjured a blanket and placed it over her and then belted her in.

He flashed back to her car and grabbed her purse and phone that he'd noticed sitting on the passenger seat, just in case.

Once on the road, he pulled away from the curb and constantly looked in his mirrors. He had a sense of foreboding that whoever had hurt Rowena would be back to finish the job.

His phone pinged from the holder.

Rowena: Call Jack

The text had come from Rowena's phone. The phone that he had shoved into her purse and that was sitting on the floor in his back seat. It didn't take a genius to figure out that someone was helping Rowena, or him. The text messages, along with the door being ripped off, were big signals.

Connor spoke to his phone. "Call Dad."

The phone only rang once before his dad's voice floated through the SUV's speakers. "Hey, Connor, what's up?"

"I need you to come to my house. I'm just over an hour away, and I have Rowena Williams with me. It looks like someone tried to run her off the road and she's unconscious.

I don't know how badly she's injured, and my healing skills are passable at best."

"Where are you now?"

"Just passing the falling-down homestead."

"Okay, see you soon." His dad hung up before Connor could say anything else. He expected his dad would flash to him and then he'd have to pull over for his dad to get in the car. That would waste time.

He glanced at the speedometer and pressed a bit more heavily on the gas pedal. "Rowena?" Looking in the rearview, he saw she didn't even stir at the sound of her name. In one of this books, he'd created a character with a concussion and had done just enough research to know that the longer she was out, the worse it could mean for her.

Pull over.

At his dad's voice in his head, Connor peered at the side of the road up ahead through the darkness. Three people stood on the gravel shoulder. He could just make out his dad, but he couldn't identify who the other two were.

Once he was closer, one man looked familiar, and he guessed it was Jack Knight, but it had been a long time since he'd seen him. Jack had aged, of course, as they all had, but in his mind, Jack was still the teenage boy he'd last seen. The man in front of him looked bigger, more muscular, and had a hard sense about him. Not surprising, considering what the man had been through.

As soon as he stopped, his dad opened the front passenger door and stuck his head in while Jack and the other man each went to one of the back doors.

The stranger glared at Connor from where he'd twisted in his seat to see Rowena. "What the hell did you do to her?"

His dad sent a look to the stranger. "Javier. Cool it." The comment and look were enough to silence Javier, but he still glared at Connor.

"How long has she been unconscious?" Jack asked without any preamble.

"I found her almost fifteen minutes ago and texts from her phone came in about two hours ago now."

Jack looked up. "She was able to text you before she passed out? That's a good thing."

Connor looked down at Rowena's pale face. "I'm not sure it was Rowena who texted me."

"Why do you say that?" his dad asked.

Jack picked up Rowena in his arms, and something in Connor wanted to tell him to let her go. He knew he was being irrational since he didn't have the skills to help her, but it didn't change the way he felt.

"We can sort that out later. Rowena is our priority right now. I'm going to flash with her to your house."

"Okay, I can—" Jack was gone before Connor could finish saying he would leave his car and follow.

Javier turned to his dad. "Frank, can you give me a memory of Connor's property so I know where to flash?" His dad must have done it because Javier left almost as quickly as Jack.

Connor focused on his dad. "Who was that?"

"Javier Cano. He's one of my agents. Actually, he reports to your uncle. He was with Jack when I called him, and he's quite close with Rowena."

His dad's last piece of information gave Connor a bitter taste in his mouth. He hadn't seen Rowena in years and had even turned her away from his door, but he didn't like the thought of someone else being close with her. He was such a fucking hypocrite. "How did Jack flash with Rowena? I didn't think anyone had the ability to flash with another person for more than a few feet. I know I certainly can't."

His dad huffed out a breath. "Me either. Jack and Meredith, and I'm assuming some of the other council leaders around the world, are the only ones who can. The leadership ceremony gave them extra power, but they haven't been really open about everything new they can do."

There seemed to be a lot that Connor didn't know lately. "I'm going to flash home. I'll come get my car later."

His dad walked over to the driver-side door and opened it. "I can drive it back. Rowena's in good hands with Jack. You don't need to worry."

Maybe not about Jack. But Javier seemed to be marking his territory, and Connor suddenly wanted to stake his own. He picked up Rowena's bag from the backseat, said goodbye to his dad, and flashed home, wondering what he was up against.

7

Connor flashed into his foyer and looked around. Not even Doyle was around. Hearing voices coming from the back of his house, he found everyone and his dog in his bedroom. Rowena was on the bed, her face now clear of blood. She looked peaceful but pale, her blond hair spread around her like a halo as she lay on his dark blue comforter.

Connor grit his teeth as he took in the others in the room. Javier was sitting on the bed beside her, his back against the headboard, looking too fucking comfortable, while holding her hand. Jack was on Rowena's other side, standing over her, his eyes closed. Doyle was curled up on the foot of the bed, his body half-draped across Rowena's legs.

Dropping Rowena's bag on the end of the bed, Connor flicked his hand toward the chair in the corner of his room and magically pulled it over. Flopping into it, he laid his forearms on his knees and let out a sigh.

Jack passed his hands over Rowena and kept his eyes closed. "Connor, can you tell me what happened?"

"Rowena left my place and I worked for a bit before going

for a walk. When I got back, someone texted me from her phone."

Javier lifted his chin and gave Connor another glare. "Why do you think it wasn't Rowena texting you?"

Connor glared back. Yes, he felt like Javier was suddenly encroaching, but Connor refused to be intimidated. And if he was honest with himself, he had to acknowledge that he could be the one wanting to encroach on Javier's territory. Not that a woman was territory, but in his mind it made sense. "The text said 'help me,' and it must have been sent over twenty times, but when I called her number, there was no answer."

"Maybe she couldn't reach the phone but was able to use voice-to-text," Jack said as he continued to work on Rowena.

"True. But too many other things were strange. Her car looked like it had rolled over the cliff, and yet it was sitting on the side of the road. And when I couldn't open her car door, something pushed me out of the way and ripped the door off the hinges. Then I got a text from her phone saying to call you."

Jack looked up. "The door is a mystery, but could someone else have her phone?"

Connor shook his head and reached for the bag. Pulling out Rowena's phone, he tossed it on the bed. "No, I retrieved it from her car and threw it in her purse." Doyle lifted his head at the disturbance and then snuggled back into Rowena's feet. Connor's king-size bed was crowded, and not in a good way.

Javier lifted Rowena's hand and softly kissed the back. Connor didn't know if the man truly cared for Rowena as more than a friend, but it sure looked like it.

"What do you mean by something pushed you out of way?" Javier asked, still holding onto Rowena's hand.

"That's just it. I don't know what it was. Some kind of

magic energy, but I didn't see anyone. It would have taken tremendous strength to rip the door off like that and to chuck it behind the car."

Jack looked up at Javier. "Why don't you go check it out? See if you can find anything. Treat it like a crime scene and call in Lisa or another agent if you need to. Let Ben know too."

Javier placed Rowena's hand gently on the cover and stood. "Where was her car?" As soon as Connor explained, Javier glared at him once more and then flashed away.

"Don't worry about him. He cares for Rowena a lot, and he doesn't know you well enough yet to trust you."

Connor's gaze met Jack's. "Neither do you."

Jack stood and stretched his back. "I'd give my life for your dad and uncle so I'm thinking you're likely a decent guy. And I liked you when we were younger. Anyway, Rowena had some internal injuries that I've repaired, but she'll still need some time to recover."

"You're a gifted healer." Connor made it a statement, not a question.

Jack's features hardened for a fraction of a moment. "From necessity, not DNA." He shook his head as if to clear it. "I'm sure she'll be fine here with you; just watch over her. She'll probably sleep for a while. Not only from the injury, but because I've noticed she's been stressed more than usual lately. I don't think she's getting the rest she needs. I'll make sure I don't go out of town in the next few days just in case you need me." Jack conjured a piece of paper and handed it to Connor. "Here's my number."

"Thanks. I appreciate everything you've done."

"And Connor…" Jack hesitated for a moment and then faced him head on. "No one blames you for what happened. Not even Ben and Stella. This seems like a great place, and it's been good for you." He smirked. "I love your books, by the way. But maybe it's time you came back to the land of the living now and then. Just drop in. Weekly dinners at The Magic Plate are on Thursdays after seven."

Connor nodded but the knot in his throat prevented him from speaking. Jack gave him a single nod and left with a flash.

Scrubbing his hands over his face, he wondered what to do next. He stood and called to Doyle. After letting the dog out, they both went back to the bedroom and Doyle didn't hesitate to climb back on the bed and curl up against Rowena's feet again. If only Connor felt that secure in his actions.

He went to the bathroom and brushed his teeth to get ready for bed before grabbing a blanket out of the hall closet. A few years back, he'd donated heaps of blankets to a local charity because he'd conjured one every time he needed one in the living room or on the back deck instead of getting one from the closet he kept shoving them into. These days he tried to use what he had.

Curling up in the big armchair, he pulled the blanket over himself and leaned his head back but didn't close his eyes. He watched Rowena sleep as the events of the night played through his mind. Something or someone had played a part in helping him rescue Rowena. If the person or thing hadn't helped him get the door off, Rowena could have died. That would have been one more person's blood on his hands. And one more reason he was right to hole himself up and cut himself off from society—people got hurt when they were around him.

For years he'd lived like a hermit in what was originally his dad's and uncles' place before he'd made enough money from his books to buy them out. He thought no one would be harmed by his actions if he lived far away from everyone.

But even that hadn't worked tonight. If the damage to Rowena's vehicle was anything to go by, someone had wanted her dead. At least that's what he'd have hinted at if the entire incident had been a scene in one of his books.

As much as he didn't want to think about the guy, he hoped Javier would come up with some answers.

Connor conjured a stool and put his legs on it, getting settled for a long night, and closed his eyes to rest them for a moment.

Flinging his eyes open, he looked around. He must have dozed off and something woke him. Pushing the blanket aside, he walked over to the bed. Doyle lifted his head and Connor gave him a pet before moving around to the side of the bed. He got a better look at Rowena in the moonlight streaming in through the slit in the curtains.

He sat on the bed and lifted his hand to move the curls out of her eyes, but hesitated. She must have moved some time in the night as she now lay on her side, one hand tucked under the pillow and the other on top.

Screw it. He gently pushed the stray hair off her face, and let his fingers linger for just a moment on her soft skin. Her face scrunched up and she moaned in her sleep. He couldn't tell if she was in pain or having a nightmare. "Shhh… go back to sleep. You're safe," he whispered. It must have been enough. She settled again, her face more restful now.

Hopefully, Jack was right and she was healed and just needed to rest. Connor went back to the chair and settled in.

The second time Rowena woke up, Connor moved his chair and foot stool over to the side of the bed so he could see her face and reassure himself that she was alright. She stirred a few more times in the night, and each time, he whispered to her, telling her she was safe and he was there. Chances were she didn't register his words or would know in her sleep who he was, but each time, she stopped moving and went back to a peaceful sleep.

Sometime in the night, Connor realized that he liked not being alone.

8

leep clawed at Rowena as she tried to shake it off. She opened her eyes, squinting in what seemed to be early morning light, and saw Connor asleep on a big chair beside the bed. Her sight traveled over the room—not her apartment, but someone's bedroom. The colors were masculine, dark yet still inviting. The dresser was a deep brown and matched the night table beside her.

She moved her feet and encountered a lump. Lifting her head just enough to peer down the bed, she saw Connor's dog half-sprawled on her feet. The huge animal lifted his head, and she would swear he smiled at her before laying his head back down and closing his eyes. She tried to remember the dog's name—something to do with mystery. Doyle, like Conan Doyle, that was it.

Rowena let out a sigh and curled further into the warm blanket. She didn't know how she'd gotten to Connor's place, but she felt safe. Closing her eyes, she let sleep claw her back under.

The next time she woke, Doyle and Connor were both gone. Stretching her arms above her head, she groaned and dropped her arms back. Every muscle in her body protested against her movement. She'd never been this sore before, not even when Meredith guilted her into working out with her.

Gingerly sitting up, she flung off the blankets and swung her legs over the side of the bed. Dizziness hit her, and she curled her hands into the blanket for purchase until her head cleared.

There was an open door at the back of the bedroom, what she hoped was a bathroom, and she slowly made her way there. She flipped the light on and looked at herself in the mirror. Except for some bedhead and some bags under her eyes, probably from working too much, she looked fine.

She used the toilet before washing her hands and face, and then used her magic to make sure her teeth were clean and minty fresh. With one hand on the wall to steady herself, she walked out of the bedroom and down a short hall.

Voices were coming from the other side of the house, and as she got closer, she recognized Javier's and Connor's. The conversation sounded heated.

"It's not safe for her to be here with you. What if Jack hadn't been able to get here right away? She could have died!" Javier said, the words an angry hiss.

Rowena rounded a corner and came face to face with both men in a large kitchen.

"I'm fine."

"Rowena." Javier spun and had her in his arms in a moment.

"Ow."

He pulled back and gently held her upper arms. "Are you hurting? I can call Jack back to heal you. Or I could do it myself, but he'd be better."

She eased herself out of his grip and patted his arm. "I'm a bit sore, but really, I'm fine. I think I'd like to sit down, and I'd love a cup of the delicious coffee I smell."

Connor pulled a mug from a cupboard and filled it three quarters of the way with coffee. "Milk or sugar?"

She smiled up at him. "Just some milk, please." He walked around the kitchen island and placed the mug on a table with six chairs seated around it. Then he pulled out a chair for her and waited.

"Thank you." She sat and reached for the coffee, cradling the warm mug between both her palms. "Javier, what are you doing here? Did you get here last night?" She looked between the two men. "With the sun coming in, I'm assuming it's morning? Or afternoon?"

Connor's eyes crinkled at the corners as he sat across from her with his coffee. "Yes, it's just after nine a.m. Javier got here a few minutes ago. He thinks I'm going to kill you."

"For fuck's sake, Davis, I didn't say that." Javier gripped the back of the chair beside Rowena and flipped it around, straddling it. "Ro, I was just concerned about you. You've never mentioned Connor before, and then you come here out of the blue and someone tries to run you off the road. I wanted to check on you."

Rowena reached for Javier's hand resting on the back of the chair and gave it a quick squeeze. "I'm safe here with Connor. I'll call you in a few days, okay?"

"I don't like it, but I can't stop you. Just be careful." He righted the chair and leaned over, giving her a soft kiss on the forehead before he gave Connor a pointed glare and flashed away.

"Good morning." Connor smiled at her and it lit up his entire face. "Sorry, didn't get to say that earlier."

"Good morning. And thank you for coming to get me last night." She took a sip of her coffee to give herself some time as she thought about last night. She couldn't remember everything, but she'd doubt she'd ever forget the man flashing in front of her car and pushing it. "How did you know to come to my rescue and how did you find me?"

"Now, that's a story. Would you like some breakfast while we talk?" Connor used his magic to float over a plate of sliced fruit. "I was going to make some eggs. Scrambled okay for you?"

"That would be lovely. Thank you."

He put plates, utensils, and napkins on the table before getting the eggs out of the fridge. Rowena felt spoiled. She had cousins who cared for her, but no one special. She'd lived on her own for years now, having moved out of her aunt's place when she left for college. She'd lived with her aunt Elise and Meredith after her mother died years ago and they'd cared for her too, but it didn't feel like this. Thoughts of her mother brought back thoughts of Taren. He'd been silent since she'd woken up and she was worried about him, saying his name before thinking. "Taren?"

Connor turned around with a spatula in his hand. "Hmm? Did you say Taren? He was your brother, right?"

I'm here.

Rowena forced herself to keep her gaze on Connor and not turn her head to where she expected Taren sat beside her. "Yes, he was my younger brother, but he's always with me. And sorry, I need to learn to talk to him in my head."

Good cover up, Ro.

"That's really nice. Ah… I mean that's he always with you, not that you talk in your head," he said before turning back to the stove.

Rowena watched the muscles in Connor's back and arms ripple with his movements as she drank her coffee and he finished making breakfast. She would never complain about being waited on and enjoying such a gorgeous view.

When breakfast was ready, Connor brought it over to the table on two plates. Rowena hadn't touched the fruit yet and spooned some onto her plate with the eggs. "Thank you. This looks wonderful and I'm hungry." She took a bite of the fluffy eggs and almost groaned.

Rowena finished the eggs and looked up to see Connor smiling at her. "Sorry, I was hungrier than I thought."

He returned her grin. "Don't apologize, it was good to see you eat."

She raised her brow in question. "Really?"

"Sure. It means my cooking didn't suck."

"I can attest to you scrambling a mean egg."

"Good to know. More?" He took the plates to the counter and brought the coffee pot back, topping off both their mugs.

"Thank you. You don't conjure your food and coffee?"

He put the pot back on the warmer and took his place across from her. "Sure, sometimes. But cooking is rewarding, especially if I don't have to do it too often."

"Well, I'm glad you were up to the task this morning." She smiled at him. "And thank you for watching over me last night."

He smiled. "No worries."

"You were going to tell me how you knew to look for me."

"I got a text message from you. Well, actually about twenty of them, all saying the same thing."

"What did it say?"

He leaned back in the chair, his arm balanced on the back of the chair beside him. "The fact that you're asking proves my suspicions that you didn't send them."

She remained silent, not yet ready to confirm what he knew.

"You texted 'save me.'" She knew Taren had somehow sent the messages. She glanced at the chair beside her, trying to make it look like a casual glance.

Yep, it was me.

"And you flashed or drove to find me?"

"I drove, worried that I'd miss you if I flashed. I think your car is totaled but it was sitting on the side of the road the last time I saw it."

"And you drove me back here?"

Connor leaned forward on his forearms. "No, I called my dad and Jack came with him and he flashed back here with you. What's going on, Rowena?"

"What do you mean? I came here last night to talk to you and then was in an accident. Thank you for rescuing me." She hoped he caught the sincerity in her voice.

"You're welcome. But I wasn't talking about you coming to talk to me… Actually, I think that's part of it. You show up here out of the blue. I could have sworn you were talking to someone in your head, and unless it was someone really powerful like Jack, I don't know how you were communicating telepathically over such a long distance."

Connor's stare was intense as he focused on her.

"Then you get in an accident but there were no signs of it on the road. I was too worried about getting to you to pay close attention to the scene, but Javier said there were no skid marks, and no broken vehicle parts on the road. Just a cave-in on part of the embankment where your car went over the cliff, and yet your car was sitting on the side of the road when I got there, with you unconscious in the driver's seat. Javier was here with Jack last night and went to the scene while Jack healed you."

You need to tell him.

She remained quiet and didn't look in Taren's direction.

"On top of that, you somehow managed to text me while you were unconscious and again when you were still unconscious on the back seat of my SUV and your phone was in your purse."

"What did I text the second time?"

"'Call Jack'. I'm guessing you knew he was a gifted healer."

He took a sip of his coffee without taking his eyes off her. "You don't seem surprised about the texts."

She shrugged. Taren was quiet beside her and she appreciated the time to think of a response. It took her only a few moments to know there really wasn't much she could do now except tell Connor the truth and see how he reacted. She wished she was sitting at the breakfast table in front of Connor for a completely different reason than to tell him he had to look into his past that he wanted to forget and that she could talk to her dead brother.

He already knew something was up. The only thing she was truly surprised about was how her car came to be sitting on the road. She'd never been more terrified than when it started to tip off the edge of the cliff. She must have lost consciousness when it fell.

"Oh, one more thing... When I couldn't get to you... something or someone ripped the driver's side door off the hinges."

Rowena felt her eyes widen and couldn't stop herself from looking to the side.

I was worried you were dying.

"Thank you," she said softly as her eyes welled with tears. She blinked them back and faced Connor. "Okay, I'm ready to explain."

9

*R*owena sat on the edge of the couch, twisting her hands in her lap. After they'd cleaned up breakfast, Connor had suggested they move into the living room so they were a bit more comfortable. Doyle followed them and curled up on the floor beside the couch.

Connor stood and faced the fireplace. She watched him absently run his finger over the large ornate iron rings. They were cemented into the brick for holding the fireplace utensils and she couldn't tell if he was fascinated by them or using the time to think. Perhaps the sturdiness of the rings helped ground him for the conversation.

"When you showed up yesterday, I hesitated about bringing you in here to talk because I didn't want any bad news to taint this room." He turned to face her. "Now, I think that no matter how bad it is, I have to hear it."

"I don't know if it's bad."

He frowned as he sat on the end of the same couch she was on. "How can you not know?"

It's okay.

She took a deep breath and let it out before she forged

67

ahead. "Because I don't know what it is I have to tell you. Someone is going to give me the information and I'll give it to you."

"Someone is coming here? Who?"

"No, no one, ah..."

Just spit it out, Ro.

Taren was right, she just had to say it. "No one is coming here. I can talk to my brother, Taren, and he'll tell us what he knows."

Connor ran his hands through his hair, pushing the long bangs off his forehead. "Taren? The brother who died over twenty years ago?"

"Yes. I can talk to ghosts. Well—I can talk to his ghost, at least."

Connor leaned forward and gave her one of his penetrating stares as if he could see right through her and was trying to see if she was delusional—and definitely not in a clinical sense. It took a lot of her willpower to meet his gaze head on and not squirm.

"I know it sounds unusual—"

"Unusual?" He coughed a laugh. "That's what you're going with?"

Rowena jumped to her feet and paced in front of the sofa a few times before turning to him, her hands on her hips. "I'm not 'going' with anything. It's the truth. After the spell was broken on me and my cousins, I started to hear noises. At first it was static and then words, although I couldn't make them out. I thought I might be having a psychotic break and maybe even lose my practice. I had test after test done, and when nothing showed up, I saw a psychiatrist, but none of my symptoms read as a clear neurological disorder." She walked over to one of the large windows and looked out at the beautiful day. It was so calm and peaceful, unlike the turbulence in her mind.

Telling everything to Connor was more difficult than she thought it was going to be. Finally, she turned back around and looked him in the eyes. "A week or so ago, after the spell broke on Morgana— you know about my cousin?"

Connor sat back on the couch, with one arm on the back and his legs crossed, giving her his full attention. "Yes. Keep going."

"Well, after the spell on her broke, the static in my head got worse. I was in my apartment and a photo album flew off the shelf. When I picked it up, it flipped to a picture of my older brother, Mirek."

He leaned forward, his forearms on his knees. Rowena was starting to think of it as his thinking position. "Like your car door flew off the hinges for me yesterday?"

She garnered hope; maybe he would believe her after all. "Yes, like that, but probably not as violent. When I looked at Mirek's picture, I heard a voice in my head, but this time it was totally clear. The voice said 'alive'."

"It was Taren?"

"Yes. I didn't know that at first, but the other day Taren said he was finally able to break through and talk to me." Rowena sat on the couch and turned sideways, lifting her knee onto the cushion, almost touching Connor's. She was suddenly exhausted, as if telling someone that she could talk to Taren had drained her of all her energy.

"You were talking to Taren yesterday, weren't you? When you were here. You kept turning your head."

"Yes… well… really, I was just listening to him. I haven't figured out how to talk to him in my head yet. I have to speak to him out loud and he answers in my head."

"He told you to come see me. Why?"

"I'm not sure, except that I have to help you look into your past and it has something to do with what's happening now."

I want to tell you what I heard and you can tell Connor.

Rowena repeated what Taren said.

Connor sat back and crossed his legs again, one knee touching Rowena's. For a moment, that was all she could think about, until Taren spoke.

When we were taken, when you thought we'd died, Drew sometimes came to visit his dad.

Rowena continued repeating Taren's words. It was like translating. Taren would at least know if she forgot to say something.

One day I walked by Snake's office and I heard Drew talking to his dad. He was talking about you, Connor.

Drew caught his dad alone in the back office of the large house. "Hey, Snake." He only ever referred to his father by his nickname. Then he sat down across from his dad's desk and waited for him to look up.

"Is it done?"

"Yes, and Connor has the power that the seer said he did."

Snake played with a coin, rolling it between his fingers. "Tell me how you know."

Drew leaned back. "We were standing in the room watching over the little shits... That's what Drew said, I didn't call them that. Taren said quickly.

"I know, it's okay, Taren."

"Okay. And then Drew said Connor put his hands on the fireplace mantel and then jumped back. He said he felt something. He told me about a Christmas that had taken place in the house, with people gathered around the fireplace. He was able to repeat their conversations. Connor even knew the year— 1947."

"Only that year?"

Drew shook his head. "No, and that's the amazing thing. When Connor placed both his hands on the mantel, he was able to go forward and backward in time, telling me about every year. There was only one year where he couldn't feel the Christmas."

Snake absently tossed the coin from hand to hand. "Maybe there wasn't a Christmas around the fireplace that year."

"That's what we thought."

"Could he do the other thing the seer said?"

"I don't know. That's when things went to shit."

"Okay." Snake stood and turned his back on Drew as he spoke. "Did you work your magic?"

"Yes, he won't remember anything."

Snake turned back around. "Good, then when the time comes, he won't be able to interfere in our plans."

Rowena repeated Taren's last words and watched as Connor stood and rubbed his hands over his face while he walked to the fireplace. He tentatively reached out, laying his hand on the mantel.

When he finally turned around, he ran his hands through his hair and fisted the strands before shoving his hands into the front pockets of his jeans. "This is kind of hard to believe. You could just be making shit up. I can't see anyone you could be talking to and I remember the events of that day much differently."

Rowena twirled a lock of her hair around her finger as she replayed Drew and Snake's conversation in her mind. "Is it true that you can feel memories and know things when you touch something?"

"Yes. It's one of the reasons I collect first edition books, mostly signed ones. I can sense the author and sometimes hear snippets of conversation. It doesn't happen with everything, and sometimes I get the impression that something is missing from the memory."

Rowena scrunched up her brows. "Missing? As in, you don't have all the information, or something is missing because you feel like what you see isn't adding up?"

"The latter. Taren said 'could he do the other thing.' I have no idea what other thing Drew could have meant."

Drew didn't say, but the seer told me you need to combine your magic with Rowena's.

Rowena repeated Taren's words before looking over at the other couch where she thought he was sitting. "Is it the same seer Drew and Snake were talking about?"

I don't know. She just told me to talk to you and get the two of you to work together. I didn't ask her what that meant. I kind of thought you would know.

When Rowena relayed Taren's comment, Connor sat on the couch beside her and turned so they were facing each other. "I don't know if you're feeding me a line of bull, but just the fact that you know I can feel memories from the past is something."

From an outside perspective, it probably did look like she was making things up. "As far-fetched as it sounds, I'm telling you the truth."

"Well… there's only one way to find out. I don't know how to join our powers, but let's try something." He took both of her hands in his. His warmth seeped into her, warming places she hadn't realized were cold. It was as if a long broken-connection had suddenly welded together.

She looked up from their joined hands. "How?"

"I have no idea." He let out a humorless laugh. "We know your specialty is talking to ghosts… or at least to Taren. So when you talk to Taren, I'll push my magic into you. I won't push too much until we get an idea of what will happen."

Rowena turned her head toward the other couch. "Taren, are you good with that?"

Oh yeah!

"He's ready. Let's do this." Rowena felt laughter start to bubble up inside her and swallowed. She hoped her hands weren't sweaty and pushed a bit of magic to her palms to dry them.

Connor must have felt the change in her hands because he raised his eyebrows at her in question. She shrugged.

"I'm starting," Connor said.

With a soft push and lightness, Connor's magic gently flowed into hers. "Taren, talk to me. I don't know what you need to say."

I'm nervous. I've been invisible for a long time.

"It's normal to be nervous. Anything new, especially something as different as this, is going to be scary. Why don't you tell me about something you remember? How about your favorite episode of *Teenage Mutant Ninja Turtles*?"

As Rowena listened to Taren, she felt her magic flowing through her arms and connecting to Connor's, as if it had a mind of its own.

After several minutes, she began to worry that nothing was happening. She'd disappoint Taren, and Connor would think she'd lied. More than anything, she wanted to help both of them. Of course she wanted to help her brother because she loved him, but Connor… there was something different. Already she felt drawn to him.

"Something's happening," Connor whispered. She looked up from their hands, and he tilted his head toward the other couch.

She sucked in a breath. A shadow appeared; it was subtle at first, but in less than a minute, it darkened and she could see the shape of a person. As the person became clearer, she could see they were sitting on the couch, lounging back against the cushions with their arms around their knees.

For the first time in over twenty years, she could see her baby brother.

10

Connor watched as the shadow on the couch continued to deepen and take shape until it filled out into the image of a young boy. He looked to be about ten or twelve and had the same blond coloring as Rowena. His hair was a riot of curls, like his sister's, only shorter.

Rowena pulled her hands from Connor's as she stood. "Taren? I can see you!"

The boy jumped up from the sofa. "You can see me?"

Rowena took a couple of steps closer to her brother and Connor walked around to her side so he could see both their faces.

"Yes, Curly Bear," she said, calling him by a nickname he must have gotten when he was little. He hadn't heard her use it before. Maybe now that she could see him he was all that more real for her. "I can see you and hear you, and not in my head."

"Awesome!" Taren clenched his hand into a fist and pulled it down in a show of child-like exuberance.

"Can I touch you?" She reached forward tentatively.

Rowena's fingers slid through Taren's form and she dropped her arm.

Connor watched as she noticeably fortified herself, and seemed to push her disappointment aside—she straightened her shoulders, plastered a smile on her face, and shoved both her hands into the pockets of her long skirt.

"You're older," she whispered, almost reverently.

"I'm twelve. Well… I was twelve when I died."

"Curly Bear, how did you die?"

"I don't want to talk about it."

Taren's image faded, becoming more transparent, and Connor worried he'd leave before they got more answers. "Taren, I'm Connor."

Taren snorted a laugh and rolled his eyes. "I know."

"Right." Connor almost rolled his own eyes. Not his most stunning comment ever, but then, he'd never talked to a ghost before. Nor to someone who'd been watching him, without him knowing, at least that he knew of. "Can you tell me what my other power is? The one that Drew was talking about?"

"Nope," he said popping the 'p'. "You're going to have to look at it yourself. That's what the seer said."

Taren's hair flopped forward and he shook his head to clear it out of his eyes. Rowena reached forward with one hand and then shoved it back in her pocket. He'd bet the royalties from his next novel that she used to take care of Taren a lot, and pushing the hair out of his eyes was something that she'd done often.

Connor couldn't imagine what she must be going through. She was going to have to talk about it, but he wasn't a counselor—that was her job. And since he hadn't been able to deal with his own mess, there would be no way he could deal with someone else's.

"I'll come back tomorrow." Taren faded away on his last word.

"Don't go!" Rowena stepped forward, one hand reaching out, but Taren was already gone. "Oh my god!" Rowena pulled her other hand from her pocket and covered her face. Her body seemed to collapse in on itself as her shoulders shook. He heard her sniff and knew she was crying. No matter how much he wasn't qualified to deal with someone else's emotions, he couldn't leave her alone with her grief.

"Come here." He wrapped one arm around Rowena's shoulders and guided her back to the couch. "Let's sit."

She leaned against the arm of the sofa and pulled her legs up in front of her, wrapping her arms around them. It was the exact position Taren had been in when he appeared before them.

Rowena laid her head on her knees and her body continued to shake as she cried. A sense of helplessness settled over him like an uncomfortable blanket. He conjured two tissues and held them out to her. "Here."

She looked up and took them from him, wiping her eyes. "Thank you."

"I'm sure that wasn't what you expected when you woke up this morning." Using his finger, he pushed a curl so like her brother's, behind her ear. "You've had a lot of firsts in the past twenty-four hours."

Rowena gave him a weak smile. "True. You too."

She was right; they'd both been through a lot. He lifted her chin with his fingers so he could look her right in the eyes. "I'm sorry for everything you've been through, but I'm not sorry that I was here with you."

Seeing Taren was probably a lot to comprehend. Even for him, and Taren wasn't his dead brother. Connor had heard about a lot of different kinds of magic specialties from his dad and uncles, but he'd never heard of anyone who could talk to ghosts. Or see them. They'd have to pursue it some more, to see if it was his magic that made Taren visible, or only the combination of their two magics. He wondered if he could make a ghost visible on his own. Would he even want to? If he could talk to ghosts, he could get all kinds of ideas for his novels. Especially, if the ghosts had died in different decades and by different means.

"It was so strange to see him. And he was so much older than I remember. And taller."

Rowena's words pulled Connor out of his musings. She had whispered the words, but they'd been loud enough to hear in the quiet of the room. "How old was he when he died?"

"Six and Mirek was ten." She disappeared her tissues and met his gaze. "When Taren had pulled the photo album off the shelf, he said that Mirek was alive. Maybe whatever you and I are supposed to figure out will give us clues to where Mirek is." She shook her head. "I can't even imagine him being alive. But then, I never would have thought I'd see Taren as a ghost."

Connor shifted on the couch, moving closer to her. Her curl had popped loose again, as if it wanted his touch to put it back. And he did. He halted with his hand caressing her hair when he realized what he'd done, but he didn't want to pull away.

Their gazes locked and it wasn't rejection he saw in her eyes. She parted her lips and licked them, and her lids lowered just a fraction. "Even with everything that's happening, I'm attracted to you, Connor," she whispered and leaned forward.

Her lips met his in the barest of touches before she leaned back. He wanted more than that. From the moment he'd seen her standing on his front step, something about her spoke to him. No other woman had elicited the kind of protective instinct and lust that he felt for Rowena.

He lowered the hand that still rested by her ear and moved it to the back of her neck, bringing her closer as he leaned in again. His mouth opened against her lips, and she responded, their lips and tongues dueling in a slow dance.

The couch moved as she shifted. He pulled back only long enough to pull her sideways onto his lap, and with one hand on her lower back and the other wrapped around the back of her neck again, he pulled her closer. It was such a possessive move, but he loved the feeling of holding her to him.

She cupped his face in both hands, her palms soft against his scruff. Connor couldn't have said how long they kissed for as the world fell away and it was replaced with only the taste and feel of Rowena.

His cock hardened where she sat on him and she wiggled against him. With her hands still on his face, she pulled back to look into his eyes and gave him a sly smile.

"You like this?"

"Definitely." He kissed her again and wondered if it wasn't too much with everything that had happened. Was it just heightened emotion? He was about to pull back when a cold nose butted in between them.

They pulled apart and laughed at Doyle trying to get in on the action.

Rowena used his chest to push herself back and stand up. "I think someone wants attention. Maybe we should take him for a walk."

Cockblocked by his dog. "Sure." He held out his hand, palm up, and the leash from the hook at the front door landed on it. "Let's take a walk around the lake."

Connor wanted to see where his feelings for Rowena could go and enjoy their time together for as long as it lasted. He'd then cherish those memories, when she eventually left him, which she would, because he wasn't worthy of staying with long-term.

THE LUNCH DISHES were washed and put away; there was nothing else to procrastinate with. Connor turned to Rowena. "Ready to do this?"

She smiled at him. "Actually, I am. It was a good idea to go for a walk and eat—I'm relaxed. Although I am still a bit anxious from seeing Taren this morning, I want to find out what you can do."

They walked into the living room and sat on the same couch. Connor smiled to himself. He now had good memories of the couch, and after their little magic session, maybe they could make more.

Even the walk around the lake created some good memories this morning. They'd talked about everyday things, getting to know each other a bit better, and as if by unspoken agreement, they didn't talk about Taren or Drew.

"Like this morning, I'm not sure how to do this, but let's start the same way." They faced each other, both with one leg bent under them, and Connor inched closer so their knees were touching. He took her hands in his and gave her a cheeky smile before closing his eyes. "I'll push a bit of magic into you and you do the same to me, then I'll think of the day Julia died." Just saying the words aloud made him want to pull away and bury himself in work or a book so he wouldn't have to think about that day.

Thinking back over twenty years ago, he pictured the house he'd gone to with his dad, Joel, Ben, Stella, and Julia. Drew had shown up at the same time the other people his dad were meeting with had started to arrive—a seer and some senior advisors to the fractured council, as well as the two remaining council members his dad trusted.

It was an old, well-kept farmhouse just outside of Blue Mountain that the seer had recommended they go to. At sixteen, Connor hadn't thought to ask who owned it or any other details; he was just happy to skip a day of school on a beautiful early fall day.

As he walked through his memory, he pushed the images into Rowena.

"Beautiful," she whispered as she saw the property in his mind's eye.

He skipped to the part where he and Drew were in a large family room, watching the kids, and let the memory play out and continue to flow into Rowena.

"One more Barbie, please Connor, and some clothes." He smiled at his cousin and conjured one more doll for Julia and another for Sarah, the daughter of one of the advisors.

He bent down and handed the dolls to the girls. "Okay, Little Pony, you sure you wouldn't rather have a chemistry set or something?" Julia was the most intelligent person he knew, and although playing with dolls was normal for most five-year-olds, he couldn't remember her ever playing with one. Reading university textbooks and conducting science experiments, yes. Dolls? No.

Julia patted his knee in a motherly way. "No, Connor, dolls are more appropriate for us right now."

He bit the inside of his cheek to hold back a smile and nodded at her as solemnly as he could muster. "Right." He straightened and looked down at her as he pointed to the fireplace. "Drew and I will be just over there."

He turned around and chuckled to himself. She was definitely going to be a handful one day.

Drew elbowed Connor as he walked up. "Sooooo... you have a lot of familiarity conjuring Barbie dolls?"

He grinned at his friend. "Fuck off."

Drew laid one arm on the fireplace's low mantel. "Have you studied for the physics exam next week? I fucking hate that shit."

"Not really, but I think I've got a good grasp of it. Watch." He turned around and faced the room, holding his hand up. A ball of magic glowed on his palm and he waved his other hand toward the lights, dimming them. There was still plenty of sunlight streaming in through the large windows on the far side of the room.

He tossed the bright orb from one hand to the other and conjured another and tossed both before adding a third. He juggled all three. He glanced over his shoulder at Drew while he continued to juggle. "See, simple physics. That test should be a breeze."

"Fucking show off." Drew scoffed good naturedly and conjured his own glowing orbs. They faced each other and continued adding orbs and juggling until they each had ten. They had to fling them up higher and higher to keep them all in the air at the same time.

His arms were tiring as he tossed them, and one didn't go as high as he needed. Bending to catch one as it fell, it suddenly flew to the right toward the couch and behind Julia and Sarah.

The couch went up in a burst of flames, sending sparks flying. Julia and Sarah stood up, Barbies clutched in their fists as they screamed. The drapes caught fire with a strong woosh.

He dropped his arms, extinguishing the rest of the orbs as they fell. Rushing to the couch, he threw out his arms, sending cool air toward it to try and distinguish the flames. "Drew, get the drapes!"

"No, Connor. Baking soda." He looked down to see Julia standing beside him, barely reaching his hip. "Conjure baking soda." She conjured some in her little hands and threw it at the couch. He did the same, but it wasn't enough. The flames were getting higher and they were coming toward them.

He scooped Julia in his arms and was reaching for Sarah when Julia screamed. Her face and neck were engulfed in flames. He bent to his knees, trying frantically to put out the flames, and called to his dad. It felt like forever as Julia struggled to breathe, and then he knew it was too late and she was dead.

Connor pulled his hands from Rowena and scrubbed his face before pushing back his damp hair. He felt dampness on the back of his shirt as well. He didn't know when he'd broken out in a cold sweat, but it wasn't his only reaction. His heart was racing and a restlessness had overtaken him.

He got up from the couch and paced back and forth in front of the fireplace.

Rowena leaned back into the corner of the couch and looked up at him. "That wasn't right."

He stopped pacing and turned to face her. "What do you mean? That's the way I always remember it."

"Maybe, but if that's everything, it doesn't make sense. I can't see the ball of light flying to the couch the way it did. And suddenly Julia is on fire and you're not? And what about Sarah?" She shook her head. "No, something's wrong."

Connor conjured a glass of water and downed the entire thing before disappearing the glass. "That's the way I've always remembered it," he repeated.

"I understand, but I think something's wrong with your memory. Perhaps you've suppressed something. Or… and I don't know how, but maybe someone altered your memory."

He walked to the couch, sat so he was facing Rowena, and took her hands in his once more. Taking her hands wasn't needed for magic or memory transfer. He just needed her touch. In less than a day she had become a touchstone for him. "I don't know how it would be possible to have altered my memory, but if I suppressed something, it was probably the part where I watched Julia die."

"Maybe, but I think there's more." She squeezed his hands and leaned forward, kissing him softly on the lips. Dropping her hands, he did his own leaning and deepened the kiss. When she pulled back, she grinned at him. "I thought you needed a distraction for a moment."

"Oh, did I? Maybe I need another one." He reached over

and pulled her onto his lap like he'd done that morning. It just might become his favorite position. Connor snaked one of his hands under the weight of her long curls and gently grasped the back of her neck, pulling her toward him. They kissed for a long time, as he let any thought that wasn't of Rowena fall away.

When they finally broke apart, she rested her forehead on his and spoke softly. "I really like distracting you."

He chuckled. "I like you distracting me too."

She pushed off from his chest and stood up. "Now, I think we need to figure out what's wrong with your memory."

"Maybe nothing's wrong with it."

With her hands on her hips and the afternoon sun streaming in behind her, she looked like a goddess. He wished for a moment that she could be his goddess. Except what goddess would want someone whose carelessness had led to a small child's death?

He stood and shook off the thoughts. It was a habit he'd had a lot of practice with over the years. "What do you have in mind?"

"I think we should go back to the house where it happened and see if being there will help jar any memories."

Connor hadn't been back since the accident. A lot could happen to an area in a couple of decades, and it might not be what they needed to do, but it couldn't hurt. Except for the nightmares it might bring back, but he wasn't going to tell Rowena that. "Uncle Ben bought the property years ago, and it's now just an open field for wildlife.

"Can you tell me how to flash there?"

"Sure. I can give you a memory that should guide you. I'll just let Doyle out for a short run around and then we can go."

"Great. While you do that, I'll just pop to the little girl's room." She grinned at him. "You'd think with everything we can do with magic that we could solve this little biological problem."

He barked out a laugh and watched her walk down the hallway.

When they were ready to go, he gave her a memory and they both flashed to the field. There was nothing left of the burned house, only wildflowers growing in masses where it had once been. As he looked at the different colors of flowers, he vaguely remembered his aunt Stella saying something about planting colorful wildflowers for Julia.

Rowena turned around in the field, her arms out and her skirt flowing in the wind as she spun. "It's beautiful here."

She looked so young and carefree. In reality, she was less than ten years younger than him, but he felt ancient in comparison to the goddess in front of him.

He walked over to her and she stopped spinning. She grasped his shoulders to steady herself and he pulled her into his arms and kissed her. He just couldn't seem to get enough of her, and she kissed him back. No games, no pretense.

They were both breathing hard when they finally pulled away. He wanted more with her, but not here. Not with the memories that clung to the place.

He looked down at her. "Should we try again?"

"Connor. It's been a long time."

Connor spun around, pushing Rowena behind him as he faced Drew for the first time in decades.

11

Rowena moved to Connor's side so she could see the man walking toward them. She hadn't seen Drew in months, not since he took off after it was discovered he was the mole in the FBI's magic task force. He still looked the same, except for his eyes. They had a piercing glare and there was just something about him that wasn't open, like he was hiding something malicious inside. Her job had taught her to read people, and the vibes she was getting off Drew were sinister.

Connor put his hand on her arm. To make sure she stayed close to him or because he needed her touch, she didn't know, but she suspected the latter. Drew stopped about twenty feet away from them. "How'd you know we'd be here, Drew?" Connor called out.

Drew's lips turned up in a semblance of what should have been a smile, but it was too sly to be sincere. "I had someone put a spell on this place years ago. It alerted me as soon as your feet touched down. There's only one reason why you came back here."

She felt Connor's hand tense on her arm. "Oh yeah. And what is that?"

"Come on, Connor, it's obvious. You want to relive the memories of that day." Drew tilted his head to the side as if he was trying to look around Connor. "Hey, Rowena. It's been a while. You're looking lovely."

A shiver ran down her back at Drew's comment. His creepiness factor had just grown. Responding to him would only egg him on, so she stayed quiet as she tried to get a better read on him.

"Soooo, I heard that Morgana finally realized she was Molly Williams." Drew puffed out his chest, like he thought he was something special. "Not the smartest one, that girl. Took her long enough to remember. Meredith may have her sister back, but you don't get your brothers, do you, Rowena? Poor little Taren. He was pathetic. Always whining and crying. His death was a blessing. Finally shut him up."

Connor moved his hand down her arm and gripped her hand, giving it a light squeeze. Rowena knew Drew was just goading her, but it was working. Taren was never pathetic, but the fact that Drew saw her brother die, or worse—he was responsible for Taren's death—made the ever-present ache of losing him grow.

Connor shoved his free hand in the front pocket of his jeans and relaxed his stance, as if he was bored, but the grip he had on Rowena's hand said otherwise. "Cut the bullshit, Drew. What do you want?"

"I wanted to talk to you. See if you remembered anything from that day. Didn't expect to see Rowena here, though. Heard she had an accident last night."

Rowena glared at Drew. "Really? And how did you hear about that? From the guy you sent to kill me?"

Drew shrugged again, and Rowena wanted to slap the guy up the side of his head to get rid of his attitude. She didn't condone violence and it would do no good, but she was so angry at Drew, she figured that if she was a cartoon character, she'd have steam coming out of the top of her head. Drew clearly didn't care about the people who'd died. She wouldn't be surprised if he was a sociopath.

"Yes, I sent Eddie to do a little damage. He said your car went over the cliff, and yet you look fine to me. I'll have to have a talk with him."

Rowena had heard the name Eddie before. He was the one who hurt Jo and Simon. She stepped further from Connor, so she was facing Drew head on. "What have I ever done to you?"

"Nothing yet. But I was told you might be a problem in the future, so I was trying to be proactive and eliminate it. Maybe I was a bit hasty in thinking you were only a small problem. After all, you managed to get Connor here and no one else has done that in more than twenty years."

"What are you up to?" Connor asked.

Drew gave a sly smile. "Oh no. My nickname might be Bullseye, which I heard you know, but I'm not a stupid TV anti-hero who'd stand here and monologue all my sinister plans."

"You seem pretty stupid approaching us right now," Connor taunted. "Considering you just admitted you put a spell on private property. I'm sure the new council would like to hear about that."

Drew laughed and bent forward, slapping his hands on his thighs. "Really? You think that will stop me? Fuck, Connor, you're more stupid and gullible than when we were teenagers. And to think that I was jealous of you." Drew waved his hand up and down in front of Connor. "And look at you now—a pathetic hermit hiding away in the middle of fucking nowhere because you're too afraid to face the past."

Connor's hand stiffened in Rowena's before it relaxed.

"You always were a blowhard, Drew. Get to the fucking point."

"Well, I guess I can tell you my plans since you won't remember them."

Rowena didn't understand, but it didn't sound good. Drew had already killed someone for what he wanted and had tried to kill her. She didn't want to wait around for him to make it a trifecta.

"What do you mean?" Connor asked

"Just like I said. You're not going to remember this. I can get you to do whatever I want. Like how I'm going to get you to help me find the magic box."

Connor squeezed Rowena's hand and she knew he was planning something.

Two hundred yards north. Flash now.

Connor's words telepathically landed in her mind. He must have been thinking the same thing. She didn't waste any time and flashed.

As soon as Connor's feet touched down on the forest's undergrowth, he looked for Rowena. She was about twenty feet ahead of him. He flashed to her. "You okay?"

"I'm good. How did—watch out!"

Connor spun around, his hands up, ready to fight. Magically or physically, it didn't matter.

Drew threw his head back and laughed. "Oh, I love a good chase."

Four hundred yards northeast.

Connor threw the thought into Rowena's head and saw her flash from the corner of his eye. He faced Drew. "I'll ask one last time. What the fuck do you want?"

Drew tsked. "Wow, Connor, a bit touchy today? I want you to help me find something. I thought I didn't need Rowena, but since she was able to evade Eddie, maybe she's a bit more powerful than I thought. She'll come in handy and—"

Connor didn't wait for Drew to finish because Drew could go on forever. He'd been like that when they were kids and Connor hoped it would give him the advantage. He flashed one mile to the west and his feet barely touched down when he flashed four hundred yards to the north. Not waiting, he flashed again one mile to the east.

Not many people could follow a flash signal, but Drew had been able to follow the first, so Connor wasn't taking any chances. This time when he landed, he counted to ten to see if Drew had followed him. When Drew didn't appear, Connor flashed two hundred yards to the east.

Rowena had flashed northeast from their original location, so he hoped he was in her general vicinity. *Rowena?* He tried throwing the thought into her mind. If she was further than a hundred yards or so away, she wouldn't receive it.

I can see you.

Connor let out a breath of relief when he heard her. Turning in a slow circle, he looked around the meadow. He'd known there was a large clearing and had directed her here so she wouldn't flash into a tree. Doing so wasn't usually life threatening, but it wasn't fun either. He knew that from another dumb experience in his youth.

The sun had started to set and it was getting difficult to see. Pushing some magic to his sight to enhance his vision, he took another slow look around the field. He caught sight of her where the grass met a grove of trees. She walked toward him and he almost swallowed his tongue. Her long flowing skirt was gone and in its place were dark leather pants and a green camouflage-print long-sleeved shirt.

He couldn't hold back his smile. "Nice outfit change. Sexy."

"I know, right?" She looked down at her pants and then smiled at him. "My skirt got caught on some bushes after the second flash and I thought this would protect me more and maybe not stand out so much."

"Whatever you wear, you're sexy and beautiful."

She walked right into his arms and he held her like she was the most precious thing in the world. In the last twenty-four hours, she had started to feel like she was. Maybe it was just that she'd come at a time when the loneliness was catching up with him but it felt like more than that.

"I was worried when you didn't show up right after me."

"I needed to make sure we lost Drew, so I gave myself a bit of a detour. Speaking of which, we should get out of here." He let her go and pushed another memory into her mind. "This is Joel's cabin. It's only ten miles from here. Joel built it a few years after Julia died, and although Drew was still around, we were no longer speaking, so he shouldn't know it exists. Can you get there?"

"Yes. Meet you there."

She was gone a second later, and he followed right behind her.

He made it to the two-story log cabin at the same time as Rowena and he took her hand as they walked up the steps.

Joel had spelled the door instead of locking it, using a homemade spell that only family knew about. Connor unspelled the door and magically scanned the interior just as a precaution. He wasn't taking any more chances today. "It's clear; I don't sense anyone." He held the door open for Rowena. "You go in and I'll go around the back to get the generator working. Be right back."

Connor flashed to the back of the cabin and made quick work of starting the generator before flashing inside.

Rowena was sitting on the couch with her head thrown back on the cushions and her eyes closed. He sat beside her and wrapped an arm around her shoulders, pulling her into him. It was hard to believe that she'd only come to his house yesterday. He felt more comfortable with her than some women he'd dated for months. The other women were magic too, so it couldn't be that. Perhaps it was Rowena's professional skills that made her see him for who he really was. Made him comfortable enough that he didn't hide from her. Whatever the difference, she just felt right. He ran his free hand down her hair. "You okay, sexy?"

She laughed. "Yes, it's just been one hell of a day."

"It has." He felt drained from the last couple of hours and he wasn't the one who'd been in a car accident the night before. "I'm sorry for everything you've been through. Jack said I was supposed to make you rest." He sighed. "I guess I failed on that front."

She turned into him and lifted her chin and gave him a kiss before she cuddled back into his chest. "That's okay. In the last year and a half, I've learned to go with the flow."

The cabin was chilly, but Connor didn't want to let Rowena out of his arms. He waved his hand toward the fireplace, where the kindling and wood were ready to light. A spark caught the paper stuffed in the kindling, and within a few minutes, a fire was warming the room.

"Do you know what Drew wanted?" Rowena asked quietly from against his chest.

"Before I flashed the second time, Drew said that he wanted me to help him find something. I flashed before he could say anything else, but I wonder if he was talking about the other magic specialty that Taren mentioned."

"That would make sense, but how do we figure out what it is?"

"Taren said he would come back tomorrow; maybe he'll

know." Connor couldn't imagine how he'd have another skill without knowing about it, but then, he hadn't known the full extent of the first one. Maybe if they combined their magic again, they'd figure it out.

They sat quietly for a while and then his stomach growled, the sound loud with the only other sound the crackling of the fire. He smirked. "I guess we should eat something."

Rowena pulled away from him and sat up, rubbing her hands together. "I'm a master at conjuring a charcuterie board." She put her hands out and stopped, glancing at him over her shoulder. "Unless you need something more substantial."

"As long as it's got some meat and bread, I'll be good. But while you do that, I'm going to flash home and let Doyle out and feed him."

"Sounds good."

When Connor flashed back a few minutes later, a conjured feast waited for them on the low table. A large board held pieces of meats, cheeses, fruits, vegetables, olives, crackers, nuts, and chocolate. Beside it, a bottle of wine stood with two glasses. Rowena looked back at him again. "Wine good?"

"Perfect. You weren't kidding about being a charcuterie master. I think there's enough food here for four people." He conjured two plates and handed one to her.

They piled their plates high and sat back on the couch, each leaning against an arm, facing each other. It seemed to have become their go-to position.

They ate in silence for several minutes. It wasn't the type of food he'd normally eat for dinner, but it was tasty and hit the spot.

When Connor finished what was on his plate, he piled it

up again. Rowena put her plate down and picked up her wine glass, settling back into the cushions again. "Do you remember the first thing you conjured?"

He looked up from his plate. "Like, when I was a kid?"

She nodded and took another sip of her wine.

Magic was such an integral part of him that he couldn't remember never being able to perform it. "I can't remember, but maybe my dad would...but I do remember trying to conjure beer. Drew—" So many memories of his teen years were tied to his former best friend.

"Were you going to talk about a memory with Drew?"

"Yes. I met him when I was about twelve and we were inseparable for a few years."

"Tell me the memory anyway. It doesn't matter who it was with; the important part is that it's yours."

The corner of his mouth ticked up in a smile as he remembered the trouble they'd gotten into. "I think I was about thirteen and thought I was so cool. My dad was at work, so we went to the backyard and sat underneath our second floor deck. It was out of sight, so I thought no one would catch us."

Rowena's eyes twinkled as she laughed. "You got caught, I take it?"

"Oh did we. But not before we threw up. The beer we conjured tasted like horse piss—not that I've ever had horse piss, but I can imagine. Since we'd never had beer before, we couldn't imagine it well enough to conjure it. But, being boys, neither one of us wanted to admit to the other that it was horrible. So we each drank three full bottles."

"Were you drunk?"

He snorted a laugh. "I don't know. I was so sick puking my guts out that I couldn't tell. That's when my dad showed up. He had a meeting canceled and came home early. When he couldn't find me he came outside and heard us retching. What about you? What was the first thing you remember conjuring?

"I was spellbound when I was young, so I don't remember if I'd been able to conjure anything then." She gave him a sly smile. "But when the spell was broken, the first thing I learned to conjure was a tissue."

"That's not very exciting," he teased.

"No, but the second and third things were chocolate and alcohol. I think conjuring alcohol must be a rite of passage for magics coming into their powers since you conjured beer."

He slapped his leg and laughed. "It must be. Now it's my turn to ask…did you get drunk?"

"I was with my cousins Meredith and Jo, and wow, did we ever. Luckily, we Jack, Damon—you remember him?"

When Connor nodded, she continued. "Anyway, Jack, Damon, and Javier flushed our systems when we passed out so there were no hangovers."

They shared more stories until they'd made a huge dent in the food and the wine was gone. At some point, Rowena had curled up against him as they talked. He couldn't remember the last time he'd enjoyed himself so much.

He watched the fire, it was almost out now, and waited for Rowena to respond to his latest question. When she didn't, he tilted his head and saw that she was asleep. It'd been a long day for her and she was likely still feeling the effects from the accident.

Easing away from her, he repositioned himself on the couch so he could stretch out and nestled her length alongside him. He waved one hand toward the fireplace and floated three logs from the stack beside the hearth onto the glowing embers, then conjured a blanket. He pulled it over them both and pulled her tighter into his embrace.

Tomorrow he'd have to think about Drew and the past and eventually Rowena would walk away when he endangered someone else, especially since she'd already been hurt because of him. But right now, he would enjoy holding Rowena while they slept.

12

The first thing Rowena felt was warmth, and the second was a hard body pressed up against her back. She opened her eyes and looked at the fireplace in front of her, the fire burned only to ashes, then her eyes traveled down to the muscular arm draped over her middle.

The events of the last two days came back to her in a rush. She rolled over in the tight confines of the couch and looked up at Connor as he leaned over her. His eyes opened and the corner of his mouth hitched up in a lopsided smile.

That was a first for her. She'd had boyfriends before, but her relationships had always been a really slow burn. Never the chemistry she felt with Connor and never had she slept with a man after only knowing him for two days. Well… she hadn't had sex with anyone so soon, but then, she and Connor had really only slept together, not *slept* together. Normally she wasn't a risk taker, wanting to make sure she considered how any action she took would affect others. But Connor made her want to jump first and just hang on to see what was possible.

She pulled on her magic and used it to freshen her breath before she spoke. "Good morning."

"Yes, it is a good morning." Connor braced himself on an elbow and lowered his head. His breath was minty fresh too as it meshed with hers. The kiss was slow and sensual, like a morning kiss should be.

When they broke off, she smiled up at him. "I guess we should get going."

"We should, but we're not in a rush. It's still early. Doyle will be fine for a little while longer, and Drew doesn't know where we are right now."

She reached up and cupped her hand behind his neck, pulling him to her. His weight settled deliciously on hers and they kissed again, exploring each other's mouths and letting their hands wander.

After a few minutes, they both stopped as if by some unspoken agreement. Connor pushed some bedhead curls behind her ear. "You ready to get up, sexy?"

She laughed. "I'm not going to live that name down, am I?"

"You don't need to. You *are* sexy." He kissed her again. It was a while longer before he repeated his question. "So… ready to get up?"

"Ready? No. But we should."

They took turns using the bathroom and then sat at the small kitchen table and conjured some breakfast. Eating breakfast with Connor yesterday had been an anomaly, but such a domestic scene two days in a row caught her off guard. It had been a long time since she'd been this comfortable with a man, and she hadn't dated anyone since the unbinding spell more than a year ago. Finding out she was magic had more implications than just learning she didn't know about magic. She now had a secret to keep from non-magics. Dating in the future would mean being with her own kind. Not only because of the secrecy to protect all magics, but because she'd learned that most magics were not attracted to non-magics. It was a neat little nuance from Mother Nature, or so she'd been told. And she was seeing it was true—not just with herself, but with her cousins matching up with magics as well.

Rowena conjured more coffee and refilled her mug and Connor's. "What do we do now? We can't continue to hide out."

"Thanks." Connor took a sip of his coffee. "Since Drew sent someone after you the other night, I'm guessing he knows where I live and was somehow able to track you. He wants us to find something for him. But I don't know if he'll come after us again so soon or not. He wasn't patient as a teenager, and I'm sure he hasn't changed."

"But you're sure he'll attack us again?"

"Yes. I don't know when, but he will. We're going to have to be careful."

Rowena finished her coffee and used her magic to clean the mug. "I should head home today. I really need to contact my patients."

"I've got to get home too and check on Doyle, but I don't know if we'll be safe at either of our houses. Drew knows where they both are."

"I won't be long, and I'll make sure I'm always in a position to flash away." She sensed he wanted to protest, but instead he finished his coffee. Reaching out, she placed her hand on his. "I'll be careful. And you need to be too. After yesterday, I think Drew is more concerned with you than me." She wasn't sure how deep her feelings were tangled up with Connor yet, but she already knew that losing one more person would gut her.

CONNOR HADN'T MADE a single step after touching down in the foyer of his house before he was almost bowled over by Doyle. He gave Doyle some attention, got him some food, and then grabbed his leash.

He took Doyle for about a thirty-minute walk around the lake, before throwing Doyle's favorite stick back and forth for a little while. He had just gotten into the house when he heard a knock on the front door. Unleashing Doyle, he let him go, watching him climb onto this favorite spot on the couch, and turned toward the door.

Connor sent some magic to the front of the house to get a sense of who was out there. He couldn't identify the person per se, but he could only sense one person and there wasn't malevolence pouring off them. Which meant it wasn't Drew.

When he opened the door, Javier was standing there with a frown on his face. "Where's Rowena?"

"She's not here. Have you checked her apartment?" Connor knew Javier cared about Rowena, but he was getting fucking sick of the guy's attitude and didn't feel like being nice today. "What do you need?"

"I just wanted to check on her. She's been acting a bit strange lately. Then, out of the blue, she has to visit you, even though she's never mentioned you before. Next thing I know, she's in a mysterious car accident and it was right after she came here." Javier squinted at Connor. "Everything seems to revolve around you." It was an accusation if Connor had ever heard one.

Javier turned, as if searching the horizon, before facing Connor again. "Look. I'm coming across as an ass, and I don't mean to be. Jack said he could vouch for you, and I have nothing but respect for your old man. But my instincts are damn good and I know something's not right. If you're interested in Rowena, that's cool, man. She's more like a sister to me. I just want to make sure she's okay."

Connor's anger fizzled out faster than a sparkler dumped in a swimming pool. He couldn't hold anything against the guy. Connor stepped back and waved his arm into the foyer. "Wanna come in for a cup of coffee?"

Javier only hesitated for a moment. "Sure."

Connor led the way to the kitchen and got down two mugs. The corner of his lip twitched up in an almost smile as he realized he'd had more people visit his place in the last week than he usually had in six months. He wasn't sure he liked it. His writing was definitely suffering because of it, but at least he hadn't been lonely.

"Thanks," Javier said, and his coffee turned a lighter brown and swirled. "I'm a coffee fanatic but can't drink the damn stuff without milk and some sugar."

"Black myself, but I get it."

Javier took a sip of his coffee and put the mug down, his fingers playing with the handle. "Do you know what's going on with Rowena?"

"Yes. But I'm not sure it's my place to say."

"Then there is something?"

"Yes. What I can tell you is that Drew paid us a visit yesterday."

"Drew Bartley?"

Connor sighed. "That's the one."

"I take it you know he was our mole in the FBI's magic task force?"

"Yes, my dad told me. He also told me that Drew and his dad recently killed for one of the ancient magic books."

"I heard that from Ben and Jack. Why did Drew show up yesterday? That's kind of risky, considering he's a wanted man."

Connor could picture Drew standing in the open field, the place where Julia had died, and where he'd taunted them. "He admitted he was responsible for Rowena's accident the other night. Said someone named Eddie caused it, but I'm not sure exactly what happened. It sounded like he pushed her car off the road; we still don't have the details."

"Whoever helped her and texted you from her phone will know."

Connor expected Taren had helped, but he wasn't going to reveal that to Javier, no matter how close he was to Rowena. That was her story to tell. When Taren disappeared yesterday, he said he was going to show up again today, but he hadn't yet. He hoped for Rowena's sake that he did. "I'm more concerned with Drew."

Javier downed the last of his coffee, magically cleaned the mug, and pushed it toward Connor. "Thanks for the coffee," he said as he stood. "I should get back, but I'd appreciate it if you'd keep me in the loop with Rowena."

"She's a grown woman who can look after herself."

Javier's shoulders visibly dropped. "Yes, but I care about her. I don't mean for you to spy on her for me, just let me know if she needs anything I can help with."

"Will do." Connor stood and shook Javier's hand before Javier nodded and flashed.

Flopping back onto the stool, Connor picked up his coffee and finished it. Following Javier's lead, he magically cleaned the mug and put both of them away. That was an interesting conversation and not one he'd expected.

Javier didn't seem like he'd be competition for Rowena's love, and wasn't that the kicker? When did he start thinking that way? He'd only really known her a short time, and he was still of the opinion that a relationship wouldn't work out in the long run. He'd been on his own for so long and loved the seclusion, even if he was lonely. He was the complete opposite of Rowena, who had an entire family with apartments all in the same building. They were tightknit and he was a loner.

Just the thought of living back in the city and surrounded by so many people made him want to shiver.

Connor went to his bedroom and packed a small bag before heading to his office and packing up his computer. He needed to get in a bit of work over the next couple of days while they looked into the past or he'd get behind on his deadlines. "Doyle. Car."

Doyle was at the door faster than his usual couch potato speed and they headed to his SUV. Anything he forgot he'd conjure, along with whatever Doyle needed.

On the drive back to Joel's cabin, where he and Rowena had agreed to meet after they'd gone to their respective homes, his mind floated over the events of the past two days. He was falling for Rowena, and it didn't matter how long it'd been; it'd been easy. Letting her go would be the tough part. And he would let her go; the only question was if she'd walk away first when they found out exactly what had happened the day Julia died.

$\mathcal{L}$ooking around her apartment, Rowena tried to figure out whether she'd forgotten anything. She had her laptop, a few days' worth of clothes, toiletries, and a paperback book she'd been planning to read, all placed in a backpack. It wasn't too much that she couldn't flash with it easily enough.

You going back to Connor's?

Rowena looked around the room, expecting to see Taren before reality crashed in. If only she and Connor could find a way for her to see Taren on her own. "Where are you sitting?"

The kitchen stool on the right.

She turned and smiled in her brother's direction. "I thought you were going to come back to talk to me and Connor today."

I didn't want to join you if you and Connor were kissing. Yuck, mind bleach.

She chuckled at the statement that was so like something Taren would have said when he was younger. "Couldn't you just talk to me first or something before you showed up?"

I'm not sure, but I can try. So...are you going back?

"Yes, but to his uncle's cabin, not to Connor's house. I just needed to grab a few things first. Are—wait… do you know where we'll be?"

Wherever you are, I can get to. See you later.

Taren was so different from how she remembered him, but of course he would be. She flopped on the same stool Taren had used and closed her eyes, rubbing them with her fists. Her little brother was really dead. She'd known it for years, but hearing him, and now seeing him, was surreal. Somehow, she knew he would disappear again. She just didn't know if she could stand to lose him twice. She didn't know how she knew, but she did. Taren hadn't been around for however long it had been since he'd really died, so this was probably just a blip in time, and soon he'd leave her again.

She was the only one left of her immediate family and that wasn't going to change.

You home?

Meredith's voice penetrated Rowena's mind. It was so different from how Taren spoke to her. Someone communicating with her telepathically almost sounded like she was hearing the person calling from another room. Taren felt like he was in her head. *Yes.* She threw the thought back to her cousin and turned toward the living room since that's where Meredith usually landed.

Meredith appeared as expected in the living room and stalked toward her.

"Where have you been?"

"Hello to you too."

"Ro, skip the pleasantries." Meredith pulled her in for a hug and held on tight for a moment before they both let go. "I've been worried sick about you. Jack said you were in a car accident and he had to heal you. Why were you at Connor Davis's?"

Rowena tapped her phone that was still on the kitchen island—three in the afternoon—was it too soon for wine? Screw it. It was five o'clock somewhere, as the saying went. "Pull up a stool, let's have a glass of wine. I can con—wait. I've never tried flashing after I've had wine. Can you flash drunk?"

Meredith sat and grinned at her. "Really drunk? Probably not, but I have had a couple of glasses and flashed. I missed landing in our foyer and ended up in the living room, but close enough."

Rowena conjured two glasses of wine and passed one to her cousin.

"Ro, why are we drinking wine? Not that I'm complaining… but what's going on?"

Rowena took a sip of her wine and remembered when she'd conjured a glass a couple of weeks ago, right before she heard Taren's voice for the first time in years. She played with the stem of her glass and looked at Meredith. "The night Morgana's spell broke, Taren spoke to me."

"What the—Taren? He's alive, like Morgana?"

"No." Rowena took a sip of her wine for courage and filled Meredith in on everything—talking to Taren, going to Connor's, the car accident, running into Drew, and going to Connor's uncle's cabin. It sank home how much had happened in a short period of time. The only thing she'd left out were Connor's kisses.

By the time Rowena finished, they were each on their second glass of wine, and she felt good for getting the story out, but drained too.

"Oh my god! I can't believe you've been through all that in the last couple of days. And talking to Taren—wait, are

Mirek and Dylan alive? When Morgana's spell broke, you said you were sure Taren and Mirek were dead."

Rowena let out a long sigh. "Yes, because I just had the feeling that whatever I had heard in my head meant they were dead. I was right about Taren, but he thinks Mirek is alive, yet he hasn't said anything else. I'm hoping he'll tell us more when we talk to him tonight."

"Do you want me and Jack to be with you when you help Connor remember his past?"

"Thanks for the offer, but I think that might be a bit too much for Connor... and maybe for me too. I'll let you know if we need anything."

Meredith disappeared her wine glass and stood, pulling Rowena into a hug at the same time. She loved that her family was physically affectionate.

After Meredith left, Rowena disappeared her own wine glass and picked up her phone, putting it in the outside pocket of her backpack.

"Knock knock."

Rowena flipped around to see Javier walking into her apartment.

He looked around. "You alone?"

"Yes. Meredith just left. It seems to be Grand Central Station in my apartment today."

Javier narrowed his eyes at her. "Who else was here?"

Rowena waved her hand in dismissal. She didn't have the energy to explain the situation with Taren to another person at the moment. "What are you doing here? ... Not that I don't like seeing you—I mean, I'm just surprised."

Javier leaned against the kitchen island. "I just wanted to see how you were. You almost died the other night, Rowena."

"I know, but I'm fine now. I'm going to work with Connor for a bit so I just stopped home to get a few things, like my laptop."

"I think I may have been wrong about Connor. I talked to him and he seemed okay."

Rowena felt her eyebrows ascend into the curls laying across her forehead. "You spoke to Connor? When?"

A sheepish look crossed Javier's face before it quickly disappeared. "I stopped by his house again to see you because I didn't feel good how we left things yesterday and you weren't answering your phone."

Rowena stepped forward and gave Javier a hug. He'd become such an amazing friend in the last year, and she had been brushing him off recently. "I'm sorry. I should have known you'd be worried and called you. There's just been a lot going on lately that it slipped my mind."

"Connor told me about Drew showing up." Javier pushed a lock of curls off her face. "Just be careful, okay?"

"I will. So what have you been up to, except for worrying about me?"

He rolled his eyes and grinned. "I've been following up on some old cases with Jack."

They chatted for several minutes, and then Javier left after pulling a promise from her to call him if anything else strange happened.

Rowena flung her pack on her back, checking that her phone was still in the outside pocket. Taking one last look around, she called on her magic to flash just as her phone rang. She'd gotten a lot of interruptions, but at least this time it was just a phone call. She pulled her phone out and checked the display. It wasn't a number she recognized, but that happened often in her practice.

"Hello?"

"Ah, is this Dr. Williams?"

Most of Rowena's patients called her by her first name, as she wanted them to be comfortable with her and not to stand on formality. But she'd had a lot of new patients come to her through word of mouth since she'd changed the direction of her practice. She smiled to get it to come across in her voice as she answered. "This is she."

"I'm Shannon Reynolds. My brother, Tony, is a patient of yours."

"Yes." Tony was doing really well. She'd seen him the morning she went to Connor's. He'd been really positive about the future.

"Tony…ah…Tony committed suicide yesterday."

Rowena sank onto the kitchen island stool. "Losing a brother is one of the saddest things that can happen. I am so sorry for your loss."

"Thank you. My mom wanted to call, but she just—" Shannon's voice cracked and she didn't finish.

"I understand. Thank you for letting me know."

They said their goodbyes and Rowena continued to sit on the stool, her pack still on her back. She didn't know how long she sat there, going over her last conversation with Tony. He'd looked right into her laptop's camera when he said goodbye, telling her he was excited about the future. She was so sure he'd been making headway, and he had his whole life ahead of him. Making a mental note, she promised herself that as soon as she had time, she'd check her notes to see if there were any signs she'd missed and anything else she could have done.

Losing her own family was the reason she'd become a psychologist, but it was people like Tony she wanted to help so she could make a difference in the world. Every life she helped, it felt like she'd earned a bit more of hers.

She finally dragged herself off the stool and called on her magic to flash to Joel's cabin. She hadn't been able to save Tony, but she'd do whatever it took to help Connor see what she saw in him.

14

Connor paced the cabin's main room and glanced at his watch for what felt like the thousandth time. He'd give Rowena ten more minutes before he went looking for her.

He'd driven back to the cabin so he could bring Doyle with him, and they'd gone for a long walk. Then he'd gotten in a couple of hours of writing, Rowena still hadn't returned. He glanced at his watch again—screw the last two minutes. He was going to look for her. She'd flashed so he didn't have to worry about a car accident, but what if something else had happened? What if she'd already decided that he was too much work?

Giving himself an internal head shake, he flopped onto the couch beside Doyle's massive, sprawled form. Rowena would come back; he just had to give her time. Leaning his head back on the cushions, he closed his eyes, attempting to relax.

He felt a small shift in energy he normally wouldn't have if he hadn't been waiting for it and opened his eyes as

Rowena appeared. Springing to his feet, he looked her over for any signs of injury. "Are you alright?"

She huffed out a breath and set her backpack on the floor at her feet. "I'm fine. Just a long day."

"On top of two long days before that." Connor reached down and picked up her backpack, putting it on the coffee table. He enfolded her into his arms and felt all the restlessness and worry from the afternoon drain out of him. He kissed her softly and then guided her to the couch. What he really wanted to do was take her to the bedroom, strip her down, and make love to her, all while reassuring himself that she was fine.

The overwhelming protective urges were new. Maybe they both needed some rest and something to eat. He was likely just reacting to the adrenaline rushes of the past several days. "Why don't you relax and I'll make us some dinner?" he asked while guiding her backward to the couch.

"Thank you." She mimicked his position of several minutes ago—her head tossed back on the couch and her eyes closed. Doyle put his head in her lap and she absently petted him.

Connor conjured a simple dinner of pasta and they talked about random things while they ate. After a while he wanted more and broached the subject. "We've talked a lot about our likes for movies, books, and favorite foods, but what about something deeper?"

She tilted her head and smiled as if doubting him. "Like?"

"You don't want to ask the first question?" He laughed and then held up his hand when she gave him a mock glare. "Okay, fine. What achievement in life have you worked the hardest for?"

"That's easy. My job that makes it possible to help others. What about you?"

"My writing. I love writing mysteries and when I get an email from someone that says they liked my book, it makes all the hours of staring at a blank page worth it. Now, your turn to ask." He took a sip of his wine as he wondered what she would ask. He wanted to know what made her tick and thought the questions she would ask might give a clue into that.

"Hmmm, okay, what are you most passionate about?"

He grinned. "My writing. You?"

She laughed. "That's easy again. Helping others." She gestured toward him. "Back to you."

Her answers weren't quite what he'd been looking for, but he loved seeing her passion. "What do you spend a lot of time thinking about?"

"Wait for it…" She grinned again. "Helping others." She paused and her smile faded. "And lately, my family members who are no longer with me. What do you think about?"

"I was going to say mysteries." He lifted his glass in a mock toast, and then, like her, he let the grin drop from his face. "Since you've been here, I've been thinking a lot about the past."

"Did you figure anything out?"

Good question and no easy answer. "I know I need to figure out if something else happened the day Julia died, but I'm not sure I want to know."

Rowena swirled the wine in her glass, and all he could see was the caring look in her eyes when she looked at him. "It's your choice, Connor. No one can force you to look into the past. It doesn't matter what Taren or the seer said. But…" She paused and put her wine glass down. "I know it's not always easy to delve into past trauma, but sometimes it's worse when we don't. Not facing something allows it to seem like a much bigger obstacle than it actually is. I've had patients almost paralyzed with fear of past events, but when they've worked through them, they've been able to come to accept the past and move on."

"Accepting the past won't bring Julia back."

"No, but it could help you."

She was right but fear already had a firm grip on him for years. "What if we find out it wasn't even an accident? That I did something deliberate that got Julia killed?" When he started asking Rowena questions, this was not where he'd thought the conversation would go. He wanted to get to know her, not dig into his past mistakes.

"And what if you didn't?"

"I don't know." He waved his hands over the empty dinner dishes and used his magic to clean and put them away before standing and extending his hand to Rowena. "Can we lighten up the conversation for the rest of the evening?"

She took his hand and walked into his arms. "Sure," she said and went up on her toes and kissed him. Before she pulled away, he licked at her mouth and she opened to him. She tasted of wine and something that was uniquely Rowena, a taste he'd come to crave in the last couple of days. One he thought he might want for the rest of his life. He just didn't know if she would want him after tomorrow, and he knew he couldn't make love with her and then have her reject him. It could be enough to break him.

Slowly, he broke the kiss. "How about a movie? Uncle Joel has a DVD player and a bunch of movies."

"Okay." At the sight of her licking her lips, he knew if he didn't switch course soon, he'd forget all about his resolve to wait to make love with her. Taking her hand, he tugged her toward the TV to root through the DVDs. They picked an old comedy and when they settled onto the couch together, he put his arm around her, pulling her into his side. Doyle curled up on Rowena's other side and put his head in her lap.

Connor was jealous of his own dog but was determined to stick to his plan.

About a third of the way through the movie, Rowena conjured a bowl of popcorn, and he was glad she had. Eating popcorn occupied his hands; otherwise he worried they'd be all over her. The movie had become a mindless drone of noise as he couldn't focus on anything but Rowena. The feel of her breast pressed against his side and the smell of her shampoo where her hair lay on his shoulder consumed his thoughts.

She moved her hand over his chest and undid the button of his Henley and slid her hand inside the shirt's opening. When her fingers played with his nipple, he thought he was going to combust with how much he wanted her. Putting his hands over hers, he halted her movements.

"Connor?"

He looked down at her as she gazed up at him, the movie forgotten. "Hmm?"

"What's wrong?"

Playing dumb wasn't his usual MO but he worried about coming right out and telling her how afraid he was that she'd later reject him. "What do you mean?" When she pulled back so she could see him fully, he wanted to reach out and bring her hand back to his chest.

"You've been hot and cold. Do you not want this? It's okay if you've changed your mind and you're not interested in me anymore. I hope that's not how you feel, but it's alright if you do."

Hearing the hurt in her voice was worse than protecting his own heart. He pulled her back into him, wrapping his arms around her and burying his face in the crook of her neck. The position allowed him to soak in her feel and scent. "I want you, Rowena. I'm just worried about what we'll discover tomorrow when we look at that day."

She ran her fingers through his hair and once more he became envious of Doyle for having this feeling all the time. "Okay, we'll wait," she whispered against him.

"Please don't doubt that I want you, sexy," he whispered back. He shifted, laying them down on the couch like they'd been the night before, and pulled a blanket over them both. The feeling of her in his arms was one he was coming to crave and he hoped that this wouldn't be the last time he'd have it.

CONNOR WALKED to the couch and sat down. Like his living room at home, this couch now held special feelings for him. They'd spent two nights on the couch with Rowena wrapped in his arms and now he could possibly tarnish the couch memories by looking into the day he'd spent half his life trying to forget. "Are you both ready?" He looked between Rowena and his uncle Joel.

Joel nodded from where he sat on a chair near one of the couches. "I'm good. Rowena?"

They had pushed the coffee table out of the way and Rowena's chair was closer, facing the couch. "I'm good. Now, before we begin, I want to make sure you're still alright with this. Even though the testing I did said you're susceptible to hypnotherapy, that doesn't mean you have to do it."

"I need to. I have to find out why the memory I've held for all these years doesn't seem right now." He knew it could reveal things that were even worse than what he thought he remembered, but he had to know. Maybe it was the mystery writer in him, always making his characters unearth the truth. Or maybe it was time to face the past and let it go, like his uncle had said. But finding out the truth wasn't his biggest fear. It was what Rowena would think of him when everything was revealed. If she was repulsed by what he'd done, he'd have to accept that and know she would walk away.

Rowena leaned forward and laid her hand on his arm. "I'm just concerned because this is such an about face from the other day, even though you agreed last night. Until then you were adamant that you didn't want to talk about the past."

Connor looked at his uncle, who gave him a nod, before turning back to Rowena. "I know, but it's time. We have to figure out what Drew is up to. And that reminds me—have you spoken with Taren this morning?"

"I'm here."

All three of them swiveled to face the fireplace hearth. Taren was perched on it with his back against the bricks. Doyle lay sprawled at his feet, not appearing concerned at all that a ghost was next to him.

"Taren!" Rowena's smile was so wide, Connor could see it even though she wasn't fully facing him. "We can see you and hear you! How is that possible?"

"I'm not sure. I think it might be the connection between you and Connor."

"So if I..." Rowena lifted her hand off Connor's arm, but Taren didn't fade. "We can still see you."

Connor reached for Rowena's hand, wanting the physical connection with her. She gave him a smile before looking back at her brother.

"Perhaps it's not only a physical connection that will work—an emotional one will too. Taren, I don't know if you remember me, but I'm Joel, Connor's uncle. Rowena and Connor thought it would be good to have someone else here when they talked about the day Julia died. I can help transfer a visual of the memory to Rowena if needed and be a third set of eyes and ears. Are you okay to be here when they talk about the fire?"

Leave it to Joel to be sensitive and thoughtful about Taren having been in a fire.

Taren shrugged but didn't smile. "I'm okay. I didn't die from a fire."

"Okay. Just know you can leave at any time." Joel turned back to Connor. "You ready?"

Connor nodded at his uncle before turning to Rowena. "Ready?" Connor gently squeezed Rowena's hand that he hadn't let go of. "We need this. I'll be okay."

Rowena eased her hand out of Connor's. "I need both hands to take notes, but I'll be right here."

Connor leaned back on the couch, stretching his legs out in front of him to get comfortable and closed his eyes. His uncle's hand landed softly on his shoulder, for the physical connection, as they'd discussed earlier.

"Okay, Connor. We're going to start now. But remember, as I explained earlier, you are always in control. You won't reveal any information you don't want to and you will be aware of and remember everything, even when you feel like you're zoned-in or in a trance-like state."

Connor kept his eyes closed. "I'm ready."

"Good." Rowena's voice was soothing. "I want you to breathe in over a count of seven, and then breathe out over a count of eleven." Rowena talked him through the breathing and he started to relax. "Now I want you to visualize yourself walking down some stairs. Go slow. You're descending further and further into relaxation."

Connor envisioned the stairs as Rowena described and felt like he was sinking deeper into the cushions. He started the memory at the same place he had last time, skipping to the part where he and Drew were in the room with the kids.

"One more Barbie, please Connor, and some clothes." He smiled

at his cousin and conjured one more doll for Julia and another for Sarah, the daughter of one of the advisors.

He bent down and handed the dolls to the girls. "Okay, Little Pony, you sure you wouldn't rather have a chemistry set or something?" Julia was the most intelligent person he knew, and although playing with dolls was normal for a five-year-old, he couldn't remember her ever playing with one. Reading university textbooks and conducting science experiments, yes. Dolls? No.

Julia patted his knee in a motherly way. "No, Connor, dolls are more appropriate for us right now."

He bit the inside of his cheek to hold back a smile and nodded at her as solemnly as he could muster. "Right." He straightened and looked down at her as he pointed to the fireplace. "Drew and I will be just over there."

He turned around and chuckled to himself. She was definitely going to be a handful one day.

Drew elbowed Connor as he walked up. "Sooooo... you have a lot of familiarity with conjuring Barbie dolls?"

He grinned at his friend. "Fuck off."

Connor was in the memory, but Rowena was right, it wasn't like a dream. He could remember his teenage self shoving his hands in the pockets of his jeans as he watched Drew lay his arm on the low mantel of the fireplace. Next, Drew would ask him if he'd studied for the physics exam coming up.

Connor was aware of Rowena's comments and questions gently guiding him and his uncle's hand on his shoulder, but they all seemed very far away. He let himself continue with the memory.

Connor pulled his hands from his pockets and braced them on the mantel while looking down into the fireplace. "Holy shit!" He jumped back and looked at his hands.

"What happened?"

Connor took his gaze off his hands and looked at Drew. "I felt something."

Drew straightened and examined the mantel. "What? I don't see anything."

"No, not a physical thing, well... not exactly. I felt a memory, or...shit, I'm not sure. But I watched a Christmas dinner that took place here." Connor pointed to the fireplace. "Right here, with stockings hanging on the mantel and everything. It was 1947 and they were talking about the past year—the new movie Miracle on 34th Street and Jackie Robinson, the first African-American player in a major league baseball team."

Drew motioned toward the fireplace. "Do it again."

Connor reached out slowly, almost expecting the mantel to attack him. He snorted at the thought and laid his hands flat on top of the mantel. He could see the same Christmas. He watched for a moment, but wished he could see something else. And he did. The Christmases changed. He saw the different years—the topics, clothing, and hairstyles changed. There were many of the same people, but as they aged others came and went. He thought of a year and was transported to that year in the visions.

"Well? What do you see?"

Connor dropped his hands from the mantel and wiped his palms on his jeans. "I saw their Christmas dinner every year, and I could move through time and speed it up or slow it down. The only year I didn't see a Christmas dinner was 1972."

"Maybe they went somewhere else to celebrate it that year."

"Maybe." Connor stared at the fireplace, wondering if it was the fireplace that was magic and not him. He turned to Drew. "You touch it."

"I was already leaning on it and I didn't feel anything."

"Put your palms on it, like I did."

Drew faced the fireplace and placed his palms on the mantel the same way Connor had.

"Anything?" He waited and then let out a huge breath when Drew shook his head, not realizing he'd been holding it.

Drew dropped his hands and turned around. "Nothing. Touch something else."

"Like what?"

Drew looked around the room. "I don't know. Something old, I guess." He pointed to a bookcase in the far corner. "Pick an old book."

Connor's palms itched and he felt an excitement coursing through him. When he reached the bookcase, he stared at it. There were dozens of books, many of them old, but they didn't appear dusty. Someone clearly took care of them.

Tilting his head sideways, he scanned the titles and recognized The Catcher in the Rye. He'd read it in ninth grade and remembered it was written in 1951.

He grasped the spine with his thumb and fingers and tilted the book back, releasing it from its wedged position amongst the other books. A tingling started in the tips of his fingers. Grasping the book with both hands, he closed his eyes.

Images of someone signing the book appeared in his mind, then he heard a man speak. 'I hope you enjoy the book, Gerald.'

Connor's eyes flew open and he looked down. Carefully prying open the cover, he flipped to the title page. "Shit!" He whispered the word to himself when he saw the inscription made out to Gerald.

"What is it?" Drew moved closer to get a look at the book.

"I heard J.D. Salinger tell Gerald to enjoy the book."

"No way!" Drew turned toward the bookshelves. "Try again."

Connor recognized several books from the 1950's and pulled out each one... The Invisible Man from 1952, Fahrenheit 451 from 1953, and On the Road from 1957. They were all signed by the author, and each time Connor could hear the author's comments as he spoke to Gerald. Gerald would have had to travel great distances to get each of the signed copies, but then, magics could easily do that.

He knew now that the man was Mr. Gerald Mitchell and he'd built the house they were in after the Second World War in 1947, and he had four sons and a daughter. He was a magic person and a fan of popular fiction of the times. He'd been born in 1915 and died in 1995. Connor knew the year of the man's birth and death because even though Gerald had been missing from the last vision, one of his sons had read a passage from The Catcher in The Rye at Gerald's funeral. Connor recognized the Salinger quote about living humbly for a cause.

"Can you do anything else?" Drew asked when Connor shelved the last book.

"Like what?"

"I don't know... something else to do with the past."

Connor looked around the room. Only the fireplace and book-case seemed to call to him. He walked back to the fireplace and put both hands on the mantel like he'd done before. Focusing on the 1947 Christmas, he looked at each of the people around the table, then concentrated on Gerald.

"I need to know he loved me."

Connor spun around. There was no one there except for Drew, and the girls were still playing with their dolls. But Connor had heard a woman's voice as clear as day. He turned to Drew. "Did you hear that?"

Drew came up beside him. "Hear what?"

Connor ignored his friend and turned back to the fireplace, putting his hands in the same position they'd been in before.

"He was never meant to be mine," said the same voice again.

Leaving one hand on the fireplace, Connor turned around as far as he could without losing contact with the mantel. A woman stood in front of him. "Drew, do you see her?"

"See wh—" Drew turned as he spoke. "Holy shit! Is that a ghost?"

"Connor, I want you to imagine you're climbing the stairs that you first went down." Rowena's voice pulled him from

the memory. "Your breathing is too fast. Climb the stairs and breathe out slowly."

He did as Rowena asked, visualizing the stairs and breathing with her as she continued to talk to him. He came out of the hypnosis easily but knew he'd have to go back under again. The truth surrounding Julia's death had yet to be revealed.

15

*R*owena zipped her sweater up higher as they walked. The temperature had fallen once the sun went down and the night air had brought a chill, but she loved being outside. Connor held her hand and their hands swung lightly between them.

"Penny for your thoughts," he said. "Or is it a dollar now?"

"I was just enjoying being out here."

"Me, too." Connor pointed ahead of them. "And I think we're not the only ones. Doyle loves his walks."

They didn't talk as they turned around and headed back toward the cabin, but it was a comfortable silence. After the hypnotherapy session, they'd talked a bit about what they'd learned and then Joel left, saying he'd come back the next afternoon.

When they got back to the cabin, Connor wiped Doyle's feet and looked up at her from where he crouched on the floor. "What would you like for dinner?"

She tipped her head and gave him a mischievous smile. "I don't know… can you cook, or shall we conjure?"

He stood and walked over to the sink to wash his hands.

"Oh, it's like that is it?" he teased. "I'll have you know that I'm a really good cook."

"I know you can cook a mean egg. What else can you make?"

"Mean must be my specialty because I can make a mean spaghetti sauce too. And steak." He turned around and grabbed her by the hips, pulling her up against him, and she went willingly. She loved the feel of his hard body against her softer one.

"But…" He paused, a teasing glint still in his eyes.

"Oh no, what?"

"That's all I can cook. I must confess… I conjure everything else."

She laughed and went up on her toes, giving him a quick kiss before she pulled back and walked to the fridge. "We're in luck. Joel brought a lasagna that just needs to be heated up. I put it in the fridge while you were walking Doyle before our session."

"Excellent. Did he happen to bring any bread or salad?"

Rowena pulled a pan out of the fridge and set it on the counter before pulling out a bowl covered in plastic wrap. "Salad. I think Joel must be worried we can't feed ourselves." She chuckled.

"Nah, he's just a caretaker like that. I'll turn on the stove."

"Great, and I'll conjure some wine." Since Taren had made himself known and she'd realized that she wasn't delusional, she'd cut way back on her wine consumption, but a glass with lasagna would be great.

Connor lit a fire in the huge stone fireplace, giving the open concept cabin a cozy feel as they ate their dinner. They kept the conversation light, talking about favorite books and authors.

Rowena pushed her empty plate aside and picked up her

glass of wine, absently swirling it in the glass. "What are five things you could never do without?"

He chuckled. "That's kind of random."

"Yes, probably. I was just thinking about the questions we asked each other last night and thought we could continue. So… five things?"

"Hmmm, I've never thought about it, but…"

He paused to think and she took the time to look at him, something she loved doing. It wasn't that she needed someone she was with to be really hot or handsome, but there was just something about Connor that spoke to her. She loved that he was a conversationalist, which was amazing considering how long he'd been alone. And that he was caring and smart and the way he listened when she talked.

"Okay, I've got it," he said. "My computer, the internet, coffee, wide-open spaces, and quiet. What about you?"

"Ha, I guess I should have thought of things since I asked the question." She thought for just a moment. "My family, the ability to listen and pick up nuances from people, my magic now that I have it back, wine, and the memories of my brothers and parents."

He reached across the table, palm up, and she put her hand in his. "The memories are nice, and the wine doesn't surprise me." He smiled and she knew he was trying to keep things light. "Now it's my turn. How do you typically spend your leisure time?"

"I handmake cards while I listen to music." His eyes widened and she knew she'd surprised him. "It's creative."

"Well, maybe I'll be worthy of a card from you one day."

"We'll have to see," she teased and kept things light, not saying she already thought he was more than worthy. "Now you. Leisure time?"

"Not as creative as you. Doyle and I walk outside."

They continued to volley questions back and forth until they had cleaned up and moved to the couch to watch the fire. "Connor?"

"Hmm?"

"Are you okay with everything you learned today?" She turned sideways on the couch so she was facing him as he answered.

"Yes, I actually am. It was weird to learn I can talk to ghosts too, just differently than you, but I already knew what happened when I touched old objects. I just hadn't known that I'd discovered it that day."

Studying his face, she figured he really was okay with it. His expression didn't indicate that he was holding anything back. She'd been worried that he might. "Are you ready to finish tomorrow?"

"Yes. I need to."

She agreed, but it was still his decision. "It will take time, but it might help you find the self-forgiveness you need."

He looked skeptical but didn't disagree. "We know what I need, but what about you?"

The question took her by surprise; no one had asked her that before. "What I've always needed—to help people. I'm driven to, and I can never seem to do enough."

He frowned. "Why would you say that?"

She looked down at her wine glass and conjured a little bit more before taking a sip. "I need to make sure I'm living a good life, because I'm the only one in my immediate family that gets to—live, I mean." She took a deep breath and told him about her client who had committed suicide and the guilt she felt for one more life she couldn't save.

"It seems we both feel guilt, but maybe it's time we learned to let some of it go. Maybe you need to forgive your-self for living as much as I need to forgive myself for what happened to Julia."

She felt the corner of her mouth tick up, but it wasn't really a smile. "It's not easy, is it?"

"No." He pushed a curl behind her ear and then looked down at the glass in her hand. "Are you finished with that?"

She sent the glass to the kitchen counter and felt her anticipation heighten. "Yes."

"Good." He twirled another of her curls as he gave her a heated look. "Yesterday, I wanted to wait until after we learned everything about that day before we made love, but I've changed my mind."

"Why?" As much as she wanted to make love with Connor, she had to make sure he wasn't using her to hide from his feelings.

"I think it had to do with Dorothy." He paused, "Can I pull you closer?"

When she gave a nod, he pulled her onto his lap so she straddled him, her skirt bunched up around her hips. She could feel the hardness of him through his jeans, pressed against the thin fabric of her panties. Just the touch cranked her lust up to a level ten, but it was more important that they finished their conversation first. "What about Dorothy?"

He held her by the hips, his fingers tracing small circles over her skirt. "She loved Gerald with an intensity you don't see every day, and yet they never got to be together. At least not for long."

Rowena wanted to lean forward and kiss Connor, saying that they could be together for a long time, but she didn't. First, no one could make that kind of promise—she knew that better than most—and second, she and Connor were still so new. "What does that have to do with you changing your mind?"

Connor moved his hand up to her face and cupped her cheek as he looked into her eyes. "Life can be cut short, and no matter what tomorrow brings, I don't want to lose a moment with you." He leaned forward and softly brushed his lips against hers before pulling back.

There was a question in his eyes; he was letting her choose. "Yes." She pushed off his lap and stood, holding her hand out in front of her. "Yes," she said again. "I want to make love with you." When he took her hand and stood, she led the way to the bedroom. They'd spent the last two nights on the couch, but she didn't want to make love with Connor on a couch like they were a couple of teenagers.

In the bedroom she turned on the small lamp on the nightstand, giving the room a soft glow—just enough that they could see each other, without it being too bright. When she turned back around to face Connor, she froze, not knowing what to do next. Should she initiate it? She'd had sexual partners before, but it had been a while and she suddenly felt nervous.

Connor must have sensed her nervousness because he walked right up to her and wrapped one hand behind her neck and the other around the small of her back, pulling her close. "I want to kiss you, Rowena."

"Please," she said breathlessly.

He kissed her in a way that was passionate and yet not rushed. He made love to her mouth with his own and she responded. When he finally broke the kiss he reached for the buttons on her shirt. "May I?"

"Please," she said again. Her body felt so hot with need that it seemed to have zapped her of all language except the one word. Connor lowered the shirt off her shoulders before tossing it on the bench at the end of the bed and then removed her bra, adding it to the growing pile.

"You're beautiful and sexy." He kissed his way down her neck and chest before cupping her breasts. She felt herself get wet and pushed into his hands. When he took one of her nipples into his mouth, she swore she could almost come from his touch alone.

Reaching for the hem of his shirt, she asked him the same question that he had asked her. "May I?"

He pulled off her breast, and the cool air hit the wetness left from his mouth, causing her to shiver in the best way. Helping her take off his shirt, he took it from her and tossed it with her own.

Lowering her to the bed, he followed, laying on top of her and kissing her again. She loved the slow kisses, but she wanted more. "Connor?"

"Hmmm?" He looked up from showering kisses on her stomach.

"I love your touch, but I want more. You know what my favorite position is?"

He smiled, looking up the length of her body. "Tell me."

"The missionary position. I want to see you on top of me when you pound into me." She usually wasn't so vocal about sex. Being open just seemed right with Connor, but she hoped she hadn't turned him off. The heat in his eyes told her she hadn't.

"I want our first time to be special. You deserve to be cherished." He kissed his way up her body and took her mouth in a possession that was everything she hadn't known she wanted.

"It will be special no matter how fast or slow we take it." She gasped when she felt her skirt and panties disappear and a cool breeze brush across her before the heat and hardness of his body pressed against hers.

"Sorry, I guess I should have asked," he said as he kissed along her jaw and neck.

"No, it's what I want." She reached up and threaded her hands through his hair, deepening the kiss again. "I'm ready. Please, Connor."

He lifted himself enough to hold out his palm so a condom could land on it. "From home," he said with a shy smile. He sheathed himself and then brought his body back to hers and kissed as he guided himself into her into her one slow, smooth stroke.

They both groaned at the same time, then he shifted onto his elbows and locked his gaze with hers as he slowly moved in and out. He raised her leg onto his arm and tilted his hips as he continued his slow torture.

He bent down and kissed her, the position awkward, but amazing at the same time. When he picked up the pace, she met him thrust for thrust and squeezed his length.

"Oh fuck, you feel amazing," he said against her lips.

She closed her eyes as she was overrun with sensations, so close, but not right there. Snaking her hand between them, she rubbed her clit and felt the familiar, delicious tension take hold. She screamed his name as her body tightened and the best orgasm of her life ripped through her.

Connor pumped harder, and she felt his own orgasm release inside her before he collapsed on top of her.

After a moment, when their breathing started to return to normal, he shifted to move off her. "Sorry, I'm squishing you."

"No." She grabbed onto him. "Stay for just a bit more. I love you on top of me."

He kissed her slowly, nipping at her lips. "You're amazing."

She smiled and kissed him back.

"Now I cherish you," he said as he pulled out and disappeared the condom, before moving back down her body.

16

onnor looked at Rowena and then Joel. "You ready?" He had a sense of déjà vu. Yesterday had started the same way, and once he got through the hypnosis, he'd be okay with the day ending the same way yesterday had. He even loved how it had carried on into the morning. They'd woken up and made love again, then spent the rest of the morning and early afternoon talking and taking Doyle for a walk. They'd agreed to avoid all talk of guilt and forgiveness and acknowledged that there would be time for that later.

They all sat in the same seats they'd been in the day before, even Taren and Doyle were in the same places by the fireplace.

It didn't take long for Rowena to get him into a relaxed state, and with her guidance, he was able to jump to the part of the memory where the ghost appeared.

"He was never meant to be mine."

Leaving one hand on the fireplace, Connor turned around as far as he could without losing contact with the mantel. A woman stood in front of him. "Drew, do you see her?"

"See wh—" Drew turned as he spoke. "Holy shit! Is that a ghost?"

The woman didn't look much older than Connor, maybe in her early twenties. Her hair was curly and came to just below her ears in a style that reminded him of old black and white movies he'd seen. She was wearing what looked like a nurse's uniform, but nothing like the scrubs the nurses wore today.

Connor met her gaze. "Who are you?"

Her eyes widened. "You can see me?"

Connor's arm ached from the awkward angle of holding onto the mantel and twisting to see the woman, but he worried that she'd disappear if he let go. If he sent some magic to his muscles to ease the strain, he didn't know if it would disrupt whatever magic he was using to see her. He wouldn't take the chance. "Yes, I can see you. Do you need us to do something for you?"

She blinked as her eyes watered and several tears streaked down her cheeks. "I've been waiting for years for someone to hear me. I want to know if he loved me."

"Who? Gerald?"

The woman gasped and her hands flew to her chest. "You knew Gerald?"

"No, but I felt his presence. I don't think I can talk to him, if that's what you need." Her shoulders drooped and Connor felt like he'd just kicked her puppy.

"My name is Dorothy. Gerald and I were in love and were going to get married. We joined the army at the same time because we didn't have much money. I was already a nurse, so joining the army as a nurse made sense. After the bombings on Pearl Harbor, I was sent to Manila."

Connor blinked, making sure he wasn't hallucinating. The moment was surreal. Dorothy was talking about things he'd only read about in history books. Although he'd seen the Ben Affleck movie about Pearl Harbor that came out the year before. Connor didn't know the etiquette for talking to a ghost, so he figured he'd ask the obvious. "Did you die there?"

"Yes. The hospital was bombed. Years ago I found myself here, but no one could talk to me. Throughout the years, I watched Gerald grow old. He seemed so happy with his wife and children. I thought maybe I'd see him when he died, but it's been seven years and I'm still trapped here. I wondered if he ever truly loved me or thought about me."

He felt horrible for the woman, but he didn't know what he could do.

Drew flipped the back of his hand against Connor's arm. "Hey, Con, you think you could find something that would give her an answer?"

"I don't know." He wanted to help this woman, but he hadn't explored this new talent yet. "Ah... Dorothy. Could you come over here so I can face the fireplace and still see you? My arm is aching from turning backwards."

Dorothy appeared by his side, and Connor turned his body to the fireplace, easing the strain in his arm, as he spoke to her. "I'll see if I can find out, but I won't make any promises."

"All I ask is that you try."

Connor pulled in a large breath and let it out slowly, then closed his eyes as he placed both hands on the mantel. He concentrated on 1994, the year before Gerald died.

The Christmas scene appeared in Connor's mind. An older version of Gerald sat at the head of a large table where he was surrounded by people of all ages passing food around. It looked like a noisy and happy affair.

Connor focused on December twenty-eighth of the same year, hoping to find something different, though he had no idea what.

Gerald was sitting in a big lounge chair off to the side of the fireplace, reading glasses perched low on his nose as he read a book.

Connor let his eyes roam the room. "I wish I could communicate with him somehow."

Gerald lifted his eyes from the book and searched the room. "Who's there?"

Connor gripped the mantel harder. "Wow! You can hear me?"

"David, is that you? Come here where I can see you. I'm too old to play games."

"This isn't David. I'm Connor Davis and I'm communicating with you from the future."

Gerald took his glasses off and rubbed his eyes before replacing his glasses. "Well...I've seen a lot of different types of magic, but that's a new one to me. What can I do for you, Connor?"

"I see him," Dorothy whispered.

"Damn, I can see him too. Gerald, I'm Drew, and I'm here with Connor. Can you see us?"

Gerald grasped a cane and stood, putting all his weight on the handle as he turned to the fireplace. "Oh my lord!" He reached out and grasped the mantel. "Dorothy, love, is that you?"

"Y—yes." Connor swiveled his head between Gerald and Dorothy. Tears were streaming down her cheeks, but she didn't wipe them away. "I've been stuck here. I— did—"

Gerald leaned closer to the fireplace. "It's okay, my love. You say what you need to say."

Connor gripped the mantel so hard his fingers were white, terrified he'd lose the connection between Gerald and Dorothy. He couldn't imagine a love like the love between these two people, even after all the years apart.

"Did you love me?" Her words were quiet, but Connor could see the moment Gerald heard her. He blinked and waved his hand in front of his face, perhaps to magically dry his tears.

"I've always loved you, Dorothy. I never stopped, even when I remarried." He held up his hand. "Wait, I'll show you." Leaning heavily on his cane, Gerald walked to the desk on the far side of the room. He hooked his cane on the desk's edge and sat in the chair before pulling open the bottom drawer. His hand shook as he *reached in the drawer and pulled out a bundle of envelopes tied together with a string.*

Gerald swung his chair toward the fireplace and held up the bundle. "Can you see this?"

When Dorothy didn't say anything, Connor turned his head to see her holding her fingers to her mouth as she nodded, more tears streaking her cheeks.

"Yes, she can see you," he told Gerald.

"Dorothy, I've never been perfect, but one of the perfect things I did was loving you. Will you forgive me for loving someone else after you were gone?"

Dorothy dropped her fingers from her mouth and twisted them together as she nodded. "Yes, I forgive you. Do you forgive me for wanting to help others? You hadn't wanted me to join the army. You said I could help people at home. I thought... I wondered if you hated me for the choices I made, and I've always wondered."

Gerald picked up his cane and used it as he slowly made his way back over to the fireplace. He looked right at Dorothy. "Yes, I forgive you and I could never hate you, Dorothy. You had to help people, but not because you owed anyone anything. Just because you were a kind, giving person, and it is one of the things I love about you. I will love you until my dying breath."

"I love you too."

Connor turned to Dorothy in time to see her fade away. When he looked back at Gerald, he was sitting in his chair reading his book, just as he'd been before.

Prying his fingers from the mantel and opening and closing his fists to stretch them out, Connor felt a sense of peace. He had helped someone today.

Drew knocked his shoulder against Connor's. "That was fucking crazy, man!"

"Yeah, freaky, that's for sure. I think I'm going to need to digest what just happened."

Connor glanced over at Julia and Sarah where they continued to play. Thankfully, they'd been oblivious to everything that had happened. Good thing, he didn't know how he'd explain ghosts to a couple of five-year-olds.

He and Drew sat in silence for several minutes, but he was itching to talk to his dad. Connor couldn't wait to show his dad that he had a magic specialty. Not everyone got one, and his was definitely cool. He tilted his head in the direction of the front room of the house where the adults were gathered. "Do you know what they're discussing in there?"

Drew shrugged one shoulder, his go to response for a lot of questions. "Not exactly. I'm guessing it's something to do with the council. Since Thomas Williams and his two brothers were killed in that fire this summer, and that other council member, Edward Hughes, and his wife, died in a car accident, I think they're concerned about the council since none of the council members are here, including my dad. But my dad wasn't worried that he wasn't invited to the meeting."

Connor frowned, "What do you mean 'your dad'? I thought you lived with a foster family."

Drew flopped down on the hearth, stretching his legs out in front of him, and conjured a coin. He absently flipped it between his fingers. "No. My dad made me say that."

Connor narrowed his eyes at his best friend. "Why and why tell me now?"

"Because we're not kids anymore. My mom and dad were never married, and I lived with my mom. She died in an accident when I was ten and I went to live with my dad's parents. They're fucking brutal. They don't like magics and talk shit about their own kind. I guess they raised my dad that way too until he could escape. When he found out where I was, he came and got me, brought me here."

Connor shook his head. "I don't understand. Why the lies?"

"It was what my dad wanted. But now that the plan is coming together, you can join us. Your specialty rocks and will be able to help us."

Drew wasn't making sense. "What plan?"

"There are rumors of a magic box, that when opened, will release epic powers to those who open it. Daniel Knight might have his own agenda as council leader, but he's also looking out for all magics. It's the non-magics we should be worried about. They're the ones who want to suppress us."

Connor snorted and knew that Drew had glossed over the fact that he'd lied about his dad. "How can they want to suppress us when they don't even know people with magic exist?"

Drew flipped the coin up high and caught it in his hand, making a tight fist. "Exactly. That's the problem. We can't tell non-magics about us because they'll freak out and want to experiment on us or something equally fucked up. So that means we have to hide from them. They're oppressing us, even if they don't know it."

Connor was beginning to think that Drew and his dad were the fucked up ones. Their logic didn't make sense. Connor eyed Drew. "Who's your dad?"

"Andrew Skalbeck."

"What?" Connor popped to his feet and looked at Julia and her friend. They had both stilled and were staring at him. He rolled his eyes. The little girls hadn't noticed a ghost, but they stopped playing when he spoke too loudly. He waved a hand in their direction. "It's fine. Drew just told me a story. Play with your dolls." The little girls picked up their Barbies and Connor turned back to Drew. "Your dad is a member of the council and you've lied about it this entire time?"

Drew shrugged one shoulder again, like he didn't care at all. "I told you my dad didn't want me to say anything. But now that the Williams men and Edward Hughes—the goody-two-shoes of the group—are all dead, the others, like my dad, can go forward with their plan to find the magic box."

"My dad and uncle are in charge of magics for the FBI. They're not going to let your dad and the others open this so-called magic box, if it even exists. And you're forgetting that there are still three other council members left."

Drew flipped the coin from hand to hand again and laughed. "Yeah, Andrew Copeland and Forest Sharpe are on our side. And my dad says not to worry about Curtis Stone."

Connor flicked a glance to the little girls to make sure they were still playing and lowered his voice. "My dad will stop you."

Drew shoved the coin in his pocket as he stood, his hands on his hips. "Ya think? No, Connor, you'll join us or end up with the same fate as the Williams."

That was a threat if he'd ever heard one. If what Drew said was true, Daniel Knight or Drew's dad might have been responsible for the deaths of the council members and their families. Connor shook his head at his friend—ex-friend—and turned toward Julia and Sarah. He'd take the girls to his dad and tell him and his uncle what was going on.

Drew yanked on his arm, spinning him back around. "Where the hell do you think you're going?"

"I'm taking the girls."

Drew shot him a death glare. "No, you're not ratting us out. I thought you'd realize that getting the magic box and shutting up non-magics is the right thing to do. Especially now that you have a power that can help us. I should have figured my dad was right and that you're a fucking pansy-ass."

Connor didn't care what name Drew called him. He needed to let his dad know what was going on. He took a step toward Julia and Sarah, but Drew flashed in front of him, blocking his path. "Step out of the way, Drew."

"Make me."

Connor lifted his foot to step to the side when he was lifted in the air. He flew backward, crashing into the fireplace. Pain flared up his hip and shoulder. Using the chimney as a support, he stood and faced Drew.

"I won't let you stop us." Drew raised his hands. A ball of fire sat in each of his palms.

Connor had a fleeting thought that Drew had gone crazy when Connor lowered his shoulder and plowed into his friend. His momentum sent them both backward. They hit the ground with a breath-stealing force, and Connor rolled to the side.

Julia and Sarah stood in front of the couch, their Barbies forgotten in a pile on the floor. "Drew, the couch!" Julia screamed and pointed behind him. One of Drew's balls of fire had landed on the couch.

Connor rushed forward, calling on his magic and conjuring a tub of water to douse the flames.

"No, Connor. Baking soda." He looked down to see Julia standing beside him, barely reaching his hip. "Conjure baking soda." She conjured some in her little hands and threw it at the couch. Sarah did the same. Connor conjured heaps of the powder, tossing it on the flames. The fire was only smoldering embers when it sprang back to life and the flames roared higher.

Connor scooped up Julia and Sarah in his arms and turned toward the door. Drew was fanning the fire, feeding it.

Drew turned away from the fire and held up his hands. "No, you can't leave. You know too much. I really thought you'd see it the way I do."

"Drew, we don't have time for this. We have to get out of here." Connor could feel the heat of the flames at his back and he pulled on his magic, conjuring water to soak his clothes and Julia's and Sarah's. The girls cried and wiggled in his arms.

"No!" Drew yelled. "You won't ruin this for me! My dad is going to let me help find the box, and you can't stop me!"

Connor couldn't listen to Drew anymore; he had to get the girls to safety. Pushing by Drew, he held each girl tightly and aimed for the door. He'd gone two feet when he hit an invisible wall. Drew had thrown up a spell that was blocking the entrance. Connor knew instinctively what it was and that it would block all sound *from leaving the room. No one would be able to hear a call for help or the sound of the fire. He tried to call his dad telepathically, but his voice bounced back in his head.*

Julia grabbed his chin, forcing him to look at her. "Connor, look!" He yanked his chin out of her tiny grasp and turned to see the curtains engulfed in flames. Connor dropped to his knees and shielded Julia and Sarah with his body, tucking them under him. He tried to throw up a protection spell around them, but it wasn't working. He must have drained too much of his power talking to Dorothy or Drew was blocking it somehow.

Drew's feet came into his view and then his friend bent down in front of him. The look that crossed Drew's face was one of pure hatred. "This wasn't the plan. You were supposed to join me."

Lifting his hands, Drew shoved them at Connor with what felt like all the force of his magic behind him. The girls still in his arms, they fell backward into the couch and the girls screamed as the fire caught their clothing. He rolled with both girls in his arms, trying to put out the flames.

He felt nauseous as a searing pain spread across his entire back. Taking a deep breath to push back the bile rising in his throat, he held the girls more firmly in his arms and stumbled toward the door.

"You can't leave," Drew said, blocking his path. "And you can't remember this."

"What?" Connor ignored Drew and pushed past him, aiming for the door once more.

"No!" Drew held his hand up and Connor hit a shield again.

"Drew, I have to get the girls out of here." Connor's back was a thousand pinpricks of pain and he was terrified of looking at Julia and Sarah in his arms—they were too quiet.

"I've put Sarah to sleep and because of you, your cousin is hurt."

"What?" Connor finally looked down. One side of Julia's face was red and blistered, pieces of her hair scorched. Oh my god!

What had he done? He pushed at Drew's barrier and tried to tele-pathically reach his dad.

"Connor, a seer already told us what was going to happen and we have a plan. You can't walk out of here with Julia. She'll live, but it won't look like it and you can't be allowed to remember."

"What the fuck are you talking about?"

"You can't remember." Drew waved his hand at Connor.

The memory shifted and Connor felt as if he was no longer in the memory but watching it from afar. He was scooping Julia in his arms and reaching for Sarah when Julia screamed. Her face and neck were engulfed in flames. He bent to his knees, trying frantically to put out the flames, and called to his dad. It felt like forever as Julia struggled to breathe, and then he knew it was too late and she was dead.

He didn't need Rowena to bring him out of the hypnosis. It was as if he'd been flung out when the memory abruptly changed. All these years he'd been living with guilt for what he'd done, and he'd been wrong. The deep remorse for letting Drew control him and hurting Julia was still there, but now his past had been rewritten.

17

*R*owena exited the bathroom after getting ready for the night and wondered how she was going to get through to Connor. He was already in bed with his arms crossed over his bare chest, his eyes closed, and Doyle was curled up on a rug at the end of the bed.

Connor had been withdrawing since he came out of the hypnosis. He hadn't wanted to talk about what they'd learned, saying he needed time to process. That was a normal response and Rowena gave him space, but he'd barely spoken when they'd had dinner and later cuddled on the couch.

With anyone else, she might have thought she'd done something wrong. But with Connor, she knew he wasn't pushing her away as much as he was clamming up out of self-loathing. She needed to get through to him. Although Connor wasn't like her teenage patient that she had just lost, she still wanted to save him from himself. Every person she helped made her life a little bit better to knowing she'd saved another family from feeling the loss of a loved one. Losing Connor would be so much worse than failing a patient, because he meant so much more to her.

She climbed in beside him and faced him, lying on her side. Placing her hand on his stomach, she rubbed slowly, hoping to give him some comfort. "Talk to me please, Connor."

He looked down at her. "What is there to say? Nothing's changed. I'm still the reason Julia died. It just didn't happen the way I'd always thought it had." He didn't sound angry when he spoke, just sad.

Rowena propped herself on her elbow to get a better look at him while she kept soothing his skin. "I don't think that's true."

Connor's eyes held a look of resignation. "It is true. Did you not hear what I said? You saw what happened that day."

"I did." She weighed her next words carefully. He was hurting and vulnerable and trying so hard to lay all the blame on himself. "Drew started the fire and stopped you from getting help."

Connor sat up, knocking her hand off with his movement, and leaned back against the headboard, but she didn't think he was rejecting her. Self-loathing clung to him like a blanket. "I didn't stop him. I huddled in a ball with the girls. I didn't stop Drew."

"How could you have? You would have left Julia and Sarah vulnerable."

"I fucking did that anyway, didn't I? I'm still the reason Julia died because I didn't protect her. I had one job to do that afternoon—keep those two little girls safe—and I failed."

The more Connor raised his voice, the softer she kept hers. There was a physical ache in her heart for what he was going through. "Whatever happened to Sarah? When we went over everything with Joel, I forgot to ask."

Connor looked down at his hands in his lap. "Her family moved away after the fire. My dad may know where they went, but I didn't ask."

Lifting her head off her hand, she looked up at him. "Come back and lie down with me. Please?"

He slid down the bed and lay on his side facing her. "I really like you, Rowena."

She smiled and traced patterns on his arm with one finger. "I really like you too."

"I wish we could have this"—he waved his hand in the small space between their bodies— "forever. I feel more for you than I've ever felt for anyone."

She got the feeling that he didn't think they could keep what was growing between them, but she did. Leaning forward, she placed a soft kiss on his chest. "I feel the same."

He pulled her over on top of him and kissed her with a passion that spoke of the feelings developing between them.

She wound her hands into his hair, pushing the long strands off his forehead while she kissed him back with an intensity she'd never given anyone else. The urge to give to him, to make him feel the way he'd made her feel the night before, was driving her.

Kissing her way down his body, she let her hands trail behind her lips. A moan escaped him when she showered attention on his nipple, licking and biting it before moving to the next. He pushed her hair out of her face and held it to the side as he watched her with hooded eyes.

She continued her downward descent, using her hands, lips, and tongue to pleasure him. Bypassing his groin, her hair grazed his cock as she teased him, kneading the muscles of his thighs.

"Fuck!" he said as he groaned. "Don't tease, I need you."

Her lips curved at the realization that she was making this big, strong man beg for more. Moving back up his body, she grasped his cock in a firm grip and used her tongue to tease. His hips bucked and she took pity on him, taking him in her mouth. She hollowed her cheeks and took him as deep as she could. She gagged for a moment and pulled back, then continued her assault.

She heard his breathing pick up and she matched the rhythm with the movements of her hand and mouth.

"No. Stop." Connor gripped her upper arms and pulled his body back.

He popped out of her mouth and she looked up his muscular length at him. "Don't you like it?"

"I love it." He tugged her up his body, the sensation on her breasts as she moved over his lightly haired muscles sending shivers to her core. She was wet with need for Connor, but she wanted tonight to be about him. He was struggling with what he'd learned and she wanted to bring him pleasure. "I want to be inside you and see you on top of me when we both come."

"Well, when you put it like that, who am I to argue?" She chuckled as he helped her position herself in his lap. She grasped him and squeezed lightly before lifting herself over him, then stopped as she hovered. "I don't know how to conjure a condom."

"We don't need to." He waved his hand toward the nightstand and the drawer opened. A condom landed on his palm. Watching him sheath himself and stroke his length up and down was one of the most erotic things she'd ever seen.

She took him in her hand and slowly lowered onto him. They both groaned when he was fully seated within her, filling her up in the most delicious way.

Rocking back and forth on him, he used his hands on her hips to steady her as she ground herself against him. She leaned down and kissed him, tugging his lip between her teeth and biting softly before soothing it with her tongue. "I need more, Connor."

She pulled back and sat up straight before kneading her

breasts and pinching her nipples. He snaked his hand between them and found her clit, rubbing just hard enough. She was so close and felt a burning need to come. Dropping her hands to his chest, she used him for support as she increased her rhythm. His hips rocked up to meet hers and he let out a hoarse yell as he pinched her clit. A second later, her cry of release joined his.

Rowena flopped down beside him. "That drained me, but in the best possible way." She chuckled and turned her head to face him.

"Agreed." He leaned over and placed a sideways kiss on her lips. "I still remember the day I figured out I could do this."

She lifted her head. "Do what?"

"Disappear a condom."

Closing her eyes, she cuddled into his warmth. "Hmm… that is definitely handy."

"And conjure this."

Opening one eye, she peered up at him as he braced himself on his elbow and half hovered over her. He held a washcloth in his hand and gently wiped between her legs. The cloth was warm and soft as he cleaned her. It was almost more intimate than sex. "Wow."

"Exactly." He chuckled. "It was helpful as a horny teenage boy in my room." He disappeared the cloth and laid down again, pulling her tighter into his side.

They were quiet for several minutes, and she was so warm and sated that it would be easy to fall asleep. It was probably what Connor wanted, but the psychologist and caregiver in her couldn't let the conversation from earlier go. "Connor?"

"Hmm?"

Rowena resumed her earlier position, propping her head on her hand and lightly running her fingers over Connor's flushed skin. "I think we should talk about what you said earlier."

She felt him tighten under her fingers and lazily kneaded his muscles. "How you think you're solely responsible for Julia's death."

Connor didn't open his eyes. "Maybe not solely, but I am responsible. I could have done more to stop Drew."

"You don't know that."

"I do. You showed me and Joel what happened."

Connor opened his eyes and turned his head toward her, his eyes piercing. "Do you tell yourself the same thing, Rowena?"

She frowned. "What do you mean?"

"You have guilt because you're the only survivor in your family. Are you telling me that doesn't have anything to do with why you are so intent on helping people? That it's not because you feel guilty."

His last words weren't a question and they were too insightful for her liking. "Yes, but it's normal."

"And what about the teenager you said committed suicide? Can you tell me that in the past two days you haven't mentally gone over your last sessions with him trying to figure out what you missed?"

Rowena pulled her hand off Connor and rolled onto her back. "No," she whispered. Because she had. She'd gone over every word they'd spoken and wondered if she could have done more.

Connor leaned over and kissed her forehead. "You can't save everyone, Rowena," he whispered.

She looked up at him. "I want to save you."

"I'm not worth saving." He pulled up the blanket on them both and gently rolled her so he was spooning her back, his arm draped over her waist. The feeling of him surrounding her suffused her with a sense of safety, and yet he wouldn't let her do what she wanted most—to save him.

ROWENA LOOKED up from her laptop at the knock on the door. She had just pushed her chair back and stood when Joel opened the front door to his cabin.

He tilted his head toward her computer when he walked in. "I'm not interrupting your work, am I?"

She sat back down and closed the lid of her laptop, pushing the device off to the side. "No, I'm good. Join me for a coffee?"

Joel pulled out the chair across from Rowena and sat as she conjured two coffees. "Black, right?"

"Yes." Joel took the mug from her and sipped. "Perfect, thanks."

She picked up her own mug and peered at Connor's uncle over the lip while she cradled the mug. "Just a social visit or checking up on Connor because of what he remembered yesterday?" she asked.

"A social visit… with you."

"Me? Really?" She'd met Joel over the years, and in the past year since they'd resumed the ritual of weekly family dinners in the restaurant, he hadn't been a stranger. But as far as father-figures went, she was closer to Ben, mostly out of familiarity.

"I didn't think Connor would be here." Joel smirked. "And I'm guessing he's not hiding in the bedroom?"

Rowena laughed, but it wasn't a happy sound. "No, he's not hiding. He drove home with Doyle. Said he'd take him for a long walk and then get a couple hours of writing in."

Joel nodded. "I figured. That's his comfort zone, and what

happened yesterday definitely wasn't." He took a sip of his coffee and looked like he was contemplating something before putting it down. "He's going to retreat."

"I know. He already has. Julia's death wasn't his fault, but he won't listen to me when I tell him that."

"We've been telling him that for years, and Ben and Stella have never blamed him."

"He blames himself and I won't be able to get through to him until he's willing to look at the situation differently." She understood what he was feeling better than Connor thought she did. Indirectly, she'd killed her own mother. After her dad, uncles, and the kids died in the fire, her mom and aunts spellbound her and her cousins as a way to protect them. Over the years, the spellbound magic built up and killed her mother and then her aunt. Tragedy killed her other aunt, but it all stemmed back to the fire.

"It's not your job."

Joel's comment startled her, pulling her out of her thoughts. "What's not my job?"

"Making Connor look at the situation differently. He needs to be ready to accept help first."

"I know that." Her comment sounded defensive, even to her own ears. "Sorry, that was kind of snippy. I know that a person has to want to accept help. I just wish I could get Connor to see what I see in him. He's a protector and he never would have let harm come to Julia if he could have done anything more to keep her safe."

"Funny you should say that." Before she could ask what he meant, Joel disappeared his coffee mug and pushed his chair back from the table. "Why don't we go for a walk? It's a beautiful fall day. A little crisp, but nice."

"Sure." Rowena stood and held her hand out to retrieve her sweater from the bedroom and put it on. "I haven't been outside much since Connor and I had our little jaunt in the woods to escape Drew." She looked around as they walked along a well-worn path. "It's hard to believe that was only three days ago. So much has happened."

"You have had quite the week. You almost died."

"Right. After Jack's healing and getting some rest, I don't feel the effects from it, but I haven't forgotten. There are still so many unanswered questions."

"Such as?"

"Why did Drew want me out of the picture? What hasn't my brother told us yet? What are Drew's plans?" She kicked a rock with the toe of her shoe as she walked, watching it shoot into the grass on the side of the path.

"I spoke with Frank this morning and I filled him in on what we learned yesterday."

"You were worried that Connor wouldn't say anything?"

Joel pulled a leaf from a tree as they passed and ran it through his fingers. "No, not that. Connor and Frank are really close. We all are, but I knew Connor would need time to digest everything before he told his dad. I'm glad I was there yesterday."

Rowena turned her head and smiled at the older man. "Me too. I was worried that I wouldn't remember everything correctly, so it was good having another set of ears... and eyes."

Joel hummed in agreement. "Frank is going to come by tonight, probably with Ben and Jack, to get all the details. He said he'd text Connor to let him know. He'll have too much time between now and tonight to run through everything and come up with excuses for why Julia's death is still his fault. But he'd do it anyway, regardless of how much time he has."

Rowena laughed. "That sounds like the Connor I'm getting to know."

Joel turned and leveled her with a serious stare. "It sounds like someone else too."

"Ben?"

"Yes, and you."

"Me? Why would you say that? I haven't taken on any of the responsibility for the deaths in my family." Her throat clenched after she'd said the words. They weren't a complete lie, but they were definitely a stretch.

"You may not feel responsible for their deaths, but I think you feel guilty that you're alive and they aren't. It's similar to what Ben felt when I was injured as a kid. For years he blamed himself for not doing more, like Connor does, and he felt guilty for surviving. Like I expect you feel."

"I thought you were an engineer. Did you take psychiatry classes in your spare time?"

Joel barked out a laugh. "I'm just observant. I think it came from years of struggling to speak. It was easier to listen and observe."

Rowena kicked another stone as she processed her thoughts. "Is that why, earlier, you said 'funny you should say that'? You're thinking that I feel guilty because I didn't do more to save my family, just like Connor thinks he should have."

"Pretty much. Ready to turn back?"

"Sure." Joe's comments were worth mulling over. Was she helping people and always trying to do more because she felt guilty or was she just trying to live the best life she could because she'd been granted one when her family hadn't?

When they made it back to the cabin, Joel didn't come inside. "I'm going to head out. Maybe see if I can get Connor out of his head. I'll see you tonight."

"Sounds good. I'm going to head out too. Flash back to my place for a bit."

"Keep your guard up, Rowena. We don't know where Drew is."

"I will." Joel flashed and she stayed on the porch, gazing out at the trees in the distance, but not really seeing them.

What are you doing?

Rowena spun around, her hand on her heart. "Jeez, Taren, you scared me to death. I mean—"

Taren laughed. "It's okay, I get it. I don't think I could scare anyone into dying. But maybe I'll try it one day."

She wasn't going to touch that one. She walked into the cabin and sat on the couch, pointing to the chair that was still pulled up to one end. "Can you sit there?"

I am.

"Yesterday, you left right after we finished with Connor's hypnotherapy session so we didn't get a chance to talk. Did everything you see mesh with what you heard from Drew and Snake?"

I think so.

Rowena leaned forward, focusing her gaze on the top of the chair cushion, hoping she'd be looking at Taren's eyes. "Are you ready to tell me how you died?"

When Taren didn't say anything after a minute, she was worried he'd left. "Taren? You still here?"

Yeah. It was my fault that Mirek got hurt.

"Can you tell me what happened?"

I eavesdropped on Drew... I didn't mean to, I just heard them. After... when Snake talked about his plans, I turned to leave and bumped right into Eddie. He'd been standing there, listening too. I tried to go around him, but he was bigger than me and shoved me against the wall. Drew came out and grabbed me. He dragged me into the big room where Mirek and Dylan and the girls were...

Rowena kept her eyes on the empty chair, wishing Connor was here so they could combine their magic and she'd be able to see her brother as he spoke. But then, maybe this was easier for him. Being invisible.

She began to worry again that Taren had left when he finally spoke.

Drew chucked me into the room, and I fell and hit my head on the table. I wasn't hurt bad, but Mirek got really angry. He shoved Drew, pushing him back against the wall. I'd never seen Mirek that mad before. Some of what happened is a blur, but I remember Eddie pulling out a knife. Dylan stood in front of him, but when Eddie said something to him, Dylan backed off. Drew told Eddie to 'shut the little shit up'. He meant me.

Rowena could hear the anxiety in Taren's voice, and the need to comfort him overwhelmed her. Clenching her hands into fists, she laid them in her lap and waited. It was a full minute before Taren continued.

I was still on the floor when Eddie came at me. I scooted backward until I hit the wall. Mirek flashed in front of Eddie just as he raised his hand with the knife. The knife slid down Mirek's face. Blood was pouring everywhere, but I couldn't see much. Eddie and Drew yelled at Mirek and pushed him to the floor, then Eddie came after me. I think Dylan tried to stop him, but I'm not sure. I felt pain in my chest and then it was gone. I couldn't breathe and I felt something funny in my mouth. I found out later that I'd died.

Rowena felt as if her brother had just died all over again. She couldn't see him and hold him, only visualize what it must have been like for him as he died.

Don't cry, Ro. It was a long time ago.

She felt a cool breeze on her cheek and looked at the empty chair. "Is that you?"

Yep. I'm gonna go, but I'll be back tonight when Connor's dad comes.

"Were you listening to me and Joel?"

Only a little. Bye.

Rowena sat still for a long time. She'd received so many emotional blows over the past few days; she didn't know if she could take any more.

153

18

Connor sat back in his chair and shoved his keyboard away from him in disgust. He'd been staring at his computer for over an hour and hadn't written anything. He was pathetic.

When he'd left Rowena at the cabin this morning, he'd felt like a dick. He was barely civil, telling her he'd drive Doyle home, take him for a walk, and get some work done. He could have worked just as easily from the cabin.

Swiveling in his chair, he watched Doyle sleep on the couch, his long body sprawled across the cushions, his chin jutting out on a pillow. Doyle, and Conan before him, had been his primary companions for a long time. Connor had been good at living his solitary life. At least he thought he had. Until right around the time Rowena showed up and rocked his world. Literally.

He wanted her with a passion he hadn't felt in a long time, maybe ever. But he wasn't good for her. He wasn't trying to be a martyr, just practical. Even if she was never in danger, he would always worry that if such a time came, he wouldn't be enough. On top of that, he lived with constant guilt—it ate at him and could ruin her life too. She'd have to live with a partner who constantly felt that way, with no end in sight.

Yesterday, he'd been a total ass when he'd said she was doing the same thing as him by not forgiving herself for living. Maybe she was, but she was compensating by helping others. All he did was write, and sure, he might entertain people for a few hours, but he wasn't making the kind of difference she was.

I'm outside and I'm coming in.

Connor heard his uncle Joel's words in his head only moments before he appeared in his office. He smirked at his uncle. "That wasn't much of a warning. What if I'd been jerking off?"

"I guess you'd learn to do it in your bedroom from now on." Joel walked to the couch and pried Doyle's head, shoulders, and front paws off the cusions. He sat down and draped Doyle over his lap. The dog wiggled until he was comfortable and went back to sleep.

Connor envied Doyle—walks, naps, and eating. He had a good life. No worrying about the past and how he'd have to walk away from a woman he'd come to care for in a very short amount of time. He met his uncle's gaze. "What's up?"

"Do you want to talk more about what you learned yesterday?"

"No." He really didn't.

"Did your dad text you?"

"Yeah. We're meeting at your cabin tonight. Does Rowena know?"

Joel absently ran his hand along Doyle from his head down his spine. "Yes, I had coffee with her and let her know."

"Were you looking for me?"

"No. I knew you wouldn't be there. I went to support her while you were doing your hermit thing."

Connor glared at his uncle. "I wasn't doing my *hermit* thing."

Joel raised his eyebrows. "No?"

"Okay, fine. I needed to think."

"And what conclusions did you come to?"

"I was still responsible for Julia's death, just not the way I thought I had been." He held up his hand when his uncle opened his mouth to speak. Connor didn't want to fend off any more rationalizations. "I also want to explore the other part of my specialty that I didn't know about. Which in itself is weird. Why wouldn't I have figured it out after all these years?"

"Magic is a mysterious thing. As much as we know about it and why we have it, we still know very little. Perhaps when Drew did whatever he did to you, it was suppressed."

Connor slouched back in his chair. "Maybe. So… we'll talk to Dad tonight and let him know what we found out, but I'm guessing you already filled him in a bit."

Joel lifted his eyes from where he was petting Doyle. "Yes, and I wanted him to fill in Ben and Stella as well, so nothing would come as a shock to them tonight."

"Shit." He hadn't even thought about his uncle and aunt having to relive their daughter's death when they learned the truth of what had happened.

"It's been a long time, Connor. Ben and Stella will always love and miss Julia—that never goes away—but they've grieved. It's time you moved on too. I've told you before, but I think you need to hear it again: you need to forgive your-self. You could have a future with Rowena but you have to let go of the guilt in order to do that. I saw how you looked at her yesterday. You love her."

"We haven't known each other very long. Knowing each other as kids doesn't count, so there's no way I can already love her."

Joel moved Doyle to the side and stood. "Don't make excuses. It doesn't matter how long you've been together. You care deeply for that woman and whether it's love right now or intense like that will soon turn into something more doesn't matter." Joel moved in front of him, and Connor stood. His uncle wrapped him in his arms and held tight before giving him a slap on the back and pulling away.

Connor felt his throat tighten and just nodded. He wasn't even sure what he was agreeing to. To not making excuses? To grieving and moving on?

Joel held his hands out and two framed pictures landed on his palms. "These are from my house, so I'd like you to return them later. No rush. But I want you to take a good look at them first. Ask yourself if you're doing both yourself and Julia a disservice by not talking about the past and remembering the good times. Julia was only five, but she was the smartest person I ever knew. She'd probably call you impractical for not moving on with your life." Joel chuckled. "I laughed the first time I heard that word come out of her four-year-old mouth."

Connor took the frames but didn't look down at them.

"See you tonight." Joel slapped him on the back and then was gone.

Placing the frames on his desk, Connor dropped into his chair. Resting his elbows on his desk, he dropped his head in his hands, pushing his hair off his face. Maybe his uncle was right and it was time to remember the good times with Julia.

Though there was one thing his uncle got wrong—the excuses. Connor wasn't making any. Keeping to himself and living like he did was preservation for himself and others in case the unthinkable happened again and he couldn't react in time. That wasn't an excuse, it was being responsible.

Connor lifted his head and picked up the first picture. It was of Joel and Julia leaning over a textbook. Joel must have retrieved the photo from the cabin. It was the one Rowena commented on when they'd first gotten there. Another thing Joel had been right about—Julia had been wicked smart. She'd loved to learn and could understand concepts in Joel's textbook at five that Connor hadn't at sixteen.

After putting the photo down, he picked up the other one and blinked against the tears that burned at the backs of his eyes. The photo was of him and Julia when he'd turned sixteen. Even though she was a genius, she'd still been a little girl and had loved birthdays and cake. She'd helped him blow out his candles.

The photo had been taken right after they'd blown them out. They were grinning like idiots and her little hand was against his much larger one as she high fived him.

Right then, he promised himself that from that day onwards, no matter what happened and how much he wished he could have changed that day so long ago, he would remember the amazing little things about her.

CONNOR LOOKED around the room as everyone settled. Joel's cabin was packed with people. It'd been like a mini family reunion with handshakes all around. Except for Meredith, who had acted like she hadn't seen Rowena a few days ago and checked her out from head to toe like a mother inspecting her cub.

Once that was over, there was conjuring of drinks and even a couple of extra chairs. Connor sat on the couch with Rowena on one side of him, her hand in his, and his dad on the other. Ben, Jack, and Meredith sat across from them, and Joel and Javier were off to the side. Taren wasn't visible yet, but Rowena had whispered to Connor that he was there.

Jack leaned forward, an intense look on his face, as he looked between Rowena and Connor. "Fill us in on everything that's happened in the last few days."

Connor wasn't quite sure where to start but figured chronologically made the most sense. "The morning after the accident, which wasn't an accident by the way, Rowena and I compared notes about what had happened. Someone flashed in front of her vehicle and then pushed it off the cliff."

"That explains why it looked like it had rolled, but how did it get on the road?" Javier asked.

Connor looked at Rowena. "You want to explain this part?"

Her eyes flicked to the fireplace for a moment and he expected she was talking to Taren. She gave his hand a squeeze before twisting both hands in her lap and facing the group. "My brother Taren pushed the car back on to the road. Curly, can you make yourself visible, please?"

"Hi," Taren said from his place, leaning perched on the hearth.

Exclamations peppered the air.

Meredith looked over her shoulder at Taren. "You look older. That means, you died—" She swiveled back, giving Rowena a questioning look.

Rowena paused and then nodded at Taren before facing the group. "Yes, Taren died when he was twelve. Six years after the fire. Apparently, I have the ability to talk to ghosts, but Taren couldn't get through to me when I was spellbound. It didn't happen right after the spell was broken either because I was only just coming into my magic. He was finally able to talk to me a couple of weeks ago."

"If you could see him, then why couldn't we?" Jack asked.

Rowena blew out a nervous laugh. "Because that's new. It wasn't until Connor and I combined our magic that I was able to see Taren. At first, Connor and I had to be touching, but not anymore."

Ben stood up and walked behind the chairs so he was facing the entire group. He grasped the back of the chair as if to steady himself. Connor knew his dad had given his uncle a head's up, but knowing and seeing were two different things. Ben leaned heavily on the chair back and directed his gaze at Rowena. "Can you talk to any ghost?"

There wasn't a person in the room who didn't know why Ben asked. He wanted to know if Rowena could talk to Julia. "No. From what Taren says, I have to be connected to the ghost, but I don't know if I have to be related to them."

Connor's dad stood and walked over to his younger brother. He spoke too quietly for anyone else to hear, but Ben nodded and turned to Taren. "Taren, I don't know if you remember me, but I'm Ben. I was friends with your mom and dad. Can you tell us how you died?"

Taren shook his head and his image started to fade. Connor doubted the young guy wanted to relive that event again and jumped to his rescue. "Taren, it's okay. Rowena and I will explain it later so you don't have to."

All eyes were on Taren as his form became opaque once more. Connor rubbed the back of Rowena's hand with his thumb and turned so he could see her. "Why don't you start at the beginning?"

"Sure. The same night Morgana's spell was broken, Taren pulled one of my photo albums off my bookcase to get my attention. That was the first time I was able to clearly hear a word from him. He told me that Mirek is alive."

"Did you learn about Dylan?" Meredith asked, looking between Taren and Rowena, before turning to Javier with an explanation. "Dylan was Jo and Reece's brother and died in the fire with our dads. Well... we thought he did."

Rowena lifted her shoulders. "I don't know yet, and

talking about this is tough on Taren." She glanced at Connor, and he wished he could say something to make all this easier so none of them had to rehash the past, but he couldn't.

He continued to soothe his thumb over the back of her hand and looked at Meredith. "There's a bunch we don't know yet. We've got a lot to tell you and it might answer some of your questions."

Rowena explained what she knew about the car accident and how Taren saved her. She and Connor tag teamed as they recited their initial conversation with Taren, what he'd overheard Drew and Snake talking about, and when they *saw* him for the first time by combining their magic.

They walked everyone through how they'd revisited Connor's memory of the day Julia died and why they ended up at the field, the chase with Drew, and coming to the cabin.

"Can you back up a bit?" Jack asked. "Drew said he was looking for something. Have you figured out what it is?"

Connor shook his head. "No, but I think we might be able to figure it out. But first we'll fill you in on what we learned about what really happened that day." It had been years since Julia's death, but he didn't want to keep mentioning the day she died. Everyone would understand what 'that day' meant. He'd talked more about that day in the last week than he had in decades.

Connor detailed what they'd learned when he'd gone through the memory under hypnosis, with Rowena and Joel throwing in items he missed. When they were finished, he was a mix of swirling emotions. He felt good about explaining Drew's involvement in that day but still guilty for not having done more. The full strength of his magic and the intricacies of his specialty would take a bit more time for him to fully process, but even the retelling of it had drained him.

His dad stood, stopping the questions that had been

peppered at him and Rowena. "Let's take a break. I could do with a scotch, and I know my brother keeps some good stuff around here—far better than anything I can conjure." There were chuckles around the room and people got up and refilled glasses and conjured snacks.

Rowena put her head on his shoulder. "You okay?" she whispered.

He had to think about her question for a moment. His guilt wouldn't just fall away, but it surprised him that he was feeling better with everything in the open. "I'm good. What about you?"

Connor followed Rowena's gaze as she turned toward the fireplace. He couldn't see Taren so he didn't know if he was still there. "He's still here, but just not visible," she said, like she'd read his mind. "This is all really hard on him." Turning back to Connor, she gave him a quick kiss and then stood. "I'm going to use the bathroom and get another drink."

When everyone was back and seated, Jack stood on the outside of the group and conjured a big-ass whiteboard. There were some laughs from the FBI crew, so Connor guessed they must use the whiteboard a lot.

"Jack," Joel called out. "You better disappear that thing when you're done."

Jack gave Joel a mock salute. "Yes, sir." There were more chuckles before the room sobered as Jack wrote the facts—dates and people involved—on the whiteboard. He wrote the word *book* and circled it, drawing an arrow from it to the word *map*, then another arrow to a question mark. He capped his marker and turned to face the group. "We have a copy of the map, and although we never expected an X to mark the spot, there is one on the map. But we don't know where it's referring to and we think there's something missing."

"Yes, like a key," Meredith added. "We just don't know

what the key is or where we'll find it. I expect that's what Drew wanted from you, Connor. But why would he think you have it?"

"Good question." Jack turned back to the whiteboard and added names and places, starting with the fire that killed half the Williams family.

"Jack, why are you going so far back?" Rowena asked.

"This is when it all started. Stella's brother was working with my dad and other members of the council. We know about Copeland and Skalbeck, Drew's dad, so that leaves Forest Sharpe as the only unaccounted for council member. We've heard the nickname Maverick bounced around, so we expect it's Sharpe. After Stella's brother died, a seer sought Frank out. Frank?"

Connor's dad stood and walked over to the whiteboard. "Just like home," he said, grinning at Jack as he passed over the whiteboard marker. When he turned to face the group, his expression was grim. "The seer, Helen, told me there would be many deaths, and eventually there would be a new council with fourteen members. She died shortly after the fires and I never learned anything more… I think we need to contact a seer, but I don't know of any living. I spoke with Fiona, Damon's mother, awhile back, but she said this was beyond her knowledge."

There were some names tossed around in the group, but no one knew of a powerful enough seer. His dad turned to him. "What about contacting the seer I spoke to years ago?"

"By using Taren?" Connor turned from his dad and looked at Taren, who was once again visible. "Taren, are you okay with that?"

"Yes, I think it's the same woman. She's the one who told me to talk to Rowena."

Jack disappeared the whiteboard and looked at Connor. "How do we do this?"

19

Rowena wiped her damp palms on her skirt, thankful it was dark. Taren seemed to be okay with contacting the seer, but she wasn't so sure. Her brother had been through so much already and it felt like they were asking too much of him.

She closed her eyes and concentrated on Taren, grasping on to the words he'd spoken in her mind. *Are you sure you're good with this?*

Hey, you spoke from your mind. Cool. Yeah, I'm good.

Wow, I did, didn't I? Yes, it's cool. She smiled, loving her new connection with Taren, and then grasped Connor's hand. "Taren is okay with it."

"Okay." Connor picked up her other hand and they turned at an angle so they could both see each other, Taren, and the others in the room. "I'm not sure how to do this. Taren, do you know?"

"Yes. The seer says she's ready. She wants you to push your magic into each other the way you did the other day."

Rowena didn't want to know how the seer knew what

they did. Just the thought of Taren being able to watch her without her knowing was creepy enough.

She felt Connor's magic as it seeped into her and she did the same, pushing her magic toward him.

When Meredith gasped, Rowena pulled her gaze from Connor's. A shape was forming beside Taren, just like his had done that first day that Taren became visible.

"Hello, Frank. Hello, Connor, Rowena. My darlings. I'm so happy to finally meet you both. Connor, you met my husband years ago."

"Your hus—Gerald? He was your husband?"

Helen's laugh had a husky crackle to it, like it wasn't used very often. There were so many questions Rowena wanted to ask, such as did Helen ever see her parents? Were they happy? How was Taren, really? Was Helen looking out for Taren?

Rowena didn't know how long they'd be able to speak with Helen, so she only asked what was relevant. "Helen, if you knew Connor had spoken to Gerald, why didn't you tell Frank?"

Helen's smile was wistful. "Because it hadn't happened in Connor's time yet, and by the time it did, I was dead. You see, as a seer, I must be careful what I reveal because if I mention something that hasn't happened yet, a person may choose to do something different to avoid an action if it has negative consequences."

Rowena frowned. "Wouldn't that be a good thing?"

"No, my darling. By trying to change what is foretold, something even worse could be unleashed, along with whatever was destined."

"I hadn't thought of that," Rowena said. "Do you know of an example from personal experience?"

"Unfortunately, yes." Helen's voice held a touch of sadness.

"My grandmother was a seer. She knew my grandfather was going to die in a car accident and begged him not to drive that day. He was going to drive to his brother's and bring him and his wife over for dinner. Not everyone had cars back then. Anyway… he decided to walk to his brother's instead and stay there for dinner. A huge stormfront came in. There was torrential rain and downed trees and powerlines everywhere, so instead of walking home, my grandfather decided to stay. Lightning hit the house, causing a fire. My grandfather died along with his brother and wife. Because of that, I know I can't stop fate, and so I only reveal what I absolutely need to."

Rowena's throat tightened and she swallowed against the lump. She felt a sadness for this woman, who although was long gone from this earth, must have lived with such tremendous guilt for the rest of her life. Something Rowena was all too familiar with, just for a different reason.

From behind Helen, Jack got up and walked over so he was beside Rowena. "Helen, I'm Jack Knight."

"Hello, Jack. Yes, I know who you are. I foresaw you a long time ago and knew you were a good soul, unlike your father."

"Thank you. Do you know anything about the magic box? We found one of the ancient books and were able to use a spell to locate the map, but the map isn't working."

"Because it needs a key." Helen sighed and her shoulders sloped like the weight of the world suddenly rested on them. "I think you should know the history of the magic box before I tell you about the key."

Jack conjured a chair beside the sofa and sat, giving Helen his full attention.

"Please do."

"What I know about the magic box was passed down through the generations of seers in my family. I don't know if the history of the box is written in the ancient books, as

I've never seen one. But what I do know is that the magic box was created shortly after the creation of magic people. As in all societies, there are people who are greedy and want more than they should. The story claims that a small group of some of the first magics were far more powerful than most today, and they developed some spells that when unleased would make them as powerful as deities—godlike, or so they'd hoped. They wanted the power to control other magics."

Jack leaned forward on his forearms. "Then why put the magic in a box?"

"I don't think they wanted to, but some others convinced them that it wasn't the right time to control all magics. Even knowing that they—the magics who created the spells— would never get to make use of them, they agreed to lock them away until it was time."

Jack narrowed his eyes. "When was that time?"

Helen shook her head. "I don't know. Maybe someone knew at one point, but that information didn't get passed down through my family."

Rowena gave Taren a reassuring smile and then looked at Helen. "If the magic box contains powerful magic, then how do we know it's evil? I heard the magic box contained untold evil power."

Helen smiled, the wrinkles around her eyes deepening. "That's the thing. If the box contained good, it likely wouldn't have been contained at all, but shared." She paused and her image wavered, like it was coming in and out of focus.

Rowena leaned forward. "Helen, are you alright?"

"I'm fine, darling, but I cannot stay in this realm for long, like Taren, so I must hurry. When the box was created by those that desired more power, there was nothing that could be done to reverse its creation. But some powerful magics who foresaw the destruction that the box could bring about decided to do something to counter it. That's where the key came in. They couldn't destroy the box or the map to locate it, but they were able to create a key to make it more difficult to find. They also created an object that when forged will permanently close the box."

"What kind of object?" Jack asked.

Helen sighed. "I'm not sure exactly, but rumors were passed down through the years that it is a slab of metal. I don't know if that's true or not and I don't know where it is. I expect that there are clues to it in one of the ancient books."

Frank walked over to Jack's chair, resting his hand on the back. "Thank you, Helen. Now that we know about this object, we'll look for it. But since you don't have much time, can you please tell us about the key?"

"Yes, my daughter Linda has it. She'll explain what to do." As soon as the last words left her lips, she faded away.

Rowena sat back on the couch and thought about what they'd learned. "There's no way that Drew could know this, so we have a head start."

"I think you're right," Frank said.

Jack's phone rang, startling everyone who seemed lost in their thoughts. "Knight… Where are you?... Okay, we'll be there soon…Yes, we'll bring him."

Jack hung up his phone and addressed the room. "Damon had asked for some help in Mexico and we were going to go tomorrow or perhaps the next day, but that was Morgana. Damon is in trouble. Meredith, we need to go now." Meredith stood and Jack turned to Ben. "Morgana said you too."

Ben stood. "I'll go, but I'll need to stop halfway. I won't be able to flash that distance at once."

"That won't be a problem." Jack gripped Ben's right arm, just above his wrist, and turned to Meredith. "I'm sending the coordinates of the location that I got from Damon. Let me know when you've got them."

Meredith tapped her temple. "Yes, got them."

"Great—before I go…" Jack held out his free hand and an ancient book landed in his palm. "Rowena, this is the book that Jo and Simon found. The map is tucked in the front. I trust you'll keep it safe."

Rowena took the book. "Of course."

Jack, still holding Ben's wrist, turned toward Meredith. "Let's go." Jack, Meredith, and Ben were gone in a flash.

"I'm leaving too," Taren said as he faded away.

Rowena looked down at the book in her hands and then at the four people remaining in the room. "I'm sure Jack, Meredith, and Ben will be able to help Damon with whatever he needs. So that leaves us to find the key." She turned to Connor. "You up for that?"

"Yes." He looked at his uncle, dad, and Javier. "Can you help?"

Rowena saw the love Frank had for his son as the usually serious man smiled. Her parents had been gone a long time, but the yearning for their love never went away. Just like it always did, her heart ached at the thought of the support she'd never have again.

"Of course, we'll help. Let's talk about what we need to do. Since Drew isn't a problem at the moment and can't know where the key is, I think we'll be good if we don't go first thing in the morning. I've got some meetings for the magic task force because Ben was originally going to attend them, and now I'll have to go in his place."

They went over everything that Helen had told them and Frank reached out to Linda before they decided on a course of action. By the time they were finished and Rowena and Connor were the only ones left, it was well past midnight.

Connor stood in front of her and pushed a curl behind

her ear, then took her hand and led her into the bedroom. They stripped down without uttering a word and climbed into bed. He pulled her into his arms, and when he entered her, he did so slowly, making her feel more cherished than she'd ever felt.

She wanted so badly to be everything he needed. She was falling in love with Connor and knew that no other man would ever be enough for her. If only she could convince him that he was everything she needed.

DREW FLASHED into the back stairway of Javier's apartment building, his feet landing softly on the concrete. Eddie leaned against a wall, playing something on his phone. "You're supposed to be keeping an eye out. Get off your fucking phone."

Shoving his phone into his pocket, Eddie glared at him. Drew wanted to wipe the look off the guy's face. Permanently. Not much longer and he could.

"I *have* been watching. I've been watching all fucking day. He flashed away hours ago, and I figured they were meeting at that cabin in the middle of bumfuck nowhere. I flashed there and saw a bunch of people meeting inside."

Drew was tired of following people and doing grunt work. He should be the one being waited on. "Were you seen?"

"Jesus, man. This isn't my first rodeo. No, I wasn't fucking seen. I shielded myself and although the curtains were closed, they hadn't protected the place. I could sense eight people inside. A few hours ago, three people left, but the other five stayed. I came back here to wait. Since they were all flashing in and out from inside, I wouldn't know when he left so I put an alarm spell on his apartment door. It will let me know when there's movement inside. He won't be able to detect it."

Drew wanted to punch something… or someone. His life had become all about waiting around. When he'd been a mole in the FBI, he'd been in on the action. Now, he had to hide and direct morons like Eddie. The kid envisioned himself as some sort of gangster, but he was just another one of his father's flunkies. "Did you try flashing inside his apartment?"

"Yeah, but it was spelled. The outside of the door wasn't."

"Call me when he arr—

"Wait!" Eddie threw his hand up. "I felt my alarm spell. He's home."

Drew didn't comment, just flashed to Javier's door. Standing off to the side out of view of the peephole, Drew threw up a light cover spell. Enough not to give his presence away, but not too much that it would raise suspicions. He threw out his magic, imitating a knock on the door.

When the door opened, Drew threw a blast of magic into the opening, knocking Javier back on his ass. In an instant, Javier was back on his feet. Drew was waiting for him, magic swirling in one palm and a Glock 19 in the other.

He sensed Eddie walk in behind him and shut the door, but Drew didn't take his eyes off Javier. The man was a magic and a trained FBI agent not to be underestimated, unlike Connor.

"What do you want, Drew? Shouldn't you be with dear old dad?"

If he didn't need Javier, he'd shoot the taunting asshole right between the eyes. "I need you to do me a favor."

Javier barked out a laugh. "Really? You think I'd do you a favor?" He shook his head. "Not going to happen."

"Yes, it is." Drew grinned. "In the morning, you're going to tell Connor that I have the key to the map so he has to hurry and get to the box before I do."

"And why the hell would I do that?"

Finally, he got to do something fun. Drew loved manipulating people. "Because I'm telling you to."

"I think your hearing's going, Bartley."

Javier stood with his hands on his hips—way too fucking cocky. Drew had hated Javier from the moment he'd met him at Quantico when they'd been in the same training class. Javier embodied everything Drew despised. He was a rule follower to the extreme and not willing to use opportunities to his own advantage. A goody-two-shoes just like Connor.

It was too bad Drew wouldn't get to see Javier do exactly what he wanted, but Drew would still benefit. The trade off was worth it. "You won't have a choice. You're going to wake up in the morning and do what I say."

Drew saw the exact moment that Javier started to make a move. After all, they were both trained by the same bureau. Javier moved his hand up and before he could pull on his magic or conjure anything, Drew whipped his magic orb straight at Javier's chest. It hit his target dead center and Javier flew backward, crashing into the wall behind him.

Standing over him, Drew used his magic and changed Javier's memory, making him believe that Drew had discovered where the magic box was and that if Connor didn't act soon, it would be lost. He also erased Eddie from Javier's memory.

Using his magic, Drew floated Javier into the middle of the room. He would have preferred to leave him slumped against the wall, but the position wouldn't match the memory Drew implanted.

Javier's memory was already altered, making him believe he fell asleep in the middle of the floor. When Drew pushed his magic into someone during or immediately following the memory he wanted to change, he had learned never to waste time. Whether the person was conscious or not, if he waited more than a minute to alter someone's memory, it would be too late to change it.

Drew had been twelve when he'd figured out his magic specialty. He'd come across it by accident and had celebrated the day ever since.

It had been the year before his dad had rescued him, and his grandparents had just given him another lecture about the evils of magic people. Ironically, they were going to use magic to spell his door and lock him in his room as punishment. It was a common occurrence that Drew had tired of.

Yearning to make them think he was the best grandson in the world, he wished with everything in him that he could get them off his back. He wanted them to believe he'd just gotten an A on his exam because he'd studied hard the non-magic way. Keeping the thought in his mind, he pushed his magic at them. The force knocked them off their feet, sending them both backward onto the pristinely polished hardwood floor, their heads hitting with thuds.

When they'd come to, they'd been confused but had congratulated Drew on his exam score and for finally seeing the horrible truth about magic. He'd been stunned. His wish had come true. It didn't take him long to discover that it wasn't a wish, but an ability to change a memory, and from that day onward he'd perfected the use of his gift.

He'd learned quickly how little magic he needed to push into someone, allowing his specialty to go undetected. The efficacy of the magic was another thing he'd perfected. Changing someone's memory had to be done at the time the memory was occurring or within a minute. He couldn't change a memory retroactively and had learned that the hard way. Not acting fast enough had cost him a magical beating from his grandfather.

Now, standing over Javier, he looked over his shoulder at Eddie. "I've changed his memory. He won't remember you were even here. I've also placed a light spell on him so he won't wake up before seven tomorrow morning." Stepping off to the side, he gestured toward Javier's prone form. "Do your thing. And make sure it lasts until tomorrow night."

It took Eddie only seconds to place a temporary undetectable tracking tag on the back of Javier's neck. Eddie's specialty was similar to his older sister's, something Eddie said she and their parents hadn't known. He'd only just come into his magic when he'd been recruited into the drug cartel in Mexico that Drew's father ran with another council member, Maverick. Eddie was an idiot for believing he'd ever be more than a pawn.

But as annoying as he was, Eddie's skills had come in handy. Though soon Drew would be so powerful he wouldn't need the likes of Eddie. He gave Javier one last glance. "I implanted the memory that he'd locked his door after I left, so lock the door and follow him in the morning. Call me when he goes somewhere."

Drew flashed to the penthouse he kept in one of the new high rises in Blue Mountain. As soon as he had the final piece to unlock the map, his father would meet him here and they'd get on with their destiny—controlling non-magics. He conjured himself a glass of bourbon and looked out at the skyline. It wouldn't be long before no one would be able to tell him when he could and couldn't use his magic. Soon he'd have everything he'd ever wanted.

20

*J*avier sprung awake as if his body was an alarm clock on steroids. The first thing he noticed was stiffness permeating his entire body as he pulled himself to a sitting position. The second thing? He looked down at the hardwood floor beneath him and realized he was on his living room floor, meaning he'd slept there all night.

The events of the night before came flooding back at him. He'd left Joel's cabin and flashed back to his apartment. His protection spell hadn't been disturbed.

There'd been a knock and he'd thought it odd considering the time of night. Late night calls usually only brought bad news and he'd been right—it had brought Drew. Javier hadn't sensed anyone outside the door and the hallway was empty when he'd peered through the peephole. He'd been cautious but relaxed when he'd opened the door, knowing his magic was strong and his gun was just a quick retrieval away.

Picking himself off the floor, the conversation with Drew ran through his mind as he got ready for the day. Why would Drew come to tell him he'd found the key to the map? How would he even know there was a key? And why would Drew tell Javier and not Connor? Maybe Drew had just wanted to taunt Javier as they'd been equals in the FBI, but he didn't think so. There had to be something that Javier wasn't seeing. He needed to warn Connor and Rowena that Drew was up to something.

Javier flashed to the outside of Joel's cabin where they'd all gathered the night before. At any other time, he would have loved to spend some time there, surrounded by old-growth trees, relaxing, watching the sunrise.

Connor answered his knock and held open the door for him to enter. "Hey, what's up? You're early."

"Something happened last night," he said without any preamble.

"Are you alright?" Rowena walked around the kitchen table and gave him a hug. He returned it before pulling back and letting her go. Her beauty struck him every time he saw her, both her physical and her inner beauty.

"I'm not injured, but there are some things that don't add up." Javier turned to Connor. "We need to get your dad on the phone, and probably Joel too, since he's going to be helping us."

They sat at the table and Connor called his uncle, and then connected his dad into the call. "Hey, Dad, you're on speaker. I've got Rowena and Javier with me and Uncle Joel is on the line too. Javier needs to tell us about what happened last night."

"Okay. Unfortunately, I don't have much time because I've got to be in another meeting soon, and it can't wait."

Javier launched into a bare-bones account of what happened when Drew arrived.

"Drew didn't touch me, yet I don't know how I ended up sleeping on the floor, and why didn't I wake up earlier?"

There was silence on the other end of the phone. Javier

knew from years working with Frank that he was formulating his next thought before he spoke.

"I agree, something's not right. Drew has an ego as big as his father's, but I don't know what he'd gain just by taunting you. And I think you're also right in that Drew would have gone to Connor to brag, not you… Okay, let's move up our timeline to get the key. I'll call Linda and let her know. I can postpone one of the meetings, but not all of them. We'll meet Linda in three hours if that works for her. If it doesn't, I'll get back to you. Agreed?"

When there was agreement all around and Frank and Joel disconnected from the call, Javier stood. "I've got a few things to look up for a case, so I'll head into the office and meet you at Linda's"

Rowena came up to him and gave him another hug. "Please be careful," she whispered in his ear.

"I'll be fine."

He said his goodbyes and flashed to a section of the underground parking garage in the building that magic agents had been using for years, and looked around to make sure he hadn't been seen by a non-magic person.

At his desk, he checked his email and followed up on a few leads for a case he was working on. When he was satisfied that the rest could wait until the next day, he turned off his computer and stood.

"You heading out?" Frank asked as he walked toward him.

"Yes, sir. I'm leaving now."

"I'll be right behind—" Frank's phone buzzed in his hand. He looked down at the screen. "I've got to deal with this. I shouldn't be long."

"I'll see you soon, sir."

Javier walked back to the hidden area in the parking garage and flashed to the meeting location. He'd been surprised to learn they were meeting in the field behind

Linda's house. Connor and Frank had explained that it wasn't far from Helen's original house, where Julia had died.

Doing a slow turn, Javier could just make out two of the houses in the distance. It was a massive plot of land, and he'd learned the night before that there were four houses scattered amongst the property. It wasn't so different from the field where they taught the W's magic. When Javier turned in the direction of Linda's house, Drew was standing in front of him with someone at his side. The man was Latino, like him, and Javier figured it was Eddie. He'd been mentioned several times in briefings as being one of Snake's and Drew's henchmen.

Javier stayed where he was but kept his hands loose at his sides in case he needed to use his magic or the gun in his holster. "What do you want, Drew?"

"I want the key to the magic box. I appreciate you leading me to it."

Javier held out his hands. "I don't have it." Drew's admission made his appearance last night even more strange. But now there was a bigger question. "How'd you find me?"

Drew laughed. "Oh, I've got a few tricks up my sleeve. And you may not have the key, but since you're here in the middle of nowhere, it must be close. I'll wait."

Javier weighed his options. He couldn't telecommunicate from where he was; it was too great a distance. He could pull out his gun, but as an FBI agent he needed provocation, and unless Drew pulled a gun on him first, he didn't have any. Using his magic was another option, if he was fast enough.

Eddie disappeared in a flash and Javier did the same, landing twenty feet away. He'd been taught never to let someone flash behind him so when he flashed Eddie was standing to his right.

Javier turned to his left to look for Drew, but the place he'd been standing was empty. Javier flashed again, this time to his left, where Drew had been. As soon as his feet touched the grass, he scanned the area in front of him. Eddie hadn't moved, which was a red flag that he was waiting for something.

Javier spun to look behind him and caught Drew out of the corner of his eye as something hit him from behind. Pain exploded in his head and he dropped to

the ground as his vision went black.

Burning bile in Javier's throat woke him. He swallowed against the nausea and took in shallow breaths through his nose. After several minutes, the percussion playing in his brain had lessened enough that he was able to open his eyes.

He lay sprawled on the back seat of a large vehicle—by the size and number of seats, an SUV. His hands had fallen asleep underneath him, and he had the sensation of thousands of pins and needles bursting up his arms. He bit his lip to stop the groan that bubbled up.

Turning his head to the front of the vehicle, he squinted against the blinding light streaming in through the front window and caught sight of Eddie in the driver's seat.

Javier pulled on his magic, but it wasn't there. Twisting his hands to one side, he craned his neck to get a view of his them. They were bound with magic rope, which meant his magic had been blocked.

Rolling back to his side, he caught Eddie's gaze in the rearview mirror. "Where are we going?"

Eddie laughed at him. "I'm taking you home. Right neighborly of me."

"You're just going to drop me off?" Javier doubted that. He rubbed his hands against the seat, but there wasn't any give in the rope. His hands weren't tingling just from lying on them; the rope was tight enough to cut off some of his circulation.

They drove in silence for a few more minutes. The stops

and starts alerted Javier that they'd reached the city limits. Glancing at the passing scenery visible through the top of the window, he knew he didn't have much time before they reached his apartment.

Scenarios ran through his mind. If he had his hands free, he could definitely overpower Eddie. But with both his hands and his magic bound, his options were limited. They hadn't bound his feet though. If Eddie was stupid enough to open the driver's side door where his feet were, he might have a chance.

When the vehicle pulled into his building's underground parking area, he prepared to act.

Eddie stopped the vehicle and turned to peer at Javier. "Don't try anything or I won't be nice." He waved his hand in Javier's direction, and his throat constricted. His instincts were telling him to break whatever held him captive, but without his hands and magic, he was helpless.

Javier fought for air against an invisible enemy as his vision blurred and he became lightheaded. The door opened at Javier's head and Eddie released the spell. Javier gulped air into his lungs as Eddie hovered over him. "Another handy little trick. And I'll do it again if you don't do as I say."

A strong energy force entered the vehicle, and Javier was flung backward out of the SUV. His ass hit the pavement first, and then his head did a good imitation of a bouncing ball. Stars flashed before his vision as he blinked, struggling to remain conscious.

"Get up." Eddie grabbed Javier by an elbow and hauled him up. The movement jerked him to his feet so fast that it had to have been assisted by magic. "Move."

Eddie pushed Javier forward and headed toward the rarely used stairwell and not the elevator. By the time they got to Javier's floor, he was winded and his head throbbed like a strobe light in an old disco bar.

Falling into the hallway, he stumbled his way to his apartment. He leaned against the wall outside his door and closed his eyes to stave off more nausea.

He needed to make a move. It was now or never. Taking a deep breath, he slammed sideways into Eddie, knocking him off his feet, and they both fell forward. At the last second, Javier pushed his shoulder downward so he didn't smack his face into the floor, then flipped onto his back. Putting his heels together, he bent his knees, lifting them and slamming his heels into the floor while pulling his body forward. He used the momentum to jerk his entire body forward and onto his feet.

Spinning around, Eddie was standing only a few feet away. The gun in his hand stopped Javier in his tracks. "Enough of this shit. Open your fucking door."

"I spelled the door. I need my magic to release it."

"What? You think I'm a stupid fucker? As soon as I release your magic, you'll attack."

"Probably," Javier agreed, but it was also true that he couldn't undo the spell without his magic.

"Fine. Let's do it your way, but with a twist."

Javier frowned. "What?"

Eddie shifted the gun's position and pulled the trigger. The bullet tore through Javier, sending him backward to the carpeted floor. An agony unlike any he'd ever felt before pierced his leg and rippled throughout his entire body. Between the injury to his head and the one to his leg, he was consumed by endless pain.

"Now I know you'll do what I say. I'll remove the magic rope, but if you don't want to eat a bullet this time, you won't try anything." Eddie kicked his hip, pushing him over, sending shards of pain shooting up his leg. "Move. I need to get to your hands to take off the rope."

Javier sucked in a breath and rolled to his side, giving

Eddie access to his wrists. As soon as his magic was released, Javier removed the spell on the door, but he didn't have the energy to get to his feet. He lay in the hallway bleeding to death; he never expected this would be how he would die.

"Oh for fuck's sake, you're taking too long."

Javier felt the huge blast of energy in the air before he registered that his body was airborne. Eddie's magic flung him through the doorway. He didn't have time to react as his leg hit one side of the doorframe, his head the other, before he was smashing into the far wall of his apartment.

CONNOR FLASHED to the designated meeting area and saw a house a couple of hundred feet in front of him. He knew from what his dad said it was Linda's new house—the one built after the fire, because it had been her house they'd been in when Julia died.

Turning around, he took in what he could see of the massive property. There were a couple of houses in the distance and behind them was the field of wildflowers where the old house used to stand. The rest of the area was a wide-open field with copses of trees and more wildflowers growing through the tall grasses. The mountains in the background rounded out the majestic setting.

Rowena landed by his side. "Is something wrong?"

Turning to her, he pulled her into his arms and kissed her. She melted into him like she was meant to be there; if they were at his place or Joel's, he'd take the kiss further. Instead, he let her go, and pushed one of her curls behind her ear. "No, I was just looking around."

"Hey," Joel said.

They both turned around to see his uncle a few feet away. "Hey. Did you talk to Dad?"

"No," his dad said from where he landed on the grass a couple of feet away. He looked around the vast area. "Where's Javier?"

Connor met his dad's worried gaze. "I haven't heard from him since we split up this morning. But he should be here shortly."

"Hello," a woman called out as she walked toward them. She looked to be in her late seventies but seemed fit and spry. When she reached them, she stuck out her hand to his dad. "It's been a while, Frank."

His dad shook the woman's hand before gesturing to the rest of the group. "Linda, you would have met my son, Connor, a long time ago." No one mentioned that the day they'd met was the day that Julia died. Connor shook the woman's hand as his dad continued the introductions and her messy salt and pepper bun bounced as she nodded.

"I saw this meeting in a vision. Did you reach out to my mother in the beyond and speak with her?" Linda asked, her glance passing amongst them.

Frank gave her a nod. "Yes, last night. Have you spoken to her?"

A sadness passed over the woman's face. "No, not for a long time. I know of someone who has the ability to reach out to her, but she's not of this world anymore. It's not like just calling her up for a chat."

"Understood." His dad checked his watch and frowned. "Javier should be here by now. I got detained and he went on ahead. He should have been at least twenty minutes ahead of me."

"I'll call him." Rowena had her phone out and was calling him before she even finished speaking, and he heard the faint sounds of ringing coming through the phone's speaker. "It went to voicemail," she said a few seconds later.

His dad checked his phone. "No messages. Something's not right. Javier is one of the most responsible people I've ever met. I'll flash to his apartment and see if he's there."

"Frank, I can go instead. You stay with Connor," Joel offered.

"No, I should go. He's my agent, and I need to make sure he's okay. Plus, I've got the training if needed. I'll be right back."

When his dad flashed, Connor turned to Linda. "While we wait for my dad, is there anything about the key to the map that we should know?"

Linda smiled, her wrinkles becoming more pronounced around her eyes. "Not really, but I can give you some background. I don't know what my mom told you, so I'll just give you the Cliffs Notes version of what's been handed down through the generations in my family. When the magic box was created, some magics knew the destruction it could wreak, and since they couldn't destroy it or the map, they tried to counteract it by making it difficult for the box to be located instead. They created a key to the map that will show the box's location that has been passed down through my family."

"No offense, but what if your family line no longer existed?" As if he was writing one of his novels, Connor could see plot holes in the story.

Linda chuckled. "You would think that could happen, but remember, we are a family of seers. We knew when this would happen and how large our family would become."

Connor raised his eyebrow. "You knew we would come for the key today?"

"No. We can't always see details like that, but we knew in

the twenty-first century there would be a search for the box and that it would be opened."

"Opened?" Rowena stepped forward and slipped her fingers into Connor's. "If we get the key, we won't open the box, but you know someone will? Who?"

"I don't know. Like I said, I don't always get details." Linda turned to face the open field. "And before you ask… several keys were made and are with other families around the world. How the holder of the map is supposed to find those families, I don't know. Perhaps the families know who will come for the key, as I did. I knew that someone from your family line would come some day for this key and I wouldn't need to reach out to you."

That led Connor to so many more potential problems. "I hadn't realized that there were more keys. I thought maybe if we left this key alone and Drew didn't know to contact you, the box would be safe, but that wouldn't be true, would it?"

"Like I said, I don't get all the details, so I don't know. But since you're here now, how about we just get you the key?"

Connor wondered if Linda was hedging because she'd seen something she didn't want him to know. Maybe it was like the situation Helen had mentioned the night before— telling someone could cause them to change course and that could lead to further tragedy.

Just then, his dad arrived and he looked more worried than he had when he left. "Javier wasn't at his apartment or at the office. I'm going to keep looking. Instead of calling, I decided to stop back here to make sure everything was alright and see if Javier and I crossed paths mid-flash. I also think I just needed to see that you were all okay." He looked between them all. "You good without me?"

"Yes, we've got this." Connor caught his dad's gaze before he left. "Be careful."

"I will. You too," he said right before he flashed away.

Joel turned to Linda. "Okay, how do we get the key? I'm assuming it's not as easy as you just pulling it out of your pocket?"

Linda smiled. "No, it's definitely not a key I'd want to be carrying around." She turned to face Connor. "Do you have the book Jack gave you?"

Connor didn't bother to ask how she knew Jack gave him the book; duh—seer. He held out his hands and used his magic to call for the book from the hiding spot where he'd left it. The book landed in his hands, pushing them down a touch with its weight. The dusty smell wafted up to him as he sandwiched the smooth leather between his hands.

He conjured a small blanket and spread it on the grass and placed the book on it. Kneeling on the soft grass in front of it, he almost expected the ancient book to creak as he opened it. He was a tad disappointed that it didn't.

After pulling out the map Jack had tucked inside the cover, he spread it out on the blanket beside the book. He ran his finger along one of the deep crease lines marking the entire surface, surprised it wasn't brittle considering how old it was. "I expected the map to be older and in worse condition." Connor looked at Rowena. "Do you know how Jack found the map? Was it spelled?"

Rowena knelt beside him. "Jack and Meredith used a spell within the book to retrieve the map, so I'm guessing it was protected by wherever it was stored. Simon and Jo found the book in some kind of realm." She shook her head and her lips twitched. "Some days I'm still amazed by all this."

Joel and Linda joined them on the blanket. Joel studied the map before looking up at Linda. "It's not as impressive as I expected it to be."

"My thoughts exactly." Rowena smiled at Joel. "Now what?"

"Only one person can retrieve the key because they will

need to reach into the portal and retrieve it. Who will it be?" Linda asked.

"I'll do it." Connor didn't know what would happen, but he wasn't willing to chance someone else he loved getting hurt. He paused, feeling like a romantic lead in a novel. The familial love he felt for his uncle was a no-brainer, but Rowena? He looked over at her and she smiled. His past would never change, but the solitary existence of his future that stretched endlessly out in front of him could. Feeling deep into his soul, he recognized he was falling in love with her.

"Are you okay?" she asked.

"Yes." He reached over and clasped her hand. "I'm good." And he was, no matter what happened to him. He still wasn't sure he could burden anyone with the guilt he would always carry, or if he would be enough to keep them safe, but in that minute, with Rowena at his side, he felt invincible. He felt deeply for her, and nothing was going to change that.

"Connor, turn to the right a few inches so you're fully facing north," Linda said. When he complied, Linda continued. "Place one hand on the book and one on the map near the end." She pointed to the place where the box's location would be. He smiled when he saw a small x on the map. "Now pull on her magic and envision a physical key."

"That's it?" It seemed way too simple.

Linda smiled. "Almost. The key is hidden in a realm to the north. A portal will open and you'll need to reach in and retrieve the key. Even though I'm now the keeper of the key, I've never actually seen it, but I was instructed at a young age on what to do."

"Okay, here goes nothing." Connor placed one hand on the map and one on the book. "Wait, how am I going to grab the key when both hands are occupied?"

"Oh right." Linda laughed. "When the portal opens, you

can lift your hand off the book, but you must keep in contact with the map."

Connor nodded and pulled on his magic. He'd once done research about old keys for one of his books and knew that the first keys in existence were rough and made of wood. Hoping this key had been updated over the centuries, he pictured a large, ornate brass key with a big loop on one end.

Directing his magic to the north, Connor held the picture of the key in his mind while leaning forward to keep in physical contact with the book and the map. The field of grass and the trees before him glazed over as he continued to picture the key.

"There," he heard Rowena whisper.

The air darkened as a small, gray, round cloud floated directly in front of him. It grew bigger, circling clockwise, until it was almost as large as he was, hanging in the air.

The middle of the cloud became lighter and lighter, like a white opaque door. Then all at once it dissolved, as if the door had opened to reveal a blue cloud inside. Sitting on the cloud was a key.

He'd never seen anything like it. A grin split his face as he reached to take the key. He could picture a huge guillotine coming down on his hand, causing him to snatch the key as fast as he could.

When he pulled the key free, the door closed and the cloud disappeared, leaving a clear line of sight to the trees beyond.

The key was warm and exactly as he'd pictured it.

Rowena leaned over his shoulder. "Is it heavy?"

He bounced the key in his hand. "Yes, it has some weight to it." He looked up. "We'll have to hide the key now."

Joel snorted. "Yes, which is ironic considering that's what the portal was supposed to do."

Linda stood. "Placing the key on the x on the map will

locate the magic box for you." She stepped off the blanket. "I will leave you now. I wish you luck."

Rowena picked up the map and Joel grabbed the book as Connor disappeared the blanket. "Thank you for everything, Linda." She flashed away and he turned to Rowena and Joel. "I'm not sure where would be a safe place."

"That won't be necessary, Connor. I'll take the key now."

Connor turned around to see Drew standing only a few feet in front of him, and he instinctively took a step back.

"You can't escape me, Connor. The key is mine. It was really good of Javier to tell me where you were going to be. Too bad he had to die to do it."

Connor clutched the key tight in his fist as Drew stood only a few feet in front of him. "What did you do to Javier?"

Drew took a step forward, but Connor stood his ground. "Javier was kind enough to show us where you were meeting and then he had an unfortunate accident. He was a good agent, but never as good as me."

Drew tsked and shook his head, but Connor didn't give him the response he wanted.

"I'm done playing around," Drew said, all signs of his mock congeniality dropping from his face. "Give me the key or I'll take it."

Connor knew from years of friendship that one of Drew's biggest weaknesses was impatience. He'd always suspected that one day it would get Drew into a situation he wouldn't be able to get out of, and Connor was going to use it to his advantage now.

The more Connor told Drew no, the more Drew's impatience would grow and then he'd make an impulsive move. Connor just hoped he'd be able to capitalize on it. "I'm not going to give it to you." He didn't say 'duh,' but Connor was sure Drew knew it was implied. He did have to give it to the guy—he was definitely tenacious.

Again, Drew took another step forward, his impatience already showing. "You always were a sanctimonious prick, Connor. But this time it works in my favor because I know what you're willing to do. And not do. As for me, I'm willing to do anything."

Out of the corner of his eye, Connor saw Rowena move toward Drew to address him. "I don't believe you. Javier didn't give you anything, and you didn't kill him."

Rowena was like a fierce mother bear protecting her cub, but he feared she'd underestimated her opponent. Drew was a loose cannon.

Don't aggravate him. Connor threw the thought into Rowena's mind.

Javier is not dead and Drew can't win, she threw back. Rowena was blond and beautiful and that's all guys like Drew would see. Connor would bet that's all Drew had ever seen, even though he knew her profession and what she'd been through. But Connor had seen the intelligent, brave warrior she had inside her. He loved how strong she was, but this wasn't the time to play that card. Drew's enormous but fragile ego wouldn't deal well with feeling threatened.

Connor decided to become the threat, knowing it would trigger Drew, and took another step closer to him, until they were almost nose to nose. He hoped to put the focus on him and not Rowena. Something touched his arm on the other side of Rowena, and he looked down to see his uncle's hand staying him.

Joel didn't look at him but he met Drew's gaze head on. "Drew, we're not going to give you the key. But there are other keys located around the world; go find one of those," Joel said in a patient voice.

It took a moment for Connor to understand why his uncle had mentioned the other keys. He realized his uncle's words weren't meant for Drew—they were for him. If there were other keys in the world, then Drew could get one of those. But finding one of them would take time, which might give them the time and distance they needed to stop Drew. Joel was telling him to send the key somewhere safe.

Drew squinted at Joel. "I remember you. You're Connor's fucked-up uncle. Stay out of this, old man. I don't have time for games, and I don't give a shit about the other keys. Not when Connor has one here and now." Drew turned away from Joel and held his hand out toward Connor. "Give me the fucking key now or someone else is going to end up with the same fate as Javier."

Beside him, Rowena gasped. "Oh no!"

Connor turned to Rowena and followed her gaze to the map she was cradling in her palms. The edges were slowly crumbling as if the map was self-destructing.

"Looks like you've got a little problem there," Drew taunted.

He really was an annoying ass. If the map disintegrated, did it mean the key would too? Or was the map disappearing because they now had the key? And what would that mean for the magic box? Maybe if he didn't put the key on the map before the map completely disappeared, the key would become useless to them and Drew still had his own map to use the key on.

"Connor, hurry!" Rowena held out the map. "We have to do something. The map is half gone and it looks like it's now dissolving faster."

Joel touched his arm again. "Hide the key, Connor."

"No! Give it to me." Drew lunged at Connor, his arm outstretched. He grabbed Connor's hand, squeezing his fingers, just as the key disappeared from his palm and he sent the key to the safest place he could think of.

"Where the fuck did you send it?" Drew yelled, letting go of Connor and shoving him back with both hands.

Stumbling backward, Connor managed to stay on his feet and rocked forward, sending magic through his hands and into Drew. The force sent Drew back about ten feet; it hadn't been meant to hurt him, just stave him off.

Connor turned to Rowena just as someone flashed to Drew's side. He'd never seen the man, but he expected it was Eddie, Snake and Drew's goon. Eddie flashed in front of Connor, blocking his path to Rowena.

"Kill him!" Drew yelled at Eddie as he got to his feet.

Connor pulled on his magic again, but this time he wasn't going to play nice. He sent a blast of magic straight to Eddie's chest. He must have anticipated Connor's move, since he flashed out of the way and Connor's shot of magic disintegrated in the air.

Connor flipped around, looking for Drew and Eddie. Fear crawled up his throat as he witnessed Joel and Rowena facing off with Drew. All three of them stood with balls of magic glowing in their palms, facing each other. Before Connor could help them, Eddie flashed in front of him again.

"Javier was a trained FBI agent and he couldn't defeat me. You're just a lazy fucker who sits on his ass all day." Eddie sneered at Connor and held up his hands, palms facing him in a 'come get me' gesture. "Come on, give me all you've got."

Connor had never learned how to fight. All his adult life, he'd hidden himself away, believing he was the harmful one and that if he didn't engage with anyone, he'd never hurt anyone again. How naive he'd been. Years ago, his dad and uncle Ben had tried to convince him to learn how to use his magic to defend himself, but he'd always refused. Now he would rely on everything he'd learned researching fight scenes for his books and hope that his magic would make up for his lack of knowledge.

He pulled hard on his magic and raised his hands.

"Noooooo!" Rowena screamed behind him and an image of Julia flashed in his mind. If it was between saving himself and someone he loved, he wouldn't let history repeat itself.

Ignoring Eddie, Connor flashed to Rowena's side and knocked her out of the way with his body as he aimed a shot of magic toward Drew.

A shocked expression crossed Drew's face just before the blast hit him in the shoulder and flung him backward. Connor swung toward Rowena.

He extended his hand, pulling her to her feet. "Are you hurt?"

"No, but Joel is." She conjured a ball of flame in each palm as she faced Eddie. "Can you check on him?"

It took every ounce of willpower Connor had to tear his gaze from Rowena and let her face Eddie on her own. He didn't want to but he respected her, and he had to check on his uncle.

Rowena and Eddie stood in a face-off as Connor tried to keep one eye on them while looking at Joel. He was on the ground unmoving. While still keeping an eye on Rowena, Connor pushed his magic through his fingers and he waved his hand toward his uncle in a type of magic smelling salts.

Joel groaned and covered his eyes with his arm. "I'm fine."

That was good enough for now. Connor turned and fully faced Rowena and Eddie. They were still in a showdown with magic sparking in their palms. Connor saw the moment Eddie decided to make his move. His frown deepened in concentration as he pulled one hand back.

Not waiting to see where Eddie aimed his magic, Connor flashed in front of Rowena. As he landed, he turned sideways, taking Rowena with him, blocking her from Eddie's view.

Eddie's shot connected with his shoulder, knocking the wind out of him as he toppled backward, Rowena beneath him. She cried out as they hit the hard ground and he rolled off her, jumping to his feet with his good arm raised.

Connor looked around, searching for Eddie, and saw him about twenty yards in the distance helping Drew to his feet. Turning to Rowena, he gave her a hand up. "Flash to Joel and erect a protection around you both. I'm right behind you."

Out of the corner of his eye, he saw Rowena at Joel's side as he continued to watch Drew. Connor knew Drew, and losing the key wouldn't sit well with him; his ego wouldn't allow it. Connor raised his hands and pulled on his draining magic to protect himself when Eddie disappeared.

Drew stood up straight and smiled at Connor as he disappeared. Connor spun around and came face to face with Eddie, his hand raised. Instead of magic, Eddie held a gun.

In the split second that the gun registered with Connor, he turned and pulled on his magic as Eddie pulled the trigger.

The impact of the bullet sent fire racing through Connor's arm, spinning him as he dropped to the ground.

"You're becoming a pain in the ass. Just like Javier was, but I took care of him." Eddie spit out as he stood over him.

"Connor!" Rowena flashed to his side, using her magic to stem the flow of blood.

"Eddie, he—"

"He's gone." Rowena's words cut him off and he laid back, closing his eyes. "Connor, stay with me!" she yelled at him.

Opening his eyes, Rowena looked like an angel above him. "I'm just resting. Joel?"

Rowena brushed the hair off his forehead with one hand as the other one continued to heal him, her magic a sharp sting as it closed his wound. "He's weak and needs to recharge, but I healed him. We all need to recharge. Do you have enough energy to flash back to the cabin?"

"Yeah, I think so." He didn't know for sure, but they had to get out of the field. "Joel?"

His uncle came up beside them. "I'll make it."

At the cabin they'd rest and eat to recharge their magic and then they'd have to decide what to do about the key. At least it was in a safe place.

DREW TORE through Connor's bedroom, tossing the bedding to the floor and upturning the mattress. He may not have seen Connor face to face for a long time, but he'd watched him over the years. Connor never strayed far from his house, so it made sense that he would have sent the key here.

Nothing had gone right with this plan. Not once in the more than twenty years since his father told him about it. Drew had done everything asked of him, but he still didn't have the power he craved. This afternoon he'd let his father know that he had the box—a bit premature perhaps, but he'd have it before the day was out. If he had to kill Connor and Rowena and the stupid uncle in the process, he'd just consider them collateral damage.

For so long, he'd been controlled by others—his mother; his grandparents; the FBI; his dad's partner, Maverick; and now by Connor and his stupidity. He'd make Connor pay for making him put up with all this shit.

Eddie sauntered into the bedroom. "The other rooms are empty. I've torn his office to shit and couldn't find the key."

"It has to be here!" Drew shouted. "Check the living room again."

Eddie flashed away and Drew looked around the room. "What does Connor value the most?" he asked the empty room. He turned slowly, looking at what was in the room—a bed, a dresser… a dog bed in the corner. The answer was so obvious Drew smiled and flashed to Connor's office.

His large, stupid dog was lying on the couch, the muzzle Drew had put on him firmly around his snout. The dog had snarled and barked at Drew when he'd first arrived. Drew thought about killing the dog to shut him up, but thought the ugly mutt might come in handy and now he had. Drew pulled out his phone and pulled up Connor's contact info. He held out his phone to Eddie. "Here, take this."

"Why?"

Drew was fucking tired of people questioning him. When he had the power from the box, he'd never have to worry about that again. He'd be able to control non-magics and idiot magics, like Eddie. "Because I fucking told you to."

"Jesus, man. Don't get your panties in a knot." Eddie took the phone and stared at it as if it would bite. "Now what?"

"Aim it at me and call Connor on FaceTime. Just make sure he can see me."

Eddie tapped the screen and held it up toward Drew. "Whatever."

Drew would deal with Eddie later because right now Connor needed to be dealt with first. He grabbed the muzzled dog in a headlock and held a knife to his throat.

"What do you want, Drew?" Connor answered and Drew had a bit of a thrill at seeing Connor so pale. He could just imagine how weak he was.

"I want the key."

"You'll have to find it first."

"No, you're going to give it to me. Can you see where I am? Eddie, move the camera around the room."

When Eddie moved the camera back on Drew he jerked the dog higher so he was in the shot.

"Let him go! He's an innocent animal!" Connor yelled.

Drew loved seeing the self-righteous Connor lose his shit. "No. And if you don't get here in three minutes, I'm going to slit his throat." Drew rubbed the blade against the dog's throat and wanted so much to cut him. He'd get the key, but he wanted to make Connor pay for putting him through all this shit. But not yet. He needed Connor to come to him.

"Don't hurt him. He's an innocent."

"Then you better get here. You're down to two and a half minutes now." He wasn't watching the time, so he could count down any way he wanted."

Connor's face looked red as he stared into the phone. "I can't flash. Your boy there shot me. Remember, Drew? How do you expect me to get there?"

"I don't fucking care. You'll find a way. You've got two minutes to get here or I'll kill your mangy mutt and leave his limp body for you. Eddie, disconnect."

Drew let go of the dog, but he didn't sheath his knife. He'd give Connor a minute and put the knife back to the dog's neck. Drew moved his head from side to side, needing to stretch to relieve the tension that had built from all the hoops he'd had to jump through. It had been a long day and he'd had enough. His dad should arrive tonight and he'd already told him he had the box. He wasn't going to let Connor make him a liar.

He straightened up and glanced over at Eddie. "How long's it been?"

"How the hell would I know?"

Yes, Eddie's days were numbered. Drew wrapped his arm around the dog's neck and hauled him back up. When the dog let out a whimper, Drew tightened his arm just a bit and the whimpering stopped. Holding his knife to the dog's throat, he faced the middle of the room and knew he wouldn't have to wait much longer. Connor was such a fucking goody-two-shoes, he'd make it in under the three minutes.

Right as he expected, less than twenty seconds later, Connor arrived, followed by Rowena and his useless uncle. Connor and Joel were both pale and breathing heavily. Drew loved it that the short flash had drained them. It meant that they'd been forced to do his bidding when they really had been weak, and now they were too weak to fight him.

The dog squirmed and whimpered again. It was time to show Connor that he meant business. He wanted to slice the stupid animal's throat from one side to the other but held back. He needed the key first. He used the tip of his knife and nicked the dog on the side of his neck, and he tried to pull away, but Drew added a bit of magic to his hold, just in case.

"Nooooo!" Rowena cried and the sound made Drew smile. He turned to her, flashing his pearly whites. "Convince Connor to give me the key and I'll be happy to let the dog go."

Drew knew he had to hurry things along. Even with Connor and his uncle injured, it was still three against two, and he couldn't waste any more time. He needed the box in hand before his dad arrived. "Eddie, aim your gun at Rowena."

"About fucking time." Eddie flashed behind Rowena and put his gun to her head. "If you try to flash away, bitch, I'll just kill your lover boy there."

Drew pulled the dog higher so he had to balance on his hind legs, eliciting another whimper from the pathetic animal. "Connor, I've been patient for long enough, and Eddie here has a really itchy trigger finger. Tell me where the fucking key is."

"Connor, tell him." Maybe the stupid uncle still had some smarts after all.

"Yes, Connor, tell me," he mimicked.

Connor pointed at the dog. "Look down. The key is on Doyle's collar."

Fuck. How did he miss that? It was hanging right below his arm where he had the dog in a headlock. Whatever, it didn't matter. "Eddie, if either of them moves, kill the woman."

"Right, boss."

Keeping the chokehold on the dog, he laid the knife on the arm of the couch and used his free hand to rip the key off the fucking collar. He shoved the key in his pants' pocket and grabbed his knife. He jerked the dog higher, the animal's legs scrambling for purchase, and Drew looked over at Connor. "Connor, it never had to be this way. You could have joined me years ago. If you weren't such a pansy-ass, I never would have had to change your memory."

Connor's eyes widened. "You did that? How?"

Drew couldn't hold back his smile. He'd been waiting for this moment for years, wanting to prove to Connor how inferior he was, even with his magic specialty. A specialty he didn't even know about because of Drew. His dad had been right—the Davis family was nothing. He'd finally get to prove it. "I can alter memories when they happen. As long as I'm within three minutes of the memory forming."

Rowena glared at him. "You changed Javier's memory yesterday, didn't you?"

Drew laughed again. "Yes, and it wasn't even a challenge." He looked Connor right in the eyes. "I altered your memory so you wouldn't know your own powers, and then I burned Julia. You believed you had done it. It was the perfect crime."

Connor's eyes flared with anger. "Why? She was just a little girl."

"Because the seer said she'd be important one day and I was so fucking tired of your self-righteousness. You had everything you wanted and wouldn't even consider joining me to help find the box. It's taken years to find it, but with your powers, we would have had it more than twenty years ago. You were always on your moral high horse. Well, I knocked you off that fucker. I wanted you to suffer and you did. Now, before I leave, I could change this memory, and make it all rainbows and fucking unicorns in your mind, but I want you to remember that I defeated you today. That I won."

"It's not a contest, Drew. And do you honestly think you can control what's in the magic box? There's a reason it's been locked away for centuries. No one has ever controlled power like what the box is rumored to contain."

Drew grinned. "I know I will. Eddie, pistol whip him."

"I'd love to." Eddie hauled his arm back and smashed the butt of his weapon along the side of Connor's head before he could react.

As Rowena's and the uncle's eyes were on Connor, Drew slid his knife along the dog's throat and flashed.

22

onnor's eyes fluttered open and the bright lights sent a shooting pain through his skull. Slamming his eyes shut, he groaned like he'd been on a week-long bender.

Rowena swept the hair off his forehead, and he realized he was lying on the floor with his head in her lap. "Oh my god, Connor. You scared the crap out of us." She bent down and placed an awkward, sideways kiss on his lips. "You've been out for five minutes."

"Help me up, please." Rowena stood and hauled him to his feet, and he stifled another groan. He tucked a curl behind her ear and placed a soft kiss on her forehead. "I'm fine." Facing the couch, his uncle Joel was sitting with Doyle's head and upper body sprawled on his lap. "Is he okay?" Connor flopped into the chair beside the couch and reached over, rubbing Doyle's head.

"Drew cut Doyle's throat, but Rowena was able to heal him. I didn't have enough energy to do it myself. The injury and flashing here almost drained me." Joel's voice was full of remorse.

"Uncle Joel, it wasn't your fault." Connor turned to Rowena. "Thank you."

"Of course. My healing powers aren't the best, but the wound wasn't even deep. I think Drew just wanted you to see his power over you."

Connor dropped his head back onto the chair's cushion and closed his eyes. "And now he has the key and our map is gone."

She sat on an arm of his chair and rubbed his shoulder. "It's not great, but we'll figure something out."

"Rowena, we need to face reality, the key is gone and we don't even know where the others are. On top of that, we no longer have the map. We need it for the key to find the box's location."

He knew she'd been trying to comfort him like he was doing to Doyle, but unlike his dog, Connor didn't deserve it. He'd gotten Doyle injured and it could have been so much worse. Rowena or Joel could have been hurt or killed and he'd lost the key to Drew, who probably had the box right now. Jack had entrusted him with the map and now it was gone.

He opened his eyes as another realization sank in. "Drew can change memories. At least we know now why what I've remembered for years didn't make sense—because it hadn't actually happened. I wonder how Drew altered Javier's memory yesterday."

Joel gently lifted Doyle off his lap and stood. Doyle's tongue lolled out of the side of his mouth and he jumped to the floor. Relief flooded Connor at seeing his dog back to his normal, happy self.

"There's no way Javier would have given anything away—even under duress—he's too much of a professional from what your dad's told me. My bet is that Drew made Javier believe that he had the box," Joel said. "You should probably check in with your dad to see if he's found Javier. I'm going to take Doyle for a long walk. I need some fresh air and Doyle has been inside all day. He probably needs to work out some stress too and see things are back to normal."

Connor smiled up at his uncle. "Thanks." When Joel had taken Doyle out the sliding glass doors, he reached for Rowena and pulled her onto his lap. "I'm so sorry," he whispered into her hair as he wrapped his arms around her.

"Connor, you have nothing to be sorry for."

"I failed again." He felt the weight of the guilt that had been such a constant companion for so long settle on him once again. "I gave Drew the key, and he could have killed Doyle, and we still don't know what he did to Javier. He could have hurt you too. I don't know what I would have done if he had."

She pushed his hair out of his eyes and the tender look she gave him increased his guilt. He didn't deserve her tenderness.

"Connor—"

"I need to check in with my dad." He lifted them both up so they were standing in the middle of his office. He was taking the coward's way out by not letting her comfort him, but he couldn't take it right now. He didn't deserve it. "I'll see if Dad has found Javier yet."

"Sure. I'll... uh... I'm just going to go outside for a bit." She pointed at the sliding glass doors to the back deck. The look of rejection on her face tore at him, but he didn't know what else to do.

He'd thought that maybe he could have a future with someone, but once more he'd let Drew best him. If he was a character in one of his novels, he'd call the character whiny and even verging on martyrdom. Was he? Or was he just trying to protect Rowena?

For years he'd lived on his own and being content had been good enough. Then Rowena burst into his life and made him realize he'd been lonely too. Now, even with all the shit with Drew and the magic box, Rowena had brightened his life, but would he be enough for her? She was a bright spot of sunshine in his life and he was darkness.

"Ugh!" He snorted and pushed his bangs back with both hands. His thoughts were so cliché, he'd red ink them in a manuscript, yet it didn't make them any less true.

He didn't want to be the one to dim Rowena's light.

ROWENA LEANED her elbows on the porch railing and looked up at the stars. Years ago she developed the habit of going to the patio behind The Magic Plate to stare into the sky.

She wondered if her parents and brothers could see her. "Mom and Dad, I miss you so much!"

"Did you ever say you missed me?"

Rowena's hand flew to her chest at Taren's voice. "Taren, stop doing that!"

He laughed. It was such a beautiful sound, especially hearing it out loud and not just in her head. Taren sat on the railing beside her, looking real and carefree.

"How am I seeing you without Connor in the room?"

"I think it's because you're connected with Connor now."

"Hmmm. Well… to answer your question… yes, I used to tell you and Mirek that I missed you too. I'd tell you all about my day and wonder if you could hear me."

They were silent for several minutes as they stared out into the darkness. Even though she hadn't posed a question, it wasn't lost on Rowena that Taren hadn't said whether he could hear her or not when she spoke to the stars at night.

Maybe that was for the best. If she knew for sure they could hear her, she would worry about what to say. And if they couldn't hear her, she didn't want to know because it would be too depressing to think she was talking into nothing and she'd never connect with her family again.

"I was told I could do something," Taren said quietly.

"Hmmm?" Rowena turned to her brother. She'd been so lost in her thoughts, his words hadn't fully registered. "Sorry, Taren. I was wool gathering. What did you say?"

"Ha, wool gathering. Mom used to say that."

Rowena smiled. "Yes, she had so many phrases." She'd cried the first time she'd unconsciously uttered her mother's words after her death. Now, the familiar phrases brought her comfort. "What was it you said?"

Taren moved so he was lying across the top of the railing. She had to bite her lip to stop the reprimand that sprang to her tongue. She almost warned him to be careful, that he could hurt himself if he fell.

"I was told I could do something for you."

"What's that?" She held back from asking him who told him he could do something. It was another one of those things she wasn't sure she wanted to know.

Taren sat up and swung his legs over the railing, facing her. "Do you want to talk to Mom?"

"Can I do that?" She'd never thought to ask, even though she could talk to Taren. He'd indicated that he'd been somewhere else for a while. "Has Mom been where you were before and now she's here?"

"She's still there, but I can get her for you. But I was told I can only do it this one time. I don't know why, but there's a lot of rules, just like there was in school."

Her mom had been gone for years now. If she saw her, it would be like she died all over again when she left. But it didn't matter, Rowena would never pass up this opportunity to see her mom again. Even once. She stared at the stars again before turning to her brother. "Yes. Do it."

Taren faded away and Rowena waited, wondering where to look. She shoved her hands in the pocket of her skirt and then pulled them out again and rested her elbows on the railing as she looked at the night sky while she waited.

"Oh, my beautiful girl. Look at how you've grown!"

Rowena spun around to see her mother standing by the edge of the deck, the moonlight highlighting her. A lump formed in Rowena's throat. She swallowed against it but it did nothing to stop the tears welling in her eyes. "Mom," she breathed and took a step closer. Her mother looked exactly like she had many years ago, before the magic consumed her and took her life. "So many times, I wondered what I'd say if I could magically go back in time and see you again. Ha—and that was before I knew that magic even existed."

Her mom floated closer and passed her hand over the side of Rowena's head, leaving a tingling sensation along her hairline. For years, she'd longed to feel her mom's touch again. It wasn't the same, but it was more than Rowena had in a long time and she'd cherish it.

"I expect you were angry when you discovered what your aunts and I did."

More tears welled in Rowena's eyes, blurring her mom's image. She waved her hand in front of her face, magically drying her tears before more fell. "Yes, I was a bit at first, but not like Jo and Meredith. I understood what you'd gone through. You were just trying to keep us safe."

"Yes. And I would do it again. Keeping you safe meant more to me than anything else, even my own life."

Her mother looked lovingly over at where Taren perched on the railing. She'd lost her husband and two sons and was willing to die herself to save Rowena. No mother should have to go through what she had. The image of Matt Damon's character at the grave sites in *Saving Private Ryan* popped into her head. Had she done enough in her life to make up for her mother's sacrifice? Had she saved enough people? She swallowed again as her throat burned. "I've tried to live the best life possible."

"Oh, baby girl. I didn't want that for you. I want you to just live."

"But why—" She choked on her words and tears obscured her vision. Waving away the tears, she took a deep breath. "Why me? Why not you, or Dad, or Mirek and Taren? It's not fair that I lived and—" she choked on a sob, her emotions threatening to drown her, before she tried again— "and none of you did."

"Baby girl, we don't get to decide that. No one does. All we can do is live the life we have. You can't make up for what's happened, and I don't want you to try. I want you to be happy."

"I miss you all so much!" Again, Rowena used her magic to dry her tears. They obscured her vision and she wasn't willing to miss even one second of seeing her mother. She locked her gaze on her mom and soaked her in: her blond hair, her bright blue eyes, and every single wrinkle and laugh line.

"One day you will see us again, but you have a long life ahead of you. I want you to live it with abandon. I want you to experience life to the fullest and love with all your heart, never worrying about disappointments or heartbreaks that might be in your future."

If only she was more carefree. Could she be? Could she love Connor regardless of the guilt that weighed him down? "I've met someone. You know him... Connor Davis."

Her mother nodded and her image faded enough that

Rowena could see the deck railing through her. "Yes, he's a good boy." Her mom smiled at Taren before looking back at her. "Before I go I need you to do something for me."

"Anything."

"I want you to remember that you cannot save everyone, nor is it your responsibility to do so. Everyone must choose their own path, just like I did. And your father. He knew that Daniel Knight and some others on the council were getting out of hand, and he and his brothers chose not to fight them. You cannot choose a path for someone. All you can do is point out the way. It is up to them whether they choose to follow it or not."

Rowena knew her mom was talking about Connor. She was falling more in love with him every day and she didn't know how she would walk away if he wasn't willing to follow her.

"I will always love you, baby girl."

Rowena watched as her mother faded away, then she closed her eyes and let the tears fall. She breathed in and out slowly, calming her heartbeat, while her mother's words played in her mind. She had to let Connor choose his own path, but that didn't mean she couldn't try to convince him.

Once she was composed, she turned toward the sliding glass doors to go back inside. Taren was leaning against them, his feet crossed at the ankle in front of him, and his arms folded across his chest. It was such a grown man pose, and yet he would never become one.

"Are you happy, Ro?"

Was she? She was glad she got to see her mother again, but she knew she'd think about this visit for a long time and it would bring both happiness and sadness. "Yes, Taren. Thank you."

"I'll come back later," Taren said as he faded away.

Rowena looked up at the sky, but her eyes didn't focus.

Instead of seeing the stars and moon, she saw images of her family—them laughing. That's how she always wanted to remember them. And she would. Even when she had to say goodbye to Taren.

That time would come, but right now, she needed to get Connor to see what they had to do.

23

Connor rolled his desk chair around and faced Rowena when he heard her walk in from the back deck. He'd gone to his office when he'd heard her talking to someone, probably her brother, because he hadn't wanted to intrude, and he had writing to catch up on. Before he could even get to that he'd used his magic to clean up the disaster Drew had created. The rest of the house could wait.

But the blank page had mocked him. For years he'd taken solace in his writing and then a kind, beautiful, blond woman descended upon his solitary existence and made him look into the past.

Standing up, he took the couple of steps to her and leaned down, giving her a small kiss on the lips. "Have a good talk with your brother?"

A sad smile flashed across her face. "I spoke to my mother."

Connor reared back. "Wow. Did Taren call her, like he did with Helen?"

"Yes. He said something about being given permission. I didn't ask what that meant."

Helplessness, a familiar feeling, swamped him. He wanted to take her into his arms and make love to her until the entire world fell away, but he didn't know what she needed. "Do you want to talk about it?"

She took his hand and pulled him over to the couch and sat, patting the cushion beside her. "It was so strange seeing her after so many years. I'm still—"

"Hello?" They both turned when they heard his uncle Joel call from the foyer. Moments later, he appeared with Doyle, who immediately bounded over to them.

Connor took Doyle's face in his hands and rubbed his cheek on his dog's head. "You're such a good boy."

Joel chuckled. "He might be a good boy, but he's also an energetic one. I was already drained when we went out, but the fresh air was good. Now, I'm going to go home and relax. I'm taking your car to drive Doyle to my place for the night. That okay with you since you two have to figure out what to do about the book?"

"Yeah, sure." His uncle leaving was about more than Doyle or finding the key. The man was an extremely observant person and likely knew Connor had some things to work out with Rowena.

"Good. Oh… did you get ahold of your dad?"

"Yeah. He went back to Javier's apartment and found him beaten and unconscious on the floor. He said he needed help healing him and had to call one of his agents."

Rowena gasped and he felt like a tool for not thinking about how she'd feel hearing that. "Sorry, I should have told you sooner."

"No, it's okay. I'm just upset that he was hurt."

Joel called Doyle, and he scurried over to his uncle's feet. "I'll take Doyle and check in with your dad. If he has any more news about Javier, I'll let you know."

"Thanks. And we'll let you know if we find anything."

Joel left with Doyle as soon as Connor got some things for him. This was the most time he'd spent away from Doyle since he'd gotten him, but Joel would lavish attention on his dog.

"Connor, will you come and talk to me?"

He sat next to her on the couch and turned so he faced her. She did the same and their knees touched. It was already a familiar position. He wanted more of them, but he didn't know what Rowena wanted. Would she want him long-term? He had a sickening feeling in his stomach she was about to tell him that she didn't want him.

"Talking to my mom made me realize a couple of things… I've always wanted to help people, but I wasn't always doing it for the right reasons. Well…" She twisted her fingers in her lap. "I was and I wasn't. I wanted to help people because I love seeing people succeed and find happiness. But I also wanted to do it so I could tell myself I was a good person and prove that I deserved to be alive even though my family wasn't."

Like before, Connor needed to hold Rowena. He pulled her over onto his lap, and she positioned herself so her back was against the arm of the couch. Pushing a stray curl behind her ear, he looked into her eyes. "You are one of the best people I know. You're kind and loving, and patient."

The corner of her lip lifted in a semi-smile, but there was still sadness in her eyes. "Thanks. I…" She visibly swallowed. "I think I always wondered why I lived when the rest of my family didn't. I wanted to make sure that I was worth the life I was given." She gave a self-depreciating laugh. "I always knew that if any of my patients said that to me I would have told them that they deserved to be alive just because they were. They didn't have to prove anything to anyone or be more than they were."

"And now?"

"Now, I know that I should just do what I do because I love it. Not for any other reason, and that I can't save everyone. I will always remember the teenager that committed suicide the other day, but it wasn't my place to *save* him, it was his. I could only be there to guide him, but all decisions were his to make. It doesn't mean I won't go over every session with him again to see if I could have done anything differently, but I think that's no different from what any professional would do."

She turned in his lap more fully to face him and brushed his hair off his face. Her hand lingered, cupping the side of his head. "Connor, I also realized that I can't save you."

At that moment, it felt like the world stopped turning. She was giving up on him right when he knew he had to fight for her.

"Connor, only you can save yourself. Only you can decide to let the past go. We're always going to make mistakes, but you didn't fail when Julia died and you didn't fail with Drew today. You had to make impossible decisions and you did your best. You'll only fail if you decide not to help me beat Drew."

She scooted off his lap and stood facing him. "I can get another map by reciting the spell in the book again and somehow I'll get another key and stop Drew. Are you going to help me?"

Connor leaned forward and pulled Rowena between his legs, grasping her hips. Tilting his head back, he looked up at her and saw his future. She was right, she couldn't save him, but maybe he didn't need saving. Maybe he just needed to get on with his future. "I'm not going to *help* you. We're going to do it together."

"Yes."

"But we don't have to do it right this second."

Her eyes twinkled. "No?"

"No. Soon, though. But for right now, put your hands on my shoulders."

When she did as he directed, he pushed up her long skirt, letting his hands trail along her smooth legs. He wanted to savor the feel of her but the urgency to be inside her was too strong. Lifting her, he brought her up onto his lap, her skirt around her hips.

"That's what you want, huh?" she laughed as she placed her legs on either side of him.

"No, this is." Magically removing her skirt and shirt, he left her in only her bra and panties. He cupped her ass in his large hands and ground up into her.

Her lips twisted into a sly smile. "Two can play that game."

The next instant, his clothes had magically disappeared like hers, only he hadn't done it. She'd removed every stitch of material and he felt her heat against his hardening cock. "I like this game."

He removed her bra and panties and stacked them on top of the pile of their clothes sitting on the chair.

Pushing up, he lifted her and spun around, lowering her to a slouched position on the couch, and knelt in front of her. It was awkward leaning forward and kissing her as his knees ground into the hardwood floor, but he didn't care. He kissed her until they were both breathless.

When he pulled back, she moved with him, but he wanted this to be all about her. Laying his hand on her chest, he gently pushed her back. "No, I've got this." He scooted back a bit to give himself room and bent forward, positioning one of her legs over his shoulder.

"Oh," she breathed the word out just as he bent down and licked her. He used his tongue and lips and let her sounds of pleasure guide him. Still using his mouth to pleasure her, he inserted one finger and then two. He teased and stroked while he lightly nipped at her clit. When he felt her leg tense on his shoulder, her entire body shuddered and she groaned his name.

Removing his fingers, he brought them to his mouth and licked them clean as he looked her in the eyes. Instead of crawling up her body, he pulled on her legs until he had her positioned on his lap. Later his legs might complain from the cramped position, but it would be worth it.

She gripped his shoulders. "That was… something."

He huffed out a laugh and then kissed her. She melted into him and they kissed for a long moment before he lifted her hips. It was then he realized he needed a third hand.

She laughed. "Need some help?"

He laughed at his predicament. "Ah, yeah." He looked down and groaned at both the sight and the feel as she reached between them and gripped him. She guided his cock into her core and sunk down onto his length. It was the most amazing feeling in the world.

With his hands on her hips, he lifted her up and she pushed down on his shoulders, taking him into her again and again. They found a rhythm, but the slow pace wasn't enough for him.

"I'm not going to last, Ro."

"Take me, Connor."

And he did. He pushed up with his thighs and increased his pace, pumping in and out of her. Rotating hips up he changed the angle and the delicious sensation of the friction soon had his eyes closing. He was so close to losing it but wanted her to come first. Taking one hand off her hips, he found her clit and rubbed the swollen bud.

"Yes!" Her thighs squeezed his and her core strangled his cock in the best way as she vibrated with another orgasm. He let himself go and swore he saw stars behind his closed lids.

The only sound in the room was their heavy breathing.

He kissed her again, soft and long. He wanted to stay like that forever, except his legs had other ideas. Moaning, as he moved, he lifted her up onto her feet. "My legs didn't like that position, but I sure did."

"Me too." She held out a hand and he pulled himself up and wrapped his arms around her."

Using one finger to lift her chin, he looked into her beautiful hazel eyes as he pushed an errant curl behind her ear. He swore that curl sprang free just for him, so he could touch her. "We'll do that again, but right now we've got a key to find."

She looked down and laughed. "Agreed. But let's get dressed first."

They chatted about the book and what they were going to do as they cleaned up and dressed, and he knew that no matter what came next he would do anything for this woman. Even if it meant facing off with Drew and dying in the process.

24

"You ready?" Rowena looked over at Connor from where they stood on Linda's property in almost the same spot they'd been earlier that morning.

"Yes. I just hope this will work."

She glanced at her watch—make that yesterday morning since it was already past midnight. It had been such a long day, with both highs and lows, and it wasn't even over yet. They'd gotten the key, lost the key, were attacked, rescued Doyle, she'd talked to her mom, and she'd made love with Connor.

"It will." She leaned forward and kissed him, sinking into the kiss, absorbing the taste and smell that was pure Connor.

"Yuck. Do you guys have to do that?"

She grinned at her brother when she and Connor broke the kiss. "Yes, one—" She choked on her words as she caught herself. She almost told Taren that one day he'd like kissing a girl. Blinking, she fought back the tears that threatened as she remembered that her brother would never grow older and he'd never get a first kiss. "...It's one thing I really like to do." She spit the sentence out, hoping Taren didn't catch her slip. "Thanks for coming. We're hoping you can help us, but we're not sure yet. Plus, we just appreciate you being here."

Taren smiled, but it wasn't his usual jovial response. "Okay, just no more kissing."

She crossed her eyes at her brother. "We can't promise that," she teased and got the laugh she was aiming for.

Connor conjured a blanket and laid it out on the grass like he'd done before. "Rowena, can you conjure a light? I'll get the book and map ready."

"Sure." She conjured four light orbs the way Javier had taught her, one for each corner of the blanket. As she placed the last one, her thoughts drifted to Javier—they hadn't heard if he was going to be alright. Everything bad that had happened in her life, all the loss from decades ago up to today, was because of one thing—greed for the magic box. They had to get the box and prevent anyone else from getting hurt in the hunt for it.

Just like last time, they kneeled on the blanket and Connor laid one hand on the book. He lifted his other hand to place it on the map.

"I thought you said the map disintegrated," Taren said.

Rowena looked over her shoulder at her brother. "Yes, but we still had the ancient book and were able to repeat the spell to get another copy of the map."

"So you can get another copy of the key too?"

"No. Unlike the spell which produces a map, there are only a specific number of keys, and Drew has the one that we knew the location of." She grinned at her brother. "But we have something that he doesn't."

She turned back to Connor and felt coolness radiating off Taren as he leaned over her shoulder. Holding in a shudder, she answered her brother. "Our magic specialties. We're going to go back to just before we pulled the key from the portal, and if it works, we're hoping that's where you can help us."

Taren floated around to the front of the blanket, facing them. "What can I do?"

"We're hoping you can knock the key out of the portal. We'll just have to wait and see if it's possible." Rowena turned to Connor. "You ready?"

"Yes." Connor placed his hand on the map and they looked north as Taren moved to the side.

Rowena sucked in her breath as the portal appeared like it had before, but this time it was empty.

"It didn't work," Taren said, disappointment in his voice.

"Not yet," Connor said. "That's because what we're looking at now is the empty portal in present time. We need to go back in time to just before I picked up the key."

Rowena smiled at her brother and didn't let her fear of this not working show on her face. "This is our best chance and I have to believe it will work."

Connor looked up at Taren. "As soon as you see the key, we need you to knock it out of the portal. We won't be able to do it because it's just a memory to us, but since you're an apparition in our reality, you should be able to."

Taren's face became serious as he nodded.

"Rowena, you ready?"

"Yes. Let's hope this works." They'd talked about what they could use for Connor to touch to be able to see a memory and had first considered the book. They'd quickly dismissed it since it was being used in the present to open the portal. Since the book couldn't be in two places at once, they could only use it in the present. Then they decided that Rowena might be a conduit since she'd been with Connor when they'd first opened the portal, and she had the same memory of the event. It was more her memory that would be the conduit than Rowena herself.

She placed her hand on Connor's thigh and waited.

"I'm going to go back only a few hours at a time, and then I'll slow the image to minutes."

"Okay." Rowena watched as the portal shimmered, as if coming in and out of focus, but it continued to stay empty. "Oh my god! It worked!" She clapped her hands in childlike excitement. She watched as she, Connor, Joel, and Helen appeared on the blanket in front of the portal, then the portal shimmered again and the key was still there. In the memory, Connor's hand was reaching for the key.

"Now!" Connor yelled at Taren.

Rowena held her breath as Connor's fingers in the memory were within reach of the key. If the memory finished, they'd lose the key again. And then they'd have no more options.

Taren moved in front of the portal and Rowena felt a burst of energy as the key launched from the portal, landing on the grass just as the memory faded and the portal closed.

She let her breath out in a woosh. "We did it!" She flung herself into Connor's arms.

"Hey, no kissing!" Taren called to them. She turned to see him floating above the grass, pointing to the key on the ground. A grin spread across his face.

Connor picked up the key and tossed it lightly up and down.

She leaned over and looked at it. "Does it feel the same?"

"Yes, but there's one thing I don't think we thought of."

She raised an eyebrow. "What?"

"If this is the same key, then Drew doesn't have it anymore. Essentially, we took the key before our former selves took it. Which means even though he once had it, it should have disappeared from his possession just now."

"Wow. Now what?" Taren looked back and forth between her and Connor.

"We figure out where the magic box is. If Drew knows how to use the key, there's a good chance he's got the box. He's too impatient to have waited." Connor bent over the map and placed the key on the x on the map. "I don't know —" Connor disappeared mid-sentence.

"Oh my god! Where'd he go?" Rowena jumped up and turned in a circle, searching the field, as her heart felt like it was threatening to beat out of her chest. Connor disappearing was like her worst nightmare coming true—losing another person she loved.

She stopped turning as the truth sank into her soul. Earlier, she'd told her mother she was falling in love with Connor. She'd even told herself the same thing the day before, but she'd been wrong. She wasn't *falling*, she'd already fallen right over the edge and was tumbling down the other side. She loved him.

It didn't matter how long they'd been together; she felt ten times more for Connor than she'd ever felt for a boyfriend before. She hadn't even told him yet that she loved him, but she did. Rowena looked at Taren. "Where did he go?"

"Where the magic box is, I guess."

Rowena turned in a circle again, as if wishing to see Connor would suddenly make him reappear. "But where is that?"

"I don't know. But since you're connected to Connor, let me try something."

"Yes. Anything." Rowena wrapped her arms around herself, feeling cold even in the heavy sweater she'd worn.

"You can't touch me, but I can touch you. Kneel down on the blanket and I'm going to touch you and the map at the same time and transport us to where Connor went."

Rowena knelt on the blanket. "You can do that?"

Her brother shrugged. "I've never tried it, but I've heard about it, so I don't see why I can't do it too."

Taren placed his hand on the map. His fingers looked corporeal and didn't disappear into the map as hers did when she touched him. He lifted his other hand, and as soon as he touched her, she felt a coolness on her arm and then the world went dark.

25

*R*owena was the last thing Connor saw before his world went dark. He felt like he'd been sucked into the middle of an F-5 tornado. Wind whipped around him with a deafening force and his world was devoid of all color and light. Time became inconsequential as he continued to spin.

After minutes or perhaps hours, the spinning stopped, and like the Tower of Terror at Disney World, the bottom dropped out from beneath Connor and he felt himself fall. His bangs whipped into his eyes and he braced himself for an impact that never came. The blackness receded and light appeared like it was a sunny fall day. He was upright, but he wasn't standing on anything that he could see. Not a floor or the ground, as if he was suspended in the air.

Looking around, he realized he was inside a portal, just like the one he'd opened to get the key. Testing his footing, he took a step. Although he still couldn't see anything solid beneath him, he felt it. Slowly he let his weight down and took another step.

There was a silhouette of someone ahead of him, standing

in front of something. As he got closer, he recognized the person and raised his hands while pulling on his magic. Nothing happened.

Drew turned around. "Magic doesn't work inside here."

Tilting his head to the side to look around Drew, he could make out what he'd been standing in front of. It was a low table with a box on top. The dark gray box wasn't much bigger than a shoe box. There were no markings on it to hint at what it contained. Overall, it was unimpressive, but instinct told him it was the magic box.

"Don't open it, Drew."

Drew sighed like he was fed up with Connor telling him what to do. "You just don't get it, Connor. I'm sick and fucking tired of hiding my magic. So many magics are. With the power in the box, we'll be able to rule over all non-magics and never have to hide again."

Drew was far past reasoning with, but Connor didn't know what else to do. He had to get the box away from Drew, but without his magic or weapons, he was completely powerless. It was a feeling that was becoming all too familiar.

"Wow. Oh, Connor!" Rowena landed right beside him and launched herself at him, as if reassuring herself that he was alive. He took a step back to steady them both as he wrapped his arms around her. "Are you alright?"

"I'm good—"

"Touching." Drew cut him off, drawling his word with enough sarcasm to fill an entire paragraph. "Now that you've had your little reunion, it's time for me to leave."

Rowena grasped Connor's hand, giving it a small squeeze, silently telling him that she would stand with him. Somehow, they would defeat Drew.

He gently squeezed her hand back and faced Drew head on. "We're not going to let you leave with the box."

"You will, but tell me something first. How did you get here when I had the key?"

Connor smirked, so looking forward to this part—to one-upping Drew after everything he had put him through. "Had is the right word. Are you talking about this key?" He held up the key he'd had clenched tightly in his hand the entire time he'd swirled in the portal.

"You went back in time?" Drew spit the words out like an accusation.

"I can't go back in time. I can only look at memories. But it doesn't matter how I got it." Since he had the key, Connor wondered how Rowena had gotten here. He'd had to mask his surprise when she arrived, but he wouldn't ask her in front of Drew.

"It doesn't matter now." Drew shrugged. "I have what I came for and now I'm leaving." He picked up the box and Connor lunged, knocking him backward into the table. Their momentum sent the small table flying sideways, pitching them forward into the open air. Connor braced himself for impact as the two of them slammed into the ground. Sandwiched between them, the box dug into Connor's chest.

He reached for the box to wrench it free from Drew's grasp and they struggled, neither one letting go. As Connor rolled away from Drew, holding onto the box with all his strength, he felt the ground shift underneath him.

With both of them still gripping the box, they tumbled over and over as if on a massive ski hill aiming for the bottom. Connor's fingers ached from the tight grip he had on the box, and he worried about how much longer he could hold on. His head bounced on the hill as they rolled and the box and Drew smashed into him again and again.

He heard Rowena scream his name from a great distance, but he was moving too fast to lift his head and look for her.

Sweat slickened his fingers and his grip loosened as the floor opened up. He was falling again and it felt like waves were rushing over him at the same time.

Connor looked down as the box was ripped from his grip. He couldn't see Drew, only the ground that was fast approaching. Once more he braced for a hard impact, but when the ground was only inches away, his momentum slowed and he floated down, landing in a field like the one he'd just left. The sun was starting to rise and it cast a soft glow over the ground.

Jumping to his feet, he looked around, spotting the box several feet away at the same time he noticed Drew. He and Drew were almost equal distance away from it.

Throwing his hands out in front of him, Connor called up his magic and pulled the box toward him. As soon as it landed in his hands, he conjured a protection bubble around himself.

"That won't stop me!" Drew yelled as he flashed in front of the bubble.

"Maybe not, but I will!"

Connor whipped sideways to see Rowena standing in a warrior pose, magic whirling around her. She looked exactly like the goddess he'd thought of when he'd seen her standing by the window in his house. She embodied everything he didn't think he ever deserved—bravery, kindness, passion, beauty, and so much more. To him, she was perfect and worth facing every demon in his past.

Turning to Drew, she raised her hands, her palms glowing with magic.

"No!" Connor screamed and lowered the barrier. He wouldn't let her go face to face with Drew. With the box still in his hands, he flashed to her side. "Together," he said.

"Together," she repeated. "On one."

Connor's magic wasn't at full strength yet, and his body

felt battered and worn. He didn't want to face Drew with only one hand, but he refused to let go of the box. Picturing a baby sling he'd seen on a woman once, he conjured one and sent the box into it, cradling it along his back.

Rowena lowered her voice as she counted down. "Three. Two. One." Connor sent his magic forward with every ounce of energy he had left. His knees gave out and he dropped to the ground, his breathing heavy as he lifted his head. Drew lay on the ground, unmoving.

Rowena's feet appeared in front of him and she extended her hand to him. "Let me help you up."

"Thanks." Back on his feet, he gave her a quick kiss and grasped her hand again. "Let's check on Drew. I want to make sure he's really out."

"Don't worry about Drew," a voice said from behind them. "I'll take the box."

ROWENA TURNED to see who had spoken—an older gentleman with gray hair and a bushy mustache. Since she'd seen a picture of Andrew Skalbeck, aka Snake, Drew's dad, she figured this must be Forest Sharpe, aka Maverick. He looked vaguely familiar, but she'd only been a child the last time she'd seen him.

"It's been a long time," Maverick said as he came toward them. "But you look so much like Frank; you must be Connor. And Rowena, you are the spitting image of your mother."

Connor squeezed her hand in a silent signal. She was more than happy to let him take the lead in talking to Maverick. Staying silent could help her play the role of dumb blond and just listen and observe. It provided an opportunity for

Maverick to underestimate her capabilities. It wouldn't be the first time a man saw no deeper than her looks.

"How'd you find us, Sharpe? Or should I call you Maverick?" Rowena marveled that Connor kept his voice calm, as if he was asking about something as mundane as the time.

Maverick smiled, and in some circles, he might have been considered a silver fox if she didn't know about the slime that slithered beneath his cool exterior.

Rowena slowly eased her hand from Connor's and let her magic slide to the tips of her fingers. Maverick hadn't been around for the last two decades, but she knew he'd somehow been involved in Morgana's and her brothers' disappearances, so she knew what he was capable of. No matter what he tried now, she'd be ready.

"You won't need to call me anything as I won't be here long." Maverick flicked his hand toward Connor, and Rowena tensed, her fingertips pulsing with her magic. "That's a nice sling thing you've got going on, but I'll take the box from you now."

Out of the corner of her eye, she saw Drew push himself to his feet and walk toward Maverick. "Did my dad tell you where I was? Is he on his way?" he asked, directing his question toward Maverick.

Maverick kept his gaze on Connor and the box. "Your dad told me you had the box and that's all I cared about."

Drew's nostrils flared and his face reddened as he walked up to Maverick, but he stopped a few feet away from him. "What the fuck are you talking about?"

For the first time, Maverick pulled his gaze away from Connor and sneered at Drew. "I've had enough of explaining myself tonight, and I don't have to explain anything to you. You're an annoying little pissant. And soon you won't be my problem."

Drew took another step closer to Maverick and held out

one hand. A dagger landed in his palm and he closed his fingers around it. Rowena recognized the magic dagger—it was exactly like the one Drew's father had used to pin Damon to the ground.

Smirking at him, Maverick stood his ground. "Nice trick. I know your father taught you how to retrieve those ancient daggers, but what he probably didn't tell you is that he and I both took the antidote for the poison that's embedded in them." Maverick laughed. "By the look on your face I'm guessing he didn't give it to you."

Drew raised the dagger. "You're lying. My dad would have given me the antidote too if that was true."

Maverick flicked his hand in Drew's direction, and this time it was more than just a gesture. Drew stumbled backward several feet and landed on his ass, the dagger still clutched in his fist. He quickly jumped to his feet but didn't move forward.

"Hate to break it to you, boy, but there's a lot you don't know." Maverick sounded anything but remorseful as he stared at Drew. "As I said, I've had enough of fucking explaining myself tonight—" He looked up at the sun rising on the horizon. "And this morning too. But I'll do you a favor and enlighten you, just because your father was useful to me over the years and I suppose I owe him that much. Eddie never worked for you. He's been loyal to me because he thinks he'll get power from the box. Snake's idea to control non-magics is fucking stupid, but I went along with it as I needed his resources. But now I don't. I killed him just before I blew up the building in Mexico."

"No! You're lying again!" Drew yelled.

Rowena suspected that Maverick only said what he did to Drew to throw him off. Or he was just such a narcissist that he liked to see people suffer.

Maverick ignored Drew's outrage and turned to Connor

and Rowena. As he held out his hands, she felt the surge of energy as it forced its way between her and Connor, flinging them in opposite directions. She cried out as her hands hit the grass with such force that it sent shards of pain rippling up her arms.

Sending cooling magic through her system, she jumped to her feet and turned in time to see Connor do the same.

"You alright?" he asked, reaching out to hold her hand.

She nodded and looked for Maverick. He had the box in his hands, but wasn't looking at them. Drew dove at him with the dagger and bounced off an invisible barrier, stumbling backward.

The action caused Maverick to look up. "It's just a shield, but I wouldn't recommend you using your magic to break it. You wouldn't want to disturb the contents of the box."

He was right. They didn't know what their magic would do to the box. Both the ancient book and the map had been protected by spells. Was the box? She turned to Connor. "Do you know if the box is protected and if it needs something to open it?" she whispered as she leaned close to him. "I hadn't even thought to ask Linda."

Connor dropped her hand and wrapped his arm around her, pulling her close. "Me either," he whispered. "I didn't think about it because I hoped the box would never get opened."

Maverick leaned over and placed the box on the ground before kneeling in front of it. "According to ancient lore, once you've got the book and unlocked the map, there is nothing else standing in the way." He looked up at Rowena with a sly smile and she knew he'd heard her question. "Let's find out, shall we? Oh... by the way... your cousins, and Connor, your uncle, they all died in the explosion in Mexico. Sam too. So sad," he mocked.

Rowena felt Connor's arm tense around her as she

gasped. Maverick was taunting them as he'd done with Drew. She refused to believe him. But she'd recognized that name—Sam was the friend who Morgana had recently remembered. If Jack and Meredith had been with her, then she'd hold out hope that the woman was fine, just like the rest of her family.

It was only here that she was losing hope. She watched helplessly as Maverick felt around the edges of the box before lifting the lid. A dark gray cloud, like the one in the portal, floated up out of the box.

"Yes!" Maverick walked into the mist, and Rowena watched in horror as it consumed him, obscuring him from sight for several moments. Then the mist slowly started to disappear. She thought at first it was dissipating and gasped when she realized that Maverick's mouth was open and he was ingesting it.

"No! It's not yours!" Drew yelled as he threw bolt after bolt of magic at the invisible dome surrounding Maverick. Each bolt hit the barrier and sparked before it dissolved.

Maverick picked up the empty box and laughed. "Too late." His voice was deeper than it had been before and echoed like it was coming from a tunnel. He turned to Drew. "I never agreed with Snake's plan to control non-magics. They're weak and useless. Instead, I will control all magics. That is where the power is. It's always been my destiny and now the day has come!"

Drew yelled and lunged for Maverick just as he disappeared, causing Drew to fall to his hands and knees. He jumped up and spun to Connor. "This is all your fault! It's always been your fault!"

Rowena couldn't remember a time that she had ever seen someone filled with pure hatred, but she knew that's what she was looking at now. Drew hated Connor with every fiber of his being.

"Shield!" Connor yelled.

Rowena pulled on her magic, just as Drew's hand came around her neck from behind, tipping her backward. It had all happened so fast, she hadn't noticed him flash.

"Don't move," Drew said into her ear. "In case you can't feel it, I've got a dagger at your throat. It doesn't take much, just a small nick, for the poison in this dagger to penetrate your entire body. You remember what happened when Damon was hit with one? Well, that was just his shoulder, and healers were able to get to him before it had time to fully take effect. It won't be the same for you. You make even the slightest move and I'll slice your throat. If that doesn't kill you, the poison will."

Rowena used her magic to slow her heart rate. She needed to be under control if she was going to flash. If she leaned back into Drew before flashing, she could put some distance between herself and the blade.

"Drew, let her go," Connor said. "I'm the one who ruined your plans. Take me."

Something wrapped tight around her wrist, but she couldn't look without getting sliced by the dagger.

Drew's breath was hot on her ear as he leaned even closer. "That's magic rope. I'm sure you've heard of it. It nullifies your magic, so don't think you'll be able to flash away."

Without her magic, her heartbeat picked up. She couldn't move and she dared not even swallow—the edge of the blade was cold against her skin.

"Drew," Connor said again. "Let her go. Take me instead."

"No!" Rowena felt Drew's spittle land on her cheek, but she kept statue-still. Looking at Connor, she pleaded with her eyes for him not to do anything rash.

"I'm going to make you suffer. I should have done more

than just make you think Julia died," Drew yelled, the sound almost painful against her ear.

Connor stuttered a step forward. "What?"

Drew laughed and she could feel his heartbeat speed up from where he was pressed against her back. "You're so fucking gullible, Connor. Julia isn't dead. The seer told us about her abilities, so we only made it look like she died. She's been working for me and my dad for years." He snorted a laugh and more spittle hit Rowena's cheek. "She's a fucking genius with chemistry. She's been making our drugs this whole time. But not anymore since she would have been blown up with everyone else. Poor little Sam."

Connor took another step forward, a stunned expression on his face. He questioned Drew, but she didn't hear what he asked as someone spoke into her mind.

Psst.

It's me. I didn't want to startle you, Taren whispered. She would have smiled if she wasn't so worried about moving.

I can hear you, she answered him.

If I push Drew, do you think you can get free?

Drew still held the blade tight to her neck. Depending on how Taren pushed him, he could drag the dagger across her throat, killing her in an instant. And if it didn't, the poison would.

"I'll make you suffer!" Drew shouted next to her ear, pulling her attention away from Taren. She looked at Connor as Drew shoved her sideways. Her body sailed through the air and she instinctively drove her hands out in front of her like she'd done before. This time, she rolled to her side as she landed, avoiding her hands hitting the ground with the impact's full force.

Stunned she was still alive, Rowena gave her head a small shake to clear it and pushed to her knees.

She gently probed her neck with her fingers—no pain and no blood.

Ro, you okay?

She looked up but couldn't see Taren. He was keeping himself invisible like he'd done when he'd transported her in and out of the portal. Drew still hadn't seen Taren and wasn't aware he was even around.

I'm okay, she answered Taren. Her senses must be increasing as they related to Taren because she could tell he was in front of her, even though she couldn't see him.

Hurry.

She staggered to her feet and looked up just as a bolt of magic hit Connor square in the chest, knocking him backward. She screamed Connor's name as she took off running.

Drew, with the dagger still in his hand, made it to Connor's prone form before she could. He stood over Connor like an evil sentry, but she ignored him as she dropped to her knees by Connor's side. "Connor?" She reached for him and grunted as she stubbed her fingers against something. Pulling her hand back, she shook her fingers to get rid of the pain and then reached again more carefully and touched the invisible barrier that surrounded Connor.

"He's alive, but you can't touch him, and you don't have your magic anyway." Drew held his hands over the dome for a moment before reaching down and grabbing Rowena's arms. She'd been so worried about Connor that she hadn't thought about her own self-preservation. Remembering the magic rope bound tight around her wrist, she yanked on her arm and kicked out at Drew.

With her arm still in his grip, he crouched in front of her, holding the dagger only a hair's breadth from her eye. "Stop moving!" Drew yelled.

She froze and let him pull her up. A desperate person could be extremely dangerous, and she didn't trust him. Drew hadn't said what his plans for her were, but he wanted Connor to suffer, and hurting her was a good way to do it.

Drew disappeared the dagger while dragging her to a car parked on a dirt road at the edge of the field. He ripped open the passenger door and shoved her inside.

"Drew, please, you don't have to do this. You won, you beat Connor. You can leave us now and go find Maverick," Rowena pleaded with Drew, hoping the plea in her voice would connect with his ego.

"It's not enough," he yelled at her and reached for the door, shoving it closed. She barely had time to right herself and pull her legs in before the door slammed shut.

As soon as he walked away from the door, she reached for the door handle but there wasn't one. She was trapped.

Once in the driver's seat he started the engine and turned his head to sneer at her. "You think you're so smart, but you're just as dumb and naïve as Connor. That seer you contacted? She's the same one the council leader took years ago. All it took was a little torture before she sang like a canary and then we killed her. She didn't know all the details about the box, but she knew that we'd end up here. I drove my car here earlier just in case I'd need it. Like now. I planned ahead." His voice was full of pride. He had outsmarted them, but she wouldn't give up. And neither would Connor—not after everything they'd said to each other. He'd come for her.

"Connor always thought he was so smart," he said as he pulled out onto the road. She frantically reached for her seatbelt and put it on as Drew continued his rant. "And his dad and uncles were fucking self-righteous, thinking they're better than my dad. But in the end, I got to the box first."

Rowena was getting sick of listening to Drew boast. "Did you plan on losing the box too?"

Drew slammed on the brakes and Rowena flung forward, her seatbelt catching her.

"You fucking bitch!" He yanked her shoulder back into the seat, but she didn't see the fist coming. The force of his fist on her cheek smacked her head into the side window. Stars danced behind her closed lids as she sucked in a steadying breath. She felt the vehicle move again, but she didn't look over at him.

"You stupid bitch. Keep your mouth shut, or I'll do worse next time." He went quiet and Rowena knew not to provoke him again.

"And to answer your fucking question," he said after several minutes, "No, I didn't plan on losing the fucking box. But it doesn't matter. Now that the magic is out of the box, I just have to kill Maverick to take it. Easy."

Rowena kept her mouth shut and, trying to ignore the pain pulsing in her cheek, she let her mind wander. Two weeks ago she was helping her clients and doing what she could for her family. She'd been doing everything for all the wrong reasons—trying to prove she deserved her life instead of helping others just because she loved it. Now, after talking to her mom, so much of her guilt had fallen away and she had a life with Connor to look forward to. Her life had changed in a flash, like it had years ago—it took only minutes for everything to be taken from her. No, she couldn't think that way. She wanted a life with Connor, and Doyle too. Maybe they could get another dog and she also wanted children one day. Like her mom said, she had a long life ahead of her and she was determined to live it.

She pulled herself back to the present and looked out the window. They were almost at Connor's house. Even fearing what Drew had planned, she needed to know that Connor was safe.

I'm here, Taren whispered in her mind.

Is Connor okay?

I don't know. I wanted to make sure you were okay first.

Can you check on him? Please? He's taking me to Connor's house. I'll be alright. Just check on Connor.

Okay.

After Drew pulled up in front of Connor's place, he yanked her out. "I should have made sure that Eddie finished you off. Maybe he didn't on purpose. The fucking traitor. I'm always having to fix other people's mistakes. No one ever does what they're supposed to," he muttered.

Rowena didn't respond as Drew continued talking to himself about his plans and whining about how he had to do everything himself. She and Connor hadn't put any spells on the house when they'd left, making it easy for Drew to walk right in, dragging her by her arm.

They hadn't cleaned up from Drew's earlier destruction, forcing her to step over books and cushions to keep up with him as he made a beeline for the living room.

"This is perfect."

"What is?" She looked up from watching her feet as he stopped in front of the fireplace.

"It all started with a fireplace and now it's going to end with one. When I first came here and saw these iron rings stuck into the brick for pokers, I didn't know what they were for, but now, they're going to help me."

"How?" Rowena blinked, fear rooting her to the floor.

Drew held out his hand and three pieces of rope appeared in his palm. "Did you know that you can't conjure magic rope? All the pieces in existence were made years ago. Luckily, my dad and—" He stopped abruptly as if remembering that Maverick said he'd killed Snake.

In any other circumstance, Rowena would use the opportunity to reason with a person, to get to their true feelings. But she knew it would be a waste of time with Drew. He was hellbent on destruction and didn't want to be saved.

He shook his head. "Anyway, we got a whole bunch of pieces of magic rope from someone. Not voluntarily, of course." He laughed as he tied her wrists together. She tried to keep her wrists apart, leaving some slack as he wound the rope around the piece he'd put on her earlier, but his hold was too tight. Looping more rope through the ones on her wrists, he secured her to the iron rings.

Next, he used a piece of rope to tie her ankles together. "It's funny," he said as he continued his monologue—he'd really become a chatty thing, but the longer he talked, the more time it gave Connor to get to her. "This rope has been around for centuries and there's a ton on the black market. The FBI's magic task force had been acquiring pieces for years and stocked many task force kits with it. That's how I learned about it. The FBI taught me a lot of things—like how to tie a good knot."

He stood back and surveyed his work. "That'll do." He

laughed with glee, like he was a villain out of a horror film. "Too bad Connor won't get to see you die, since he already thinks you're dead."

"No, he doesn't. He'll come for me." If there was any way that Connor could, he would. She had to hope that Taren could wake him in time.

Drew snorted and slapped his leg like she'd said the funniest joke he'd ever heard. "No, he won't. I changed his memory. He thinks he threw a bolt of magic at me and it hit you instead and killed you. He'll think the magic was so strong that your body disintegrated and there's nothing left of you to find."

She'd never labeled a person without a thorough diagnosis before, but she'd make an exception just this once—Drew was delusional. "And when he comes here and finds me tied up?"

"Finds your remains, you mean?" Drew held up his hand and a ball of flame glowed in his palm. He walked over to the window while still looking at her. "You're going to die just like he thinks Sam—er— Julia died." He lifted the curtain with one hand so the hem dangled at waist level and lowered the ball of flame under the material.

Pausing with the curtain still in the air, he shook his head and then dropped it. "I've changed my mind. Not about killing you." He laughed again. "I'm just not going to start the fire here. Doing this here will kill you too quickly and I want you to know your death is coming. Feel the fear as the flames get closer, knowing there's nothing you can do about it."

He flashed away but was back in less than a minute. "I started the fire in Connor's bedroom. It will take longer to get to you, so I hope the smoke doesn't kill you first. That would be a pity."

Drew winked at her and flashed away.

Rowena pulled at the ropes until her skin was raw. She

ignored the pain and continued to pull and twist. If she could make herself bleed more, it might lubricate the ropes enough to allow her to squeeze out of them.

She'd never been suicidal, but she'd lived with guilt for being the only immediate family member to survive. But no more, and as if by magic, she felt that guilt fall away. Like she told her patients, she deserved to live and be happy just because she was here—for no other reason than that. She wanted to live for herself and for Connor.

"Taren!" she yelled as loudly as she could. Continuing to yell, she twisted her wrists in the rope, her skin tearing with her efforts. She heard something pop and turned to look toward the hallway. There wasn't anything there, but she heard another pop and realized it was a window shattering from the heat.

Smoke was drifting into the room and she choked as she tried to yell again. *Taren!* She switched to yelling in her mind, hoping her connection to her brother was strong enough for him to hear her.

Holy cow, Ro!

Rowena looked up from the ropes to see her brother hovering beside her. *Can you get the ropes off?*

He looked down at himself and it truly sunk in that he wasn't corporeal. Taren was only an apparition. He didn't have fingers to untie the rope.

You've moved things before. Can you move me?

He surveyed the iron rings she was attached to. *I probably could since I was able to push your car back up the cliff, but if I try to pull the rings off the fireplace, I could pull the whole thing down on top of you. It could even collapse the entire roof.*

Rowena coughed again. Her throat was raw and the smoke was getting thicker. *Go get Connor.*

I tried. I couldn't wake him.

"Try again!" Rowena yelled at Taren out loud this time, but her voice was barely audible over the sound of the fire.

She continued to work her wrists inside the ropes, but they hadn't loosened. She didn't know much about magic rope, but since it was magic, it was probably impervious to regular rope properties, like slack. It didn't matter; she wouldn't give up because she didn't have any other choice. Superman had kryptonite, so there was a chance that something could loosen the rope. As her fingers continued to work, she pictured her and Connor making love, wanting to think about something besides the smoke that was filling the room.

The smoke was thicker now and she couldn't stop coughing. Tears ran down her cheeks and she could barely see her wrists and the rope in front of her. The crackling of the fire felt like it consumed her as much as the smoke. She wanted to fight, but her eyes closed as the darkness took her.

27

Pain bloomed on the side of Connor's face and he snapped awake, jerking to a sitting position.

"Finally!" Taren said. He was floating in front of Connor. "It's taken me forever to wake you. You have to hurry."

Connor stood and searched through his memories, trying to remember what happened. He walked himself through the events—they'd found the box, and he'd fought with Drew, and then Maverick had consumed the box's content. Drew then held Rowena with a dagger to her throat. "Oh my god!" He covered his face as it all came back to him. He'd thrown a bolt of magic at Drew, but he'd turned at the last minute and it hit Rowena. She'd dissolved in front of his eyes. "I killed her," he whispered into his hands.

He dropped to his knees as an ache so deep it touched his soul cut through his chest. He was sure that when he looked down, blood would be pouring out. "I killed her." Pushing his hands up into his hair, he fisted the strands and curled in on himself. He'd kept to himself his entire adult life so he wouldn't hurt anyone again. Then Rowena crashed into his life and made him feel things he'd buried long ago. She'd pulled him out of his cave with her fiery emotions and will to help others and he'd killed her.

"Connor, you have to flash to your house. Hurry up. Rowena needs you!"

He looked up at Taren and found the strength to repeat the words that would haunt him for the rest of his life. "I killed her."

"No you didn't. She's at your house and it's on fire! Hurry!"

He sunk lower onto his haunches. "No, I remember. I killed her."

"Don't be stupid, Connor. You didn't. Drew must have done something to your memory again. Hurry!"

But the memory was so vivid. He could see the bolt of magic leaving his fingers and traveling straight toward Drew. At the last second, Drew had shoved Rowena forward and she disintegrated.

He hadn't questioned the memory of Julia dying last time because there had been no reason to, but now he had to ask himself if this memory was true. He would never have sent a blast of magic if there was even a slim chance that it could have harmed Rowena. The same way he wouldn't have put Julia in harm's way. But it had taken everything that had happened recently for him to realize that.

Replaying the memory, he watched for nuances. Drew didn't have his dagger and there would have been no way Connor's already depleted magic could have killed her like it had. But the memory felt so real.

Running through the memory again, he looked at it like he had the memory of Julia's death when Rowena had questioned it. He knew Taren wouldn't lie to him, he'd have no reason to, and he would trust Taren more than his own memories right now.

He flashed to his house, right into the foyer, and smelled

smoke. The memory of holding Julia in his arms as the fire took her life was so vivid. The familiar smell threatened to transport him back to that day, but he pushed it aside in order to focus on Rowena.

The room was filling quickly. "Rowena!" he yelled as he looked around, trying to see through the darkness. He couldn't be too late; he had to find her.

He checked his office first, hoping to tick off the rooms one by one. Holding his hand out palm up with a glowing orb he'd conjured, he looked through the darkness and billowing smoke. The fire hadn't reached the room yet, which meant it had probably started at the back of the house. He prayed Rowena wasn't there.

He flashed to the kitchen and confirmed what he'd suspected. Flames consumed the back wall that connected to his bedroom. If the fire had started there, the room could be entirely consumed, but he couldn't be sure; he had to check.

Flashing into the middle of his bedroom, flames surrounded him, grabbing at his flesh like sharp knives. The heat was unlike anything he'd ever felt, but he took the time he needed to ensure Rowena wasn't there.

Using his magic, he conjured water, letting his clothes soak it up. Lifting his elbow to his mouth, he coughed into the material as the thick smoke permeated his lungs.

He flashed to the living room, and even through the darkness, relief flooded him when he spotted Rowena. Pulling on his weakening magic, he flashed to her, not willing to waste the time it would take to walk a few feet. Not with how quickly the fire was spreading.

She was slouched over, hanging from her wrists where they were tied to the fireplace. Disappearing the light globe in his hand, he leaned over her and gently cupped her face in his hands. Her eyes were closed and she didn't move. "Rowena? Ro, can you hear me?" Moving his cheek in front of her mouth, he tried to feel for her breath but the roar of the fire around him, combined with the heat and smoke, was too much.

He needed to get her outside fast and went to work on the ropes. They were wrapped around her wrists numerous times and tight, holding her firmly against the fireplace's iron rings.

Can you untie her?

Connor heard Taren in his head, but he didn't look up, keeping all his concentration on the ropes. The more he pulled at them, the tighter they became. He conjured a knife and tried to pry an end free, but it didn't budge. Slicing through the ropes didn't work either. He'd heard of ropes like these before but not that they couldn't be undone, but then, they were magic.

The sound of the fire was all consuming and the heat was intense, but he didn't stop. He knew in that moment that he loved her, and it didn't matter what was in his past —she'd helped him see that. He'd overcome anything for her.

Another minute went by and the ropes remained just as tight. His coughing was continuous now and his fingers slipped on the rope as the convulsions racked his body. Tears streamed down his face and his eyes burned, making it almost impossible to see the rope as the cacophony of sound from the fire beat at him. He was getting so tired, he wanted to close his eyes for just a minute...

Connor! Connor! He heard his name over and over again as someone shouted in his head. But he just needed to rest. *Connor!*

Something bumped into him, knocking him into the fireplace. The bricks singed his arm.

Connor!

Taren's voice in his mind finally registered and he looked

up to see him hovering above Rowena. *Can you undo the ropes?*

"They get tighter whenever I try!" Connor shouted above the roar of the fire and hoped that Taren could hear him. The fire surrounded them now, but he wouldn't leave Rowena. He looked around frantically, hoping for an answer. The fireplace was against an outside wall, which meant clean air was waiting just beyond it.

"Pull—" Connor stopped, trying to suck in more air, but he was breathing in pure smoke now. "Pull the rings out!" he yelled as loud as he could.

I can't, it could bring everything down on you.

"I know, but it's our only chance. If we don't get out now, we'll die." He swallowed, trying to stop the coughing long enough to yell once more. "Push the fireplace to the outside! I'll protect us and follow you out!" Connor blinked against the smoke and the tears clouding his vision. Exhaustion clung to him as he found just enough strength to call up his magic. Enfolding Rowena in his arms, he erected a protection bubble around them both. "Now!" he yelled to Taren.

Connor felt the field of energy first and then the force of Taren's power against the bubble as the fireplace flew from the room, the chimney and bricks arching out in all directions. He tightened his grip on Rowena and let the momentum of Taren's energy carry them out of the house with the fireplace and wall.

They tumbled to the ground, bricks bouncing off the protective bubble as the debris fell around them. He pushed at the bubble with his shoulder, forcing it to continue to roll away from the house.

"Connor!" His dad's voice came from behind him.

With Rowena still cradled in his arms, he dropped the protective shield and looked up to see his father tossing bricks aside to reach them. "Are you hurt?"

"I don't know if she's breathing." He choked the words out, not recognizing his own voice as he bent his head to her mouth. The soft puff of her breath brought new tears to his eyes. Pushing her hair off her face, he softly kissed her lips, not caring about the soot that covered them both. "I'm here. Wake up, beautiful. Please, wake up." He turned his head away to cough and felt Rowena move in his arms as she coughed too. A sound he never thought he'd be so happy to hear. "Rowena?" He brought her higher in his arms, kissing her forehead softly. "Open your eyes, sexy. I need to see you."

"Con—" Her body spasmed as more coughing gripped her.

He looked up at his dad. "Get help!"

"We're already here," Jack said as he walked toward them. Bricks disintegrated in front of him as he pushed through the rubble, creating a clear patch on the grass.

"I couldn't get the rope off." Taking a deep breath, he pushed some calming magic through his body to stop the panic that threatened to overwhelm him when he remembered the feeling of not being able to free her.

Jack knelt in front of them and whispered some words that Connor couldn't make out. The ropes fell to the ground. "It sometimes needs a spell."

The spell was one more thing he should have known, like how to fight. He made a promise to himself as he looked down at Rowena, that he'd learn whatever he could to make sure she'd always be safe. "I've got you, sexy. You're going to be okay." Connor didn't know if he was trying to convince himself or Rowena as he lowered her to the ground.

"Don't—" Her eyes popped open as her fingers gripped his wrist with surprising strength.

Shifting so he could cradle her in his lap but still give Jack access to heal her, he leaned down and kissed her forehead again. "I'm not going anywhere."

A hand landed on his back, and he felt the smoke being pushed from his lungs. "It's Meredith," said a voice from over his shoulder.

He looked up from Rowena only long enough to acknowledge her cousin. "Thanks."

"No problem," she said. "I'm going to help the others."

Connor looked up and finally noticed the absence of fire. The sounds of crackling, breaking glass, and falling debris had been replaced by voices. Several of his dad's agents, as well as Rowena's cousins, and a few other people he didn't recognize, surrounded his house. Only embers remained now, and even those were being put out. They were rebuilding his house one piece at a time.

His dad crouched to eye level in front of him. "The fire is out. Why don't you go with Rowena to Joel's cabin? I'll take care of everything here."

That sounded perfect— he needed to hold Rowena right now and assure himself she was okay, but standing was almost more than he could manage. "I don't think I can flash; I'm drained."

"Me too," Rowena mumbled against his chest.

"Let me help," Jack said. He placed one hand on Connor's shoulder and the other on Rowena's.

Connor felt a sudden surge of energy, like he'd just been given a full charge. "Holy shit. Thanks," he said to Jack and then looked down at the woman in his arms. "You okay to flash to Joel's?"

As soon as Rowena nodded, they both flashed.

CONNOR LANDED in the middle of the cabin's main room at the same time as Rowena. He pulled her into his arms, burying his face in the crook of her neck and shoulder. "Fuck. I thought I was going to lose you." The events of the last hour thundered in on him. His hands trembled as he lifted the hair away from her neck to kiss her throat. "I saw you in the fire and—"

"I didn't think—"

They spoke at the same time, but he didn't have the words to explain what had gone through his mind as he tried to free her from the ropes. He needed to feel her, to reassure himself that she was alright. He kissed her softly before he bent to put one arm under her legs and lift her. She leaned her head against his shoulder, and they didn't speak as he carried her to the bathroom.

After he set her on the counter, he kissed her slowly. The smell of smoke wafted off both of them but he didn't care. Not taking his eyes off her, he flicked his hand behind them and turned on the bathtub faucet. He wanted to kiss her forever and never let go, but he needed her to know how he felt after coming so close to losing her.

"Rowena, I—"

"Connor—"

They chuckled as they both spoke again at the same time, then Connor sobered. He put his finger on Rowena's lips and looked into her eyes. "Please, let me go first. I've hidden away for so long, but not anymore. I need to tell you how I feel."

When she nodded, he let all his feelings for her flow out. "We haven't known each other long, but time seems so trivial compared with how I feel about you. I'd only been existing and didn't even realize it until you stormed into my life and made me look at the past. You allowed me to see what it's truly like to live, and you gave me a gift by reawakening my magic. We got to see the love that Gerald had for Dorothy, and when he lost her, he got a second chance with Helen. Their love will continue for eternity." He swallowed when his throat grew tight. There were tears welling in her beautiful eyes; he hoped they were happy tears. "I want that kind of love with you, Rowena. I want us to spend the rest of our lives getting to know everything about each other. I love you, sexy."

"I love you too." She reached up and cupped the back of his neck with one hand pulling him down for a kiss. "I love you," she said again against his lips.

They kissed as the minutes passed, savoring each other until he felt Rowena shiver. Then they undressed each other and got into the bathtub. Using their magic to rid themselves of their clothes and clean the soot and dirt from their bodies would have been faster, but as if by unspoken agreement, they seemed to both know they needed the touch.

Connor sat back against the tub with Rowena in between his legs. He used a wash cloth and the body wash on the edge of the tub and washed her, taking his time to cover every inch of her that he could reach. Her wrists were unmarred now, but he would never forget the sight of the blood and her skin rubbed raw from where she'd tried to free herself.

By the time he was done, the water had turned a dark gray. It was a reminder of the fire that could have taken her from him. He refused to dwell on it and used his magic to drain and refill the tub with clean water to get rid of that reminder.

He conjured a large cup to wet her hair and squeezed some shampoo into his hands. Threading his fingers through her hair, he massaged her scalp as he washed it.

She moaned. "Oh my god, that feels so amazing."

"Good." When he was done, he rinsed her hair and made quick work of washing his own.

"Connor?"

"Hmm?"

She turned around and straddled his lap, pushing his wet bangs off his forehead. "I love you."

He'd never tire of hearing that. "I love you too." He kissed her while she rubbed herself back and forth in his lap. Taking care of her had been his top concern, but now that she was healthy and clean, he let himself fully feel everything he wanted with her. He wanted to make love to her and worship her.

Holding onto her, he lifted them both until they were standing. "Let's rinse off in the shower."

The cabin wasn't fancy and didn't have a separate shower stall, but it didn't matter. He turned on the shower and sent some magic down through the pipes to the water tank to make sure the water stayed warm.

He grabbed the body wash again and lathered it between his hands. Rowena was already clean but he wanted to touch her. Turning her so her back was flush to his front, he reached around and, starting at her neck, he rubbed his hands along her skin and then rinsed her off.

Picking her up, he stepped out of the tub and carried her to the bed. Using his magic, he dried them both as he laid her on the comforter. He crawled up her body, kissing her as he went.

"Now, Connor. You can kiss me more later."

He chuckled as he kissed her lips. "Okay, I'll hold you to that." Holding out his hand, he tried to magically retrieve a condom from his stash back home. Nothing happened. It was then that he remembered that everything he owned had burned in the fire.

Rowena put her hand on his. "We don't need it. I'm on the pill and I don't have any diseases."

"Me either." She didn't mention his house, but there would be time to talk about that later. They were both safe, and thankfully Joel had taken Doyle.

She reached forward and gripped his length and he groaned at the pleasure. "I need you, Connor."

"I need you too." He hovered over her, his hands on either side as she guided him into her body. They came together slowly, their hands moving across each other. Leaning down, he kissed her, teasing her lips and tongue, but he needed more.

Locking her fingers with his, he held their hands above her head and rocked into her, harder and harder.

"Fuck, yes!" She arched her hips, meeting him thrust for thrust as she wrapped her legs around his hips.

He wasn't going to last long, but there was plenty of time to worship her later. She tensed under him and he felt her shudder with her orgasm, gripping his cock like she was made for him. He called out her name as she took him over the edge with her.

When he'd caught his breath, he leaned down and kissed her. He would always be grateful for the day she'd knocked on his door and showed him what he needed. "I love you." In such a short time, she'd become everything to him and he'd love her for eternity.

28

onnor flopped onto his back. "Wow."

Rowena chuckled beside him. "Yes, wow." She turned on her side and ran her hand through the hair on his chest. "It's amazing what a good night's sleep and some food will do."

"True." They'd slept late, had a lazy shower, and made breakfast together before crawling back into bed. Lifting his head just enough to see the clock on the dresser, he groaned and laid back down. "We've got to get up. Joel will be here with Doyle soon."

"Rain check?"

He leaned over and kissed her. "For the rest of our lives."

She chuckled as she got up. "That's so corny, but I love you for it."

They dressed and had just conjured some coffee when Joel threw a thought into his head. *I'm coming in.*

Connor met him at the door and knelt down to greet Doyle. His dog bowled him over, licking his face, his tail going fast enough to create a strong wind.

"Your dad should be here soon," Joel said as he side-stepped Connor, still on the floor.

"I'm here now." His dad walked in the door and gave him a hand up. "I guess Doyle was happy to see you."

He laughed. "That's an understatement." Doyle had nudged his head into Rowena's lap where she sat at the kitchen table.

Joel and his dad conjured their own coffee and joined them. The look on his dad's face said he wasn't just checking up on them. "What happened?" Connor asked, looking between his dad and his uncle.

His dad took a sip of his coffee, and Connor knew he was formulating his thoughts. His dad had always weighed his words carefully as part of his FBI background. "Remember when Morgana called Jack the other night?"

"Yes," Rowena said with a nod. "But I know they're okay, because I remember seeing them yesterday at Connor's."

"Yes, everyone's back except for Ben and Stella. You saw Ben go with Jack to Mexico, but you might not know that Meredith came back and got Stella."

The hair on the back of Connor's neck stood up as he remembered what Drew had said. "Sam," he whispered, as if something in him didn't want to say it too loudly for fear of it not being true.

His dad looked him in the eyes. "Yes, your cousin Julia didn't die when we thought she did. She was taken the same time as Molly—er—Morgana, Mirek, Dylan, and Taren."

"They're alive," Taren said from where he appeared, floating at the end of the table. All heads turned in his direction.

"Yes," his dad continued. "Julia was given a new name—Sam— just like Morgana was, and—"

"They gave me a new name too. Tim. And they tried giving Mirek and Dylan new names, but they wouldn't accept them and fought back." Taren's form faded in and out as if he wasn't sure he wanted to be there. Perhaps remembering was too painful for him and he was deciding if he wanted to be a part of the conversation.

Rowena reached toward her brother and then pulled her hand back into her lap. "It's okay, Taren. You were so young, and it was an impossible situation."

Taren's form solidified again and he nodded as if that was all the reassurance he needed.

Connor raised his brows in question at his father. "Where is Julia—er—Sam?"

"She's with Stella and Ben. They're taking some time to themselves for a few days. It's a lot for them all to take in, and Sam never met her brothers."

"Shit. Right." Connor's cousins, Nate and Travis, were far younger than him, but he'd continued to keep in contact, even when he moved to the lake. He couldn't imagine what they must all be going through. And he couldn't imagine what it would be like when he saw her again for the first time. She was proof that Drew had really tricked him, and although he already knew that, this was a type of closure. He would still need to work through the guilt of not having done more to stop Drew, but he knew now it wasn't his fault.

"He's here," Taren said before he vanished.

Connor stood and walked to the door just as he heard a shout from outside.

"Connor! Get the fuck out here!"

"That's Drew." He turned to Rowena. "I won't ask you to stay inside, but I can't lose you."

She wet her lips before she leaned in and kissed him. "Together," she whispered against his lips.

He took her hand in his. "Together." Telling Doyle to stay, he opened the door and his dad and uncle followed them out.

Drew was standing less than twenty yards away, facing

the cabin, and had a gun in his hand. He leveled the gun so it pointed right at Connor's chest.

"No, Taren. That's not the way!" his dad yelled.

Connor looked over to see his dad reach up as his FBI issued gun swung up from his holster, as if on a string. Taren made himself visible as he aimed the gun at Drew.

"You killed me and now I'm going to kill you," Taren yelled across the lawn to Drew.

"Like the memory he implanted," Rowena whispered to Connor at the same time she squeezed his hand. "Together.

Connor didn't have to ask what she meant. Pulling on his magic and feeling the push of her magic into him, he flung his free hand up and directed all their magic toward Drew.

The blast hit him with such force that he disintegrated in a flash. He didn't even have a chance to scream before his body became a pile of ash.

"He was mine!" Taren said in a voice that sounded like a disappointed little boy's.

Connor turned to face the boy who would have been his brother-in-law if he had lived. "Taren, I couldn't let you do that. You shouldn't have to live with that."

"I'm not alive," he said. His shoulders dropped as his form became more translucent.

"No, but you've proven over the last few days that you still feel. I didn't want that for you."

"Me either," Rowena said from beside him. "I love you, Taren."

Taren nodded but didn't say anything as he faded away.

"Will he come back?" Rowena squeezed his hand again, and he saw her blink as she tried to hold back her tears.

Dropping her hand, he pulled her into his arms. "I don't know, but somehow we'll find a way for you to say good-bye." He didn't know how, but he would help her get the closure she needed.

29

Rowena laughed as she watched Connor walk out of the building that housed The Tower of Terror ride. He looked a little bit green.

"Oh my god! That was epic!" Taren said while he bounced on his feet. "Let's do it again."

Connor looked at her with pleading eyes, and she had to bite the inside of her cheek to stop from laughing. "Why don't we walk around for a bit and look at what else there is?"

"Sure." Taren smiled and stayed between them as they walked. Anyone looking at them would think they were parents with their child. With a little help from Jack and Meredith, they'd been able to boost their magic, strengthening Connor's connection with her. She still couldn't touch Taren, but he looked corporeal and was able to experience the rides. And no one seeing them would ever guess he was a ghost.

Taren had come back a few hours after Drew died and said it was time to say goodbye because he'd finished the job he'd been sent to do. She'd suspected that eventually he'd have to leave, but she hadn't been ready. There would never come a time that she'd be ready, but it would happen anyway and she wanted to do one thing for him first.

Before they'd decided to bring Taren to Disney World, she and Connor had talked about what to do. The rides were fine, but they avoided any talk of food for Taren's benefit and didn't bother looking at souvenirs. Taren couldn't eat, and although he could move objects, buying something for him just wouldn't be the same.

After a full day at the park yesterday, Taren had left them alone in their hotel room and they'd eaten a huge meal before making love and falling into bed exhausted. They'd eaten again this morning before meeting Taren.

She loved watching her brother laugh and enjoy himself like a twelve-year-old boy should, but it was bittersweet. Taren wasn't a boy anymore, and she had to keep reminding herself of that.

They walked for a while and then Taren coaxed them on some more rides. He didn't even mind waiting in line. They just had to be careful to surround him and make sure no one touched him because even though he looked corporeal, he wasn't. They didn't want someone pushing their arm right through him. The entire trip he'd been talking a mile a minute about everything he'd seen, just like a young boy should, and teasing Connor had become his new pastime.

Rowena loved seeing Connor dote on Taren, giving him attention, listening, and answering his endless array of questions. She couldn't remember the last time she'd laughed so much, and knowing that this time would soon end, she tried not to think about everything that had happened, but sometimes she couldn't help herself.

It had been three days since Drew had died. Frank had dealt with all the details, and with Jack's help, they were able to have everyone believe Drew had died in an accident and been cremated according to his wishes.

Normally, she would grieve for someone's passing, but she couldn't be sad about Drew's death. He'd killed her brother and kept her other brother and cousins from them. Regardless of the justice she felt, she'd woken up because of nightmares the last two nights. In the dreams she'd see Connor's still form, and then she'd be trapped in the fire.

Talking through the nightmares, she and Connor were slowly coming to grips with everything that had happened, but it would take more time. Emotional healing didn't happen overnight— she knew that from both her career and personal experience. Connor had talked more about Julia slash Sam, but he hadn't seen her yet.

No one had heard anything from Maverick, but Jack and Meredith were meeting with the other council members to come up with a plan. At the regular family dinner the next night, they were going to fill everyone in.

Rowena had expected no less, but the big surprise came when Jack informed her and Connor that he'd been told they would be the next two council members. Jack never said exactly how he learned of new council members, but she and Connor were both excited to take on the roles.

"I think we should head back," Connor said, pulling Rowena out of her musings.

Taren giggled. "Wool gathering?"

She smiled at him. "Yes, wool gathering. Are you ready to go?"

"Yes, it's time." Taren's expression sobered and he suddenly sounded far older than the child he appeared to be. But then, he was older than the twelve years he looked.

They walked out of the park, and instead of finding a place to flash, they took the monorail back to their hotel. She wanted to give Taren every experience she could before he had to leave. The last two nights, when Taren had left them after a full day in the park, she and Connor had talked about what it would be like to say goodbye to him. It didn't matter how much she'd tried to prepare herself—she wasn't ready. Whenever she thought about it, she had to take a breath and blink back the tears that continued to threaten.

Once back in their hotel room, she was at a loss for words. Connor took her hand in his and gave it a squeeze. It had become their silent form of reassurance.

"Taren, I—" Her throat tightened as she stared at her brother and blinked back tears. She didn't want his last image of her to be of her crying.

"It's okay, Ro. I'm going back to where I belong. I only came here to help you."

"I love you, curly bear." Blinking wasn't working anymore, and she waved her hand in front of her face to dry her tears.

"I know," he said and grinned from ear to ear before he laughed. "I love you too." He turned to Connor. "And you're alright too, Connor."

This time, she squeezed Connor's hand, knowing it was difficult for him too. "Thanks, Taren."

"I gotta go." Taren's image started to fade and then he solidified again. "Oh, I forgot… you'll find Mirek, right?"

She couldn't speak anymore, her throat too tight, and just nodded.

Right before Taren faded, her mother's and father's forms appeared on either side of Taren and they each took one of his hands. Even with her pain of losing them, it was some comfort that they were a family again. They smiled at her and then all three of them disappeared.

Rowena turned into Connor's chest as he wrapped his arms around her. She didn't need to hold it in anymore and let the tears come.

Connor picked her up and carried her to the couch in the hotel suite

She didn't know how long he held her as she cried, but eventually she had nothing left. She waved her hand in front of her face to dry her tears and wipe her nose. Her eyes were probably still red, but she didn't care. "I'm glad I got to say goodbye."

"I'm glad you did too." He moved her in his arms so he could kiss her, showing her without words how much he loved her. Then he stood with her in his arms and took her back to the bedroom and continued to show her.

She knew she wasn't done grieving, but she had Connor and her cousins and the hope of finding Mirek.

Reece Williams glanced at the clock on the wall and froze. Six forty-five pm—the exact same time as when he opened his eyes after coming out of the magically induced coma.

The time was a coincidence, but it also meant he had to hurry. He put the finishing touches on the tray of cupcakes before packing everything up, so he wouldn't be late for the weekly family dinner.

As he put some of the items in his bakery freezer and packed up the rest to take over to The Magic Plate, the image of a certain fiery brunette entered his mind. He couldn't wait to see her.

Isabella Garcia Flores had arrived with his cousins just over two weeks ago. Then immediately decided she didn't like him. He didn't get it. He was a likable guy. The likable-est in his opinion, and he didn't care if it wasn't a word. It was true—anyone who knew him would agree.

The bakery had closed for the night an hour ago, but he double-checked that the doors were locked, turning off the remainder of the lights. Stacking the three portable bakery holders he needed to take with him, he picked them up easily and used his magic to open the back door.

In the alley, he turned back to the door and put a spell on the door that would last for a few minutes until he had his hands free to arm the alarm system from his phone.

A good majority of magics needed to use their hands to direct their magic, but he didn't—not anymore. With just a thought he could control most objects.

A year and a half ago he'd still been spellbound and hadn't even known he was magic. During the ceremony to break the spell he was bound again with a spell meant to kill him. He'd wasted away for months until he'd been put in a magic coma while he waited for an ancient spell to be found to cure him.

While on his death he made a vow to himself that he would never be physically or magically weak again. The first vow he'd ever made.

When the spell was broken just over four months ago, he'd been too weak to even hold up his head. But he had determination on his side.

He shook off the thoughts and plastered the expected smile on his face as he used his magic to open the back door to The Magic Plate.

"Hey Jennifer," he called out to the chef, ready with a joke, as he placed the containers on the back counter. "Why did the chef have to stop cooking?"

Jennifer turned around, a spoon still in one hand as she chuckled. "I don't know and I'm not sure I want to, but okay, I'll play. Why?"

"He ran out of thyme." Reece grinned and looked around at the rest of the kitchen staff as they groaned good naturedly.

"That's so bad," Jennifer said, but she laughed again before turning back to the stove.

Reece used an app to set the alarm on his phone before chatting with the staff for a few minutes as they finished the meals and prepared to leave.

"Jennifer, are you ready for us?" Isabella said when she pushed through the doors from the front of the restaurant. He knew the moment she'd seen him— her pupils dilated as her anger surfaced and she gave him a death glare.

"Oh hey, Isabella, yes, everything is ready," Jennifer said as she smiled and pointed over her shoulder to the counter where his cupcakes sat. "You guys can start taking the dishes and we'll all be gone in a few minutes."

"Thanks." Isabella directed her smile at Jennifer and then let it fall from her face as she walked past him.

His mother had said he liked to stir up trouble, but he just couldn't let Isabella go without saying something. He walked up to the back counter, purposely standing right beside her, and pulled out the cupcake stand from the cabinet below. "Hey, cupcake," he said as he opened the containers.

He smiled when her shoulders visibly tensed. She hated the nickname, but he thought it was perfect for her. One of his signature cupcake recipes was orange creamsicle. It was made with sour cream and orange zest, which added a bit of a sour taste that was incredibly refreshing. Just like Isabella.

One day he'd caught her eating one while all bundled up in a sweater and scarf, sitting on the restaurant's back patio. The look on her face as she took a bite and closed her eyes was pure bliss. He wished he'd been the one to put that look on her face, not his cupcake.

A few days later when she'd come into the bakery, she discovered that the cupcakes were his and she'd stopped eating them. If she'd meant it as a dig, it had worked. He could still feel the sting. But now he was on a mission to get her to eat another one and enjoy it even more while knowing he was the baker.

"How are you tonight?"

"I'm fine," she said as she grabbed two dishes and gave them to a server who had come to help.

While placing his cupcakes on the stand he watched her out of the corner of his eye. She put serving spoons into dishes and passed them to the servers as they came in. Not once did she glance at him.

He finished setting up the display and turned toward her with his sexiest smile. At least, that's what a past girlfriend had called it. "Aren't you going to ask me how I am?"

Her shoulders tensed again and she passed off the last dish before turning to him. "No. I'm sure all your muscles—I mean—you, I'm sure *you* are just fine," she said as a blush stained her cheeks and she rushed out of the kitchen.

He barked out a laugh as his eyes followed her out the door. Now he knew that she'd noticed him and not just in an annoying way. That was progress. He picked up the enormous cupcake stand and pushed through the swinging doors into the restaurant.

"Reeces Pieces!" His sister's screech was loud enough to pierce his eardrum, but he didn't care. He quickly put the stand on the table with the dishes and turned, bracing himself for the attack.

Jo launched herself at him, her petite body not enough to knock him over. Enveloping her in his arms, he breathed in her natural scent, peppered with hints of coffee, felt like all was right with the world.

He finally let her go and got a good look at her. She looked happy. "Hey, Pinky Pie, it's good to have you home."

"Hey, Reece. Good to see you up and healthy," Simon said as he walked up to them and extended a hand.

With practiced ease, he gave Simon the jovial smile everyone expected from him and shook his hand. It wasn't that he didn't like Simon; he did. And he was perfect for his sister. He just hated the reminder of his withered state. "Yeah, I'm doing well."

Jo and Simon talked about their travels to find more of the ancient magic books and then Meredith told everyone to get in line to start filling their plates. Tonight's dinner was served potluck style.

Reece got in line right behind Isabella but didn't say anything as she filled her plate. When she got to the cupcakes, he watched her pause. She reached out to grab one and then pulled her hand back.

He leaned closer to her. "It's okay to take one," he whispered in her ear.

She jumped back and shook her head before walking away.

As he took a seat across from Jo and Simon, he wondered if Isabella really did hate him. That wasn't something that sat well with him. He'd have to figure out what to do about it, but not then. He wanted to enjoy being surrounded by family and friends.

There were a lot of people at the dinner tonight and the din hovered just below what was probably the safe decibel range when suddenly all conversation stopped. Reece turned toward the door to see what had everyone's attention.

Out of the corner of his eye, he saw Connor Davis, his cousin Rowena's new boyfriend, push his chair back and slowly stand. Then his eyes caught movement at the restaurant's front doors. Ben and Stella Davis came in with their two sons, Nate and Travis. They often joined them on Thursdays, so that wasn't anything new.

It was the woman standing between Ben and Stella who had everyone's attention. She had been given the name Sam in captivity, but her real name was Julia Davis.

Reece watched as Connor walked slowly up to Sam and then stopped. He couldn't imagine what the two of them must be feeling. But he wanted to know the feeling. His brother Dylan had been taken with Morgana and two of his other cousins only a few months before Sam. Morgana was safe and they'd discovered his cousin Taren had died. But no one knew anything about this brother Dylan or his other cousin, Mirek.

Connor held his arms out and Sam walked right into them. There was an audible exhale around the room. Then, as if by a collective, unspoken agreement, everyone turned back to their dinners and let the Davises catch up.

Reece dug into his meal and joined in the conversations around him. He was considering going up for seconds when he realized Simon was staring at him. He'd been doing it on and off all through dinner, but this time it was getting a little intense.

He leaned back in his chair, going for a relaxed look, and smiled at Simon. "Hey man, since you're with my sister, I know you're not my type, so you've got to let up on the lustful stares."

For a second time that evening, all conversations ceased. This time all eyes turned to him and Simon.

Simon didn't laugh or seem bothered by Reece's comments. "I've been trying to figure out all evening who you look like, and I finally did," Simon said, a frown marring his features.

"Who?" Jo leaned closer to her boyfriend. "A movie star?"

"No. He reminds me of Rocky."

Reece heard several people curse but didn't look for the sources; he was too focused on Simon. "You're talking about the guy who worked for Snake and helped capture you and Jo?"

He felt a hand on his shoulder and glanced over to see Morgana. Her twin Meredith and her husband Jack were standing behind her. Out of all the people who had been involved, only Simon had seen Rocky.

"Are you sure?" Jo asked Simon. "You think Rocky could be our brother Dylan and he knew I was his sister?"

Isabella gasped and he finally looked down the tables. Her fingers covered her mouth. Her brother Mateo was missing, but not thought to be dead like his, and he'd been working with Rocky.

"Yes." Simon wrapped his arm around Jo, pulling her into his side. "Rocky and Reece could be twins."

"Then why didn't you say anything before?" Jo asked.

"The other times I saw Reece he didn't look anything like he does now."

When he'd first met Simon, Reece had been withered and frail—just skin and bones and his skin pale, not bulked-up like he was now.

"I didn't know." Jo blinked rapidly, clearly fighting tears.

Simon turned and kissed Jo's forehead. "Of course not. Rocky didn't show himself to you." He turned and met Reece's gaze. "When he helped me, I asked him why he didn't leave. I even told him I'd help him escape with me."

A horrible feeling sank in Reece's gut. If Rocky really was his brother and he'd chosen not to leave, maybe he wasn't the same person anymore. "What did he say?"

"He said he couldn't leave or he would have years ago and never looked back. I asked him if it was because of the healer, but he didn't answer."

Jo turned to Simon. "Do you think the healer could be our cousin Mirek? He's who Dylan was staying to help?" He heard the break in his sister's voice and stood to comfort her when Simon held out his hand to him. The hand missing a finger because he'd lost it saving Jo's life.

Simon pulled Jo's chair back and then picked her up and walked out of the restaurant. The action made him smile. Jo hated anyone thinking she was weak because she was so petite, but Simon was her world.

"Let's finish dinner," Jack said to the group.

He looked at Isabella again but couldn't catch her eye. Her head was bent over her plate and she looked like the weight of the world had descended upon her. Right then, he made another vow to himself. The second he'd ever made in his life. He'd find his brother and help Isabella find hers.

Thanks so much for reading *Courage in Magic*!
NEXT IN THE IN MAGIC SERIES:
Find out what happens when the sparks fly between Isabella and Reece and if they find their brothers in
LOVE IN MAGIC
https://books2read.com/love-in-magic-kj

ALSO BY KJ WARAWA

IN MAGIC SERIES

Lost in Magic

Truth in Magic

Found in Magic

Courage in Magic

Love in Magic

Forged in Magic

Forever in Magic

CURSED TO LOVE SERIES

Cursed to Love

Cursed to Dream

Cursed to Wither

ABOUT KJ WARAWA

Paranormal romance author KJ Warawa had worked every job under the sun, including swimwear seller, switchboard operator, legal secretary, sign language interpreter, soldier, massage therapist, and process improvement advisor, before settling into the career she'd always dreamed about: Author.

She still loves processes and spreadsheets, doesn't love massaging feet, and is currently living out her own love story in Alberta, Canada.

STAY IN TOUCH WITH KJ:
Join KJ's Newsletter at
https://kjwarawa.com/free-book/
to receive a FREE book, exclusive deals, special offers, behind-the-scenes info, and learn about new releases, plus more!
www.kjwarawa.com